W9-CCT-451

WITHDRAWN

MURDER IN DISGUISE

MURDER IN DISGUISE

A Roaring Twenties Mystery

Mary Miley

BALDWIN PUBLIC LIBRARY

This first world edition published 2017
in Great Britain and the USA by
SEVERN HOUSE PUBLISHERS LTD of
19 Cedar Road, Sutton, Surrey, England, SM2 5DA.
Trade paperback edition first published
in Great Britain and the USA 2017 by
SEVERN HOUSE PUBLISHERS LTD

Copyright © 2017 by Mary Miley Theobald.

All rights reserved including the right of
reproduction in whole or in part in any form.
The moral right of the author has been asserted.

British Library Cataloguing in Publication Data
A CIP catalogue record for this title is available from the British Library.

ISBN-13: 978-0-7278-8714-6 (cased)
ISBN-13: 978-1-84751-822-4 (trade paper)
ISBN-13: 978-1-78010-886-5 (e-book)

This is a work of fiction. Names, characters, places and incidents
are either the product of the author's imagination or are used fictitiously.
Except where actual historical events and characters are being described
for the storyline of this novel, all situations in this publication are
fictitious and any resemblance to actual persons, living or dead,
business establishments, events or locales is purely coincidental.

All Severn House titles are printed on acid-free paper.

Severn House Publishers support the Forest Stewardship Council™ [FSC™],
the leading international forest certification organisation.
All our titles that are printed on FSC certified paper carry the FSC logo.

Typeset by Palimpsest Book Production Ltd.,
Falkirk, Stirlingshire, Scotland.
Printed and bound in Great Britain by
TJ International, Padstow, Cornwall.

ONE

D eath visited Hollywood about as often as it did the rest of the country. Children were carried off by polio; grandparents gave way to old age; and the influenza came shopping for victims with sad predictability. But murder? Murder dropped by a little more frequently here than it did other places.

Joe Petrovitch was murdered on a sunny Saturday afternoon in early October during the ninth reel of Charlie Chaplin's *The Gold Rush*, gunned down in the projection booth of the theater where he worked. His young assistant witnessed the crime close up, although shock muddled the story he gave the cops afterward. I had never met Joe Petrovitch, but I attended his funeral on Wednesday at Hollywood Memorial Park Cemetery because his wife Barbara worked as a hairdresser at Pickford-Fairbanks Studio where I've been an assistant script girl for nearly a year.

'I don't know Barbara very well,' I whispered to Mildred Young, my friend in Make-up who was standing beside me in the shade of an oak tree as we waited for mourners to gather at the gravesite. I scanned the crowd. 'Does she have any kids?'

Mildred had been hired at the studio just a few months ago, but Make-up and Hair Styling worked hand in glove, so she knew Barbara Petrovitch better than I did. She shook her head. 'No children, but she has a few relatives who will help her through this. That's her sister, over there, in the dark purple suit and sunglasses. And that bruiser on her left is her brother.'

I studied both siblings, looking for family resemblances. The two sisters had the same sturdy build and thick ankles. Their brother was broad-shouldered and muscular, and carried himself with the self-confidence that comes from being bigger and stronger than everyone else. As Barbara soaked her handkerchief, her siblings maintained dry eyes and tight lips. The sister clutched a black handbag in one hand and a single white rose in the other. The brother looked over their heads toward the casket with hard, narrowed eyes that lacked any pretense of grief. Suddenly, as if he sensed my thoughts, he turned his head and met my gaze with hostile eyes. Embarrassed to be caught staring, I looked away.

'Did Joe have any family?' I murmured.

'I don't think so,' said Mildred. 'None that Barbara ever mentioned anyway. They'd only been married a few years. A late marriage for both, I believe.'

Near us stood our employers, Mary Pickford and Douglas Fairbanks, the greatest stars in motion pictures. Not only were they, along with Charlie Chaplin, the best-loved actors in the whole film world, they were the only three with the business savvy and gumption to start up their own studio when everyone said it couldn't be done. A gust of warm wind lifted Miss Pickford's black veil, revealing a glimpse of her famous flawless skin, but even with her face obscured, just about anyone would have recognized 'America's Sweetheart' from her honey-gold ringlets and diminutive size. She was several years older than I, but we were so close in height and weight that she'd asked me to stand in for her on more than one occasion. From the back, with my own coppery bob covered by a wig from Barbara Petrovitch's cupboards, audiences could not tell us apart. Miss Pickford's husband, the handsome 'King of Hollywood' and my boss, turned toward Mildred and me, removed his sunglasses, and flashed us one of his famous grins.

'It was kind of them to give us the time off,' remarked Mildred.

Mourners continued to straggle over from cars parked along Santa Monica Boulevard, picking their way through the forest of tombstones, people talking quietly in small groups. The sun blazed in the clear October sky. Not for nothing had film production moved to Hollywood during the previous decade – the weather was perfect for filming almost every day of the year.

For me, lovely weather was but one of southern California's charms. Staying in one place for longer than a week ranked high on the list of luxuries I'd never experienced in my life. I'd spent every one of my twenty-six years on stage – vaudeville for the most part, although my mother and I did land a few stints in legitimate theater, and after she died, I strayed into burlesque a couple of times. But no matter if it was legit, burlesque, or vaude, the schedule was chiseled in granite: six days of hard work followed by a Sunday jump to the next town to start again.

Once I'd landed my job in Hollywood – thanks to a vaudeville friend, Zeppo Marx, who recommended me to Pickford-Fairbanks – I went hunting for a place to live. Most decent young women would have chosen a boarding house, but I'd had my fill of tawdry boarding houses and cheap hotels managed by matrons who poked their noses where they didn't belong. I lucked upon an old house shared by four other bachelor girls where I had my own room and the use of the kitchen, and for the first time in my life, I reveled in the luxury of possessions: my very own sheets, my very own blankets, my very own curtains at the window – even my very own rag rug on the floor!

Mildred nudged me and pointed discretely. Four nuns had arrived, trailed by a priest. The ceremony would soon begin.

'I pity them, having to wear those heavy black costumes,' I said.

'Spoken like a true performer,' Mildred teased. 'I believe "habit" is the word for nuns' clothing, not "costume".' Another make-up artist approached and Mildred waved her over to our side. 'Hello, Yolanda,' she said. 'You know Jessie Beckett, right?'

'Sure do. Hi, Jessie. Geez, everybody's here. The studio must be empty.'

Bob from the commissary joined us in time to hear that last remark. 'No surprise, everyone knows Barbara. She's been with Pickford-Fairbanks since they started, and she's a pip. Poor thing. A sad day, no doubt about it.'

Yolanda sniffed. 'Barbara's taking it pretty hard,' she said, keeping her voice low, 'and honest Injun, I am sorry for her, but if you ask me, it's a blessing in disguise. I know you're not supposed to speak ill of the dead, but I don't care. That

Joe Petrovitch was a mean son of a female dog. Just looking at him gave me the willies. I'm not surprised somebody killed him. I'd of killed him myself if I'd a come to work one more time and seen poor Barbara black and blue and pretending she'd fallen down the stairs. Funny how she wasn't so clumsy 'til she married that no-good bum.'

'Yeah,' said Bob. 'She's still got a cut on her lip from last week, when it was swollen up something awful. You can see it if you get closer.'

My eyes widened, but I said nothing. I hadn't been aware of anything like that going on, but my contacts with Barbara had been limited to brief fitting sessions and the occasional errand that took me to her workroom.

Two switchboard operators made their way toward us. Anybody who works for a big company knows there's no one like switchboard gals for gossip, and Patsy and Nina were veterans.

'People tried to get her to leave him, but she wouldn't hear of it,' said Patsy, picking up on the conversation.

'Once I heard her say Joe really loved her, that he just lost control sometimes,' said Nina.

'Well, I'm sorry for Barbara's loss, but I ain't sorry Joe's dead,' said Bob. 'Beating up on a nice lady like Barbara. He had no call to do that. Have they arrested anyone yet?'

'Not that I heard.'

'I heard they had a suspect—'

'No, that was someone they let go.'

'I heard the fella who did it disappeared into thin air . . .'

The conversation sank into speculation. Rumors were passed around like Christmas candy and devoured with the same enthusiasm. Of course, I'd seen the newspaper accounts of the killing, but only a birdbrain believed what was printed in the yellow press. The indisputable truth was that a man had burst into the projection booth of the Lyceum Theater and shot Joe Petrovitch, but that was about all we knew for sure. So I kept my mouth shut and listened to the comments batted back and forth like a shuttlecock across a net.

'I heard the killer shot him just after Joe had finished changing the reel—'

'He wore a red jacket, even though it's been so warm that no one—'

'The assistant said he shouted something—'

'I know the assistant. He goes to my mother's church. Well, I never actually met him, but Mom knows him and she said he was an honest person and he told her—'

'The man had a thin mustache and wore eyeglasses and a brown cap.'

'The fella plugged Joe with three shots, boom, boom, boom, point blank. Couldn't of missed. Then he said, "Don't move", and the assistant, well, he was so scared, he was frozen anyway, and couldn't so much as twitch a muscle—'

'And then he just vanished into thin air.'

'What do you mean, vanished?' I interrupted, too curious to hold back any longer. A couple of people started to answer, then Nina took center stage.

'Just that he vanished into the dark theater. Right after the shooting stopped, the assistant ran down to the lobby and got somebody to call the police. The film was almost over so they stationed a cop at each exit and waited for the end. Then they watched each person as they left, but the assistant never saw the killer come out.'

More questions rose to my lips. Had the red jacket been found, discarded somewhere inside the theater? Had the gun been found? Were there other exits? Had anyone searched the water closets? But just then, the priest lifted his hand for quiet. The crowd stilled. The nuns edged closer to the priest as we bowed our heads and began the service with a prayer.

TWO

After Joe's mortal remains were lowered into the grave, Barbara's sister handed her the rose she'd been carrying, and Barbara dropped it onto the casket with a moan. Her brother put a firm arm around her shoulder and led her away before the gravediggers could start shoveling, saving her from hearing the thud of dirt clumps on the wooden lid of the casket. The priest announced that mourners were welcome to pay their respects to the widow at the Petrovitch home where the ladies of the Blessed Sacrament had prepared refreshments. I hadn't intended to go, but curiosity called my name. I assured myself that this wasn't the same curiosity that got me into trouble before when I'd investigated some unusual murders; this time, I wouldn't get involved. I hadn't even known Joe Petrovitch. Nonetheless, something about this murder piqued my interest. How could a killer not leave the theater and yet not be discovered among the audience as people exited? How had he slipped out of the grasp of the police, a man in a red coat carrying a gun? How could they have no suspects? It was a mystery, that's for sure.

'Are you going to Barbara's house?' I asked Mildred, thinking to share the cost of a taxi.

'I, well . . . Do you want to go?'

Douglas Fairbanks passed by us on his way to his car. Mary Pickford was several steps behind, talking in low tones to someone from the studio. It was as if Douglas had read my mind.

'Do you need a ride to the Petrovitch house, Jessie?' he asked, walking closer. 'You could come with Mary and me. Or you, Mildred?'

I wavered only a second. 'Thank you very much, I'd like to go.'

Mildred gave an excuse and politely declined.

Properly speaking, Douglas was my boss, as he was the one who had hired me almost a year ago, but all of us at Pickford-Fairbanks considered that we worked for the studio rather than for a particular person. Douglas and Mary were the best employers anyone could have in the ruthless film-making business. They worked harder than any of their employees – and we worked damned hard! – but they were fair, and they didn't flinch at paying top dollar for talent. Mary was fond of saying that we worked *with* her, not *for* her, and Douglas treated everyone with respect. At the moment, I was working on Douglas's latest picture, *The Black Pirate*, which had recently begun filming.

The Petrovitches lived in Los Angeles proper, not in Hollywood, but the smooth ride in Douglas's magnificent Rolls Royce Silver Ghost was over all too soon. Traffic was light and Douglas drove with assurance. He pulled up to the curb in front of a modest bungalow just minutes behind Barbara and her family. We entered the house. A few people were talking to Barbara, who was by now seated in her living room, looking dazed. I held back for privacy's sake until others had said their piece.

No sooner did Barbara catch sight of Mary Pickford and Douglas Fairbanks than she stood up and dissolved into fresh tears. 'Oh, Miss Pickford. I'm . . . I don't . . .'

Her brother squeezed her hand and spoke the words she could not. 'My sister is honored that you came today, Miss Pickford, Mr Fairbanks.'

'All of us at the studio grieve with her,' Miss Pickford replied.

'We're very sorry for your loss, Barbara,' Douglas said. Only in moments such as these was anyone likely to see the buoyantly handsome actor without a smile on his lips.

'My name's Simon Wallace. I'm Barbara's brother. And this is my wife, Myrtle,' he added, indicating the woman at his side who was engaged in conversation with an elderly couple. When she noticed who her husband was talking to, she snubbed the pair mid-sentence and turned, star-struck, to gape at Hollywood's royalty.

'How do you do, Mr Wallace, Mrs Wallace.' Miss Pickford motioned with one black-gloved hand for me to step forward. 'This is Jessie Beckett, who also works with Barbara.'

I shook hands with Simon Wallace. He was a large man, perhaps forty, with the powerful shoulders and rough, strong hands of a manual laborer and the crooked nose of a fighter. One eye had an outward cast, making me want to shift my gaze back and forth between his eyes as I talked. With some effort, I concentrated on the straight eye while I said the things one says at a funeral.

Miss Pickford spoke again, her voice resonating with compassion. 'We were all shocked to learn of Mr Petrovitch's death. I'm so glad Barbara has her family to help her through this difficult time. Do you live in Los Angeles, Mr Wallace?'

'Yes, me and Barbara and our sister Bunny were born and raised right here. That's Bunny, over there,' he said, pointing with his thumb. 'Barbara will be staying with me and Myrtle for a while, so she won't be alone.'

Barbara bestowed a fond smile on her brother and found her voice. 'Simon has always looked after me, ever since I can remember. And Bunny too. I am so blessed . . . I don't know what I'd have done without the both of them.' She sniffed and swallowed hard. 'And thank you, Miss Pickford, for the beautiful lilies you and Mr Fairbanks sent.'

Mary Pickford took Barbara's hand and held it between her own two. Looking deep into her eyes, she said, 'You are very important to us at the studio, Barbara, but I want you to know that we will carry on without you until you are ready to return.' When Barbara dissolved into fresh tears, Miss Pickford turned to Simon Wallace. 'She's not to worry about her job, d'you hear?'

He nodded and his eyes misted up. 'Bless you, Miss Pickford. That's very kind of you. We'll see how she does. But it's true that staying busy is the best way to heal. Knowing my little sis the way I do, I think you'll be seeing her back at the studio before too long.'

As soon as they had delivered their condolences, Douglas and Miss Pickford – I could never bring myself to call 'America's Sweetheart' by her first name – got ready to leave for the studio. They offered to give me a ride back, but I declined. I had no clear goal in mind, but something was urging me to linger and talk with these people a little longer.

I thanked them and said I'd catch a Red Car back if I couldn't cadge a ride. No one was ever too far from one of the bright red electric streetcars that shuttled all over the city.

Picking up a beef croquette and a glass of orange punch, I worked my way across the room to Bunny, Barbara's older sister. She was standing in the corner with a cigarette in one hand and a glass of water in the other, sucking furtively on the cigarette between sips of something that I quickly realized wasn't really water, making me wonder if she was sneaking the smoke or the drink. Or both.

'Hello, I'm Jessie Beckett. I work with Barbara at the studio.'

'Bunny Wallace, Barbara's older sister.' So she wasn't married. I wondered briefly who she was hiding from with her cigarette and hooch if not a husband. Big Brother, no doubt. He couldn't see her from where he stood. I pegged him as the self-appointed patriarch of the family.

'All of us at Pickford-Fairbanks are so sorry about this tragedy.'

Bunny made appreciative noises about Barbara's film friends being there when she needed them, and we continued this soft, useless palaver for a few minutes while I waited for her to loosen up. People don't burst out with the truth, I've learned. They need to be coaxed. I was usually good at coaxing, not because I had any magic words, but because I listened closely and was content to be patient – traits I'd learned growing up in vaudeville where success depended on concentration, patience, and close attention to detail.

'I didn't know Joe at all,' I said, after I'd established my credentials.

'Lucky you,' she sneered, filling her lungs with smoke and blowing it out through her lips in a perfect O.

'What do you mean?'

She offered me a Chesterfield. I don't smoke very often, but I accepted, knowing that the first few draws would leave me a trifle light-headed. She flicked her lighter and held it close. 'Want something stronger than that?' she asked with a scornful glance at my punch.

'Sure.'

She sloshed a bit of her drink into mine. We were friends.

'Joe Petrovitch was a bastard.'

'How do you mean?'

She waited. I waited longer. Silence is one of the best ways to nudge someone into confidences. She gave a furtive look around, as if to make sure no one was within earshot, and took another swig of her drink.

'I thought Joe was all right at first. Nice enough looking. A decent provider, if you know what I mean. Barbara had never been married before, and she was pretty old – thirty-three – when she got married to Joe, who was a few years older. After a couple months, she started changing. Oh, I was such a simp, I didn't notice at first. When she canceled coming to Simon's house for dinner because she was sick, I thought nothing of it. We all get sick, right? When she stopped our Saturday morning movies together because she was so busy at the studio, I understood. Jobs come first, right? When she said she couldn't meet me for shopping on her birthday, I wasn't suspicious. In fact, I was such a chump that when I dropped by her house later with a birthday cake, I believed her when she said she'd fallen down the stairs and broken her arm. It wasn't until the third time I saw her face bruised that I started wondering how many times a person could walk into a door.'

She drew a lung full of smoke and let the ashes fall to the floor. I waited.

'I talked to Simon. I wanted to call the police, but he said, Are you crazy? The police aren't going to get involved in a family matter. He said let him deal with it. Next thing I knew, he'd gone over to Barbara's and beaten the bejesus out of Joe. Told him if he ever touched a hair on her head again, he'd come back and cut off his balls.'

She stopped talking, and I worried that she had finished. I took a drag on my Chesterfield and said, 'So, did that take care of the problem?'

Bunny shook her head. 'Maybe for a coupla months. But it was hard to tell, because Barbara kept dodging us, so maybe we just weren't seeing her when she was banged up. Then, a week ago, I ran into her at the butcher's and saw her split lip. She tried to tell me it was a fever blister, but by now, I've grown out of the Dumb Dora stage. She begged me not to tell Simon.'

'Did you?'

'Hell, yeah. He said he'd take care of Joe once and for all. But right about then, Joe got himself killed at the theater.'

'And the cops don't know who did it?'

She shook her head. 'They oughta pin a medal on whoever it was. Saved Simon the trouble. I hope they don't catch the guy.'

Was I the only person who wondered the obvious – whether

Simon Wallace had been the killer in the red coat? But it was obvious only if you knew Simon had beaten Joe up that one time and threatened him with worse. Maybe the cops weren't aware of that. I surveyed the crowd. There were perhaps fifty people inside the house and more spilling onto the porch and lawn. Some looked familiar because they worked at the studio, but most were strangers to me. Friends of the family, no doubt. Neighbors. People from church. Friends of Joe's. Enemies of Joe's?

Never mind, I told myself firmly. This was none of my business, and I was too busy to get involved in another murder investigation. The last time I'd played Sherlock Holmes, it had nearly killed me, and I was keen on staying alive. Crushing my cigarette in an overflowing ashtray, I excused myself and caught a ride back to Pickford-Fairbanks with one of the senior pirates, who I almost didn't recognize without his bare feet and pirate rags. But I couldn't shake the feeling that the killer had been right there all along, mingling with the mourners at the reception.

THREE

Walking through a studio's bustling back lot can play havoc with a person's sense of time and place. As I made my way through the slums of New York, past an ancient Arabian bazaar, and around a Mississippi bayou – dodging carpenters and electricians who were lugging supplies to the sets for Miss Pickford's current film, *Sparrows* – a familiar, sharp whistle pierced the din.

'David!' I called. 'What are you doing here?'

'Just come to pay a call on my favorite girl,' he said, circling my waist with his arm and giving me a squeeze. He looked like a million bucks in his Oxford bags and smart two-toned shoes. 'I haven't seen you in two whole days,' he said softly, 'and I'm getting desperately lonely . . . will you come over tonight if I dangle a bottle of French champagne?'

There were a lot of people around, so I couldn't throw my arms around his neck like I wanted to. I settled on a discrete peck on the cheek. 'I'll come even if you're serving panther sweat.'

'Never touch the stuff. I'm not in the bootlegging business anymore, remember? All my liquor sales are medicinal – lock, stock, and legal. However, in the interest of total honesty, which I know you prize above jewels, I'll confess that my real reason for stopping by the studio is to have a look at Doug's latest stunt. Rumor says it's a jaw dropper.'

'And it's a big secret, but I expect they'll let you in to see.'

He gave me that boyish grin that never fails to melt my heart. 'I expect they will, since I'm one of the investors.'

'In *The Black Pirate*?' That was news to me. I knew he'd put up half the money for Mary Pickford's last picture after he'd followed me to Hollywood from Oregon, investing some of the fortune he'd made as Portland's bootleg boss and establishing himself as a film collaborator and honest entrepreneur. I was the only person who knew otherwise, and I was no more likely to blab about his shady past than he was to blab about mine.

Even David didn't know the full extent of my wayward youth. My mother died when I was twelve, leaving me to make my way in vaudeville unsupervised, so to speak. I'd parlayed the skills I'd picked up as a magician's assistant into something more lucrative, becoming a passable thief. The few times I got caught, my young appearance usually got me off with threats and a beating. I was still playing kiddie roles at twenty-four, and it was nothing for me to pass for fifteen or sixteen; even so, I saw the inside of a jail cell more than once. I'd helped a phony Hindoo mystic con the gullible and bereaved into believing we contacted the spirits of their loved ones, and I'd narrowly missed a prison sentence for impersonating a missing heiress in a swindle to steal her fortune. But I went straight last year and planned to stay that way.

'Yes, siree bob. Do you know, I've already earned my original hundred thousand clams back from *Little Annie Rooney*? And it was only just released last month! It's tearing across the country, playing to full theaters several times a day.

At this rate, who knows how much I'll clear – three, four, maybe ten times what I put in. If I can do that again with Doug's pirate picture, well, I'll be twice blessed, as me sainted mother would say.'

He delivered that last line in a convincing Irish brogue with his hand on his heart in the familiar melodramatic pose, reminding me what a good actor he could have been. David Carr looked more like a film star than most film stars, and he had charm enough to melt icebergs, but unlike all the other handsome men who flocked to Hollywood to try their luck in the pictures, he had never expressed the slightest interest in acting. 'I aim to make lots of money,' he'd once told me, 'and acting isn't the way to do that.' His fortune had been built on bootlegging, speakeasies, gambling dens, whorehouses, and smuggling, but since coming to Hollywood, he'd gone straight.

Or so he kept telling me.

Hands clasped, we threaded our way through the construction to the back lot where Douglas Fairbanks and Donald Crisp, the film's director, had been working on the ship's rigging stunt. 'They've been going at it for the past three weeks,' I said.

'When you see a Fairbanks film, you get your money's worth, that's for damn sure. Is he doing the stunt himself?'

I grimaced. 'Of course he is! And Crisp has been giving him hell about it. Accusing him of being a show-off and taking reckless chances with his safety.'

'Ouch.'

'They've been quarreling a lot. We all pretend not to hear.'

'Isn't Crisp acting in this one too?'

'Yeah, he plays a one-armed Scottish pirate – the comic relief – who protects the princess when Douglas's character isn't around.'

'How does that work? I mean, him with two arms.'

'They pull it behind his back at the elbow. Not the most convincing one-armed man I've ever seen, but as long as the camera angles are right, it seems to work.'

I escorted David to the set where the spectacular stunt in the ship's rigging would take place. There, on the topmost spar, was Charlie Stevens, Douglas's sometime double. As we watched, he plunged his dagger into the heavy canvas sail and, holding on to its hilt, swooped down the sail with an old-fashioned rebel yell, ripping the canvas in two as he plummeted to the deck. After landing on his feet with a resounding thud, Charlie made his way over to Director Crisp, and a serious discussion ensued.

'Holy Moses!' exclaimed David.

'Charlie and Chuck Lewis and Douglas have been practicing the descent for days and Crisp still isn't happy with it.'

'But Doug's going to do the scene when the cameras roll?'

'Of course he is. You know his pride.' We all knew. Douglas Fairbanks's remarkable acrobatic skills were his trademark. Stand-ins might practice his stunts in order to spare him the exhausting repetitions, but Douglas insisted on performing virtually all of his own stunts for the actual filming.

As men began dismantling the split sail to sew the canvas together for the next trial run, Crisp snapped, 'Get that other canvas strung up pronto!' and clipped a hook to Charlie's belt to hoist him back up to the spar. I left David to his own devices and reported for work.

Back-lot sets work well enough for most scenes, but pirate films need ships and an ocean. So the next week, *The Black Pirate* cast and crew loaded up and left Hollywood for a few days on location on Santa Catalina Island.

It was my first visit to Santa Catalina, an island lying off the California coast an hour-and-a-half ferry ride from Los Angeles. Back in the days when it belonged to Spain and then to Mexico, it harbored smugglers, seal hunters, gold prospectors, and pirates, which made it an obvious choice for a swashbuckling pirate picture. Me, I think it was the long-standing rumors of buried treasure swirling about the island like sea mist that persuaded Douglas to choose this particular location. It was a simple matter for him to get permission from the island's owner, Mr William Wrigley, the chewing gum millionaire: Douglas had never met a man who wasn't a friend. Mr Wrigley even lent his private steamship to carry us and our equipment there and back.

As assistant script girl, I stood on the lowest rung of the production ladder. My supervisor, Julia Girone, held a spot somewhere in the middle. She played a key role as the director's right hand, the liaison between him and the film editor. Her main responsibility was continuity, which means making sure clothing, props, make-up, and weather stay the same from scene to scene. She also tracked wardrobe and make-up, kept notes on each scene, and took each day's film and notes to the editor. I was eager to learn everything I could about film-making so I could be promoted to script girl one day. For now, I played the assistant's role cheerfully enough, doubling as a girl Friday and doing whatever anyone asked. Growing up alone had taught me to work hard, as if everything depended on me. It usually did.

'Jessie, you help with the wigs,' said Julia, thumbing through a sheaf of papers as she muttered, 'Geez, I hope Barbara Petrovitch comes back soon. Shed number four, Jessie; you'll see it, just follow Harry. Then suitcases. You're bunking with Mildred Young and Fannie Kirchner.' She smiled and added, 'Two beds. One cot. Draw straws.' She raised her voice so everyone on the dock could hear and added, 'Hot dogs on the terrace when you need them, but we need to hustle to get everything stashed by dark. Early to bed, early to rise.'

The first day, we filmed from the shore as two dozen extras rowed a longboat past the point. Then we moved to a more sheltered spot to film Douglas doing a beach scene and walking the plank.

'He did it seven times,' I told David when I telephoned him that night from the lobby of the Metropole Hotel. 'And he needed a dry costume for each take. We also finished the on-shore scene when Douglas gallops to the rescue along the beach. This new Technicolor process makes filming a lot harder. We had five cameras yesterday filming the galley scene. But Douglas says the results will be spectacular. Oh, and I have news – Douglas fired Donald Crisp. Al Parker is going to direct now.'

'What the hell happened?'

'Rumor says they fell out over Douglas's stunts. Crisp is still here, since he's also the Scottish pirate, and they couldn't change that in the middle of the picture, but he's no longer directing.'

'That sounds messy. And you sound tired.' I liked the concern I could hear in his voice.

'I'm dead! We worked fourteen hours the first day and sixteen today. I don't think I sat down once. But I'm not complaining. Douglas works harder than anyone. Did I tell you he wrote this scenario himself? And he gets into every detail. He and Miss Pickford are on site even when he's not in the scene.'

'Mary's there? I thought she was filming *Sparrows*.'

'She took a break. When one goes on location, the other goes too. They're staying at the Wrigley mansion. You know what someone told me? They've never spent a single night apart in their entire six-year marriage.'

He probably heard the wistful note in my voice, because he said softly, 'I wish we didn't have to spend our nights apart.'

'Me too. I'm sorry to be gone all week. I'll come over Sunday night as soon as we get back.'

'We could be together every night if you moved in here with me.'

My wistful note hardened. 'David, we've talked this over before. Neither of us can risk our reputations. You'd not be welcome at Pickfair any longer, and I'd lose my job for sure.'

'That's the most two-faced—'

'No, it's business. Pickford-Fairbanks can't afford to be known as a studio with immoral employees. Their wholesome reputation is a big part of their success.'

'You could quit your job. I've got more money than you could spend if you lived to be a hundred and five.'

There was an obvious solution to this dilemma – one we carefully avoided after David told me he thought marriage wasn't a word, but a sentence. And to be frank, I wasn't sure what my answer would be if he did ask. Vaudeville vagabonds who moved to a new town every week usually dreamed of a stable life, and I was no different. I thought it would be swell to have a picket-fence house, a husband who worked an honest job, and maybe a few kids playing in the yard. I didn't really think it would ever happen – respectable men don't marry women born on the wrong side of the blanket, like me. But a backsliding, bootlegging crime boss didn't sound like a safe bet either. I couldn't help being crazy about David. But marry him? Time to change the subject.

'I like my job. Especially on days like today. You should have seen Douglas walk that plank . . . hey, why don't you come over to Catalina for the day and watch the filming? Catch one of the ferries.'

'You miss me, kid?'

'Desperately. Come over. Follow your money and make sure it's working for you.'

'I'd just be in the way.'

'Nonsense. There are always some locals standing around and a few movie-mad tourists too. You could help carry equipment and earn your lunch.'

'I may just do that.'

So all the next morning, I kept an eager eye out for David, hoping he'd catch the earliest ferry. As the sun climbed higher, my hopes sank. I was standing in front of the rope that held back spectators when Donald Crisp ambled over. He'd become almost friendly now that he was no longer directing. As if to prove it, he offered me a cigarette.

'No, thank you, Mr Crisp. But tell me, what time do you have?'

He pulled a watch out of his pocket and snapped it open. 'Eleven thirty-two.'

The morning ferry was due to dock shortly. Surely David would be on this one.

Behind us, two lanky boys in their early teens were arguing. 'Jake said it was going to be in color,' said one.

'He's a champion liar,' said the other. 'You can't believe a word outta his mouth. My dad says nobody knows how to make color film work yet.'

I couldn't resist. I turned around and took a step closer to the rope. 'It is going to be color. Technicolor, they call it.'

'Golly. How do they do that, miss?'

'Well, I don't know much about that,' I hesitated, hoping Donald Crisp would weigh in, but he stared straight ahead as if the cries of the birds and the rhythm of the sea prevented him from hearing the boys. 'But they make two separate prints, one dyed red-orange and the other blue-green and cement them together. Yellows and blues don't come out too well, I'm afraid.'

'Corking! I can't wait to see it. When will it come out?'

I shrugged. 'That's hard to say exactly. It takes two or three months to shoot a regular black-and-white picture, and color takes longer. I don't think you'll see this before early '26.'

'Gosh, I didn't know it took so long to make them,' breathed the awestruck lad.

'We're aiming to film two or three minutes' worth a day.'

My attention shifted to the tourists just off the ferry who were trailing up the hill, joining the townspeople behind the rope until hunger drove them into the little village of Avalon for lunch. To my dismay, David wasn't among them. Nor was he on the midday ferry. As the afternoon wore on, I gave up hope that he would appear today.

Late that evening, I asked the front desk clerk to place a telephone call to David's house. In a few minutes, the switchboard operator notified me the call had been put through, but there had been no answer. I tried again before breakfast the next morning, but there was no one home then either. He didn't come Friday, and his telephone rang in an empty house Friday evening.

I slept fitfully as I tried to think of reasons why David would not be home late at night and early in the morning. Any reasons at all. But my thoughts would not break free from the one most likely.

Saturday's early ferry brought the morning papers. They'd all been snapped up by the time I arrived at breakfast, so I looked over the shoulder of one of the grips as he scanned the front page. A story about Barbara's husband's death above the fold got my attention. No need to read the article; the headline said it all: 'No arrest yet in projectionist's murder.' The grip handed me that piece as he moved on to the sports section, and as my eyes fell to the bottom of the page, left-hand corner, I learned why David had not been at home.

The headline read: 'Film investor jailed on liquor charges.'

FOUR

On Sunday morning, the cast and crew began packing for the return trip to Hollywood. Mr Wrigley's steamship was again placed at our disposal, providing a luxurious ride to Los Angeles where studio trucks would meet us on the dock. Seeking solitude, I found an out-of-the-way spot on deck where I stood at the rail, the wind in my face, watching the island recede to insignificance and thinking about David. I didn't notice Douglas Fairbanks's approach until he leaned his elbows against the rail beside me.

'I saw the newspaper,' he began, without looking at me.

'They get a lot wrong in the newspapers,' I replied. 'As we both know from experience.'

We stood there for a while watching the seabirds swoop about the ship. A few people strolled past us, but it was as if someone had hung a big 'Do Not Disturb' sign on our backs. No one interrupted us. Finally Douglas broke the silence.

'The paper said "violations of the Volstead Act". Why would they arrest him for that? His drug stores sell medicinal liquor. That's legal.'

His use of the plural jolted me. Drug *stores?* I had been aware of only one: Hess's Drugs at the corner of Hollywood Boulevard and Wilcox. I'd been in that one, and I'd taken note of its real purpose. It did a booming business in medical alcohol. Legal hooch, as long as you had a doctor's prescription. But it seemed there was more than one. Evidently David had neglected to mention his growing retail collection.

'It's probably a misunderstanding,' I said. 'He's got a good lawyer. The best money can buy. He's probably been sprung by now.'

'Probably he forgot to sign some form on the dotted line.'

'Probably.'

I could feel Douglas retreating from David. Slowly, carefully. Nothing dramatic or sudden. But I could sense his

withdrawal, like someone edging away from a too-hot camp-
fire. He and Mary Pickford couldn't afford an investor or
a friend who was a felon. If everything smoothed out the
way I hoped, they would inch back and pretend they'd never
had any doubts. But for the time being, they would keep
their distance. The knowledge hurt. I understood, but it still
hurt.

Douglas remained beside me for another few minutes, then
without further comment, he pushed back from the railing
and disappeared below. The Wrigley boat docked half an
hour later. By the time we'd unloaded the equipment, loaded
it onto the trucks, and unloaded again at the studio, it was
dark. I arrived home fagged out and empty – in spirit and
in stomach.

I hadn't eaten since breakfast, but the thought of food made
me nauseous. I needed a drink more than anything – my throat
was as dry as stale bread – but I didn't have anything stronger
than orange juice. I poured myself a glass and made my way
through the kitchen.

'Jessie! You're home!' Myrna Loy danced her way down
the stairs, twirled a pirouette in the hall, and greeted me with
a quick hug. An aspiring actress, she'd had good luck since
she changed her last name from Williams to Loy, getting bit
parts at last in several MGM and Warner Bros. films, parts
that paid better than the occasional seven dollars a day she'd
been earning as an extra. Then, just two months ago, had come
her big break: Jack Warner offered her a contract at seventy-
five dollars a week.

'I heard the screen door bang,' she said. 'How was it? I'll
bet being on location is the most exciting thing in the world.
How did you like Catalina? I've heard it's very, very beautiful.
What was the hotel like? I know it's very elegant and famous.
Did you get any dinner? There isn't much food in the kitchen
– Helen's going to the market tomorrow – but I could scramble
you some eggs. And . . . oh, I almost forgot. You got a tele-
gram.' She rummaged through the mail on the hall table. 'Here.
It came yesterday.'

'Thanks, Myrna. I'm awfully tired, but—'

She grabbed my valise out of my hand. 'I'll carry your bag

upstairs. You sit and read your telegram. And how about those eggs?'

In truth, eggs sounded like something I could swallow. 'Yes, please, Myrna.'

The telegram was from David's lawyer, asking to see me the moment I came home. I took him at his word, so even though the clock said 9:00, I went to the telephone and asked the operator for his home number, Madison-7372, that he'd sent in the telegram. Mike Allenby picked up on the first ring and said he'd come right away to my house on Fernwood.

I lived in an old farmhouse that had a city grow up around it. I rented the place with Myrna, Lillian, Melva, and Helen – all great girls but I liked Myrna best. It had just three bedrooms upstairs, so we turned the first-floor parlor and the dining room into bedrooms so we each could enjoy the privacy of our own room. Since the weather was nice year-round, the front porch and back patio served as outdoor parlors, and we made do in the kitchen on those rare rainy days.

I'd never met David's lawyer, and within minutes of showing him into the kitchen, I knew I did not share David's high opinion of the man. Some call it women's intuition; others call it psychic powers. Whatever it was, I sensed an unscrupulous core to Mr Allenby's character that he covered with what he considered irresistible charm. To be fair, he'd probably been a pretty baby and a handsome enough little boy, but the once-attractive, youthful features had coarsened as he matured. He was not the ladykiller he thought he was. I reminded myself that my estimation mattered for nothing as long as he was a crackerjack lawyer.

'Mr Allenby, please have a seat and tell me what has happened.'

'Call me Mike.'

For all that he'd rushed over, Mr Allenby seemed in no hurry to enlighten me. He took a cigarette out of his silver case, fixed it into his Bakelite holder, and inhaled dramatically. Only then did he lean forward on his elbows and, fixing me with what I'm sure he thought were bedroom eyes, say, 'My client requested I see you at once and let you know the score.' He filled his lungs again, leaned back, and crossed his legs in a preening manner before exhaling. This routine could not possibly impress any female over the age of ten.

I'd reached the end of my patience. 'What are the charges, Mr Allenby?'

'Murder, robbery, insurance fraud, and tax evasion.'

I nearly fell out of my chair. Bootlegging, I expected. Failure to fill out the proper forms, I expected, or some slap-on-the-wrist charges that could be dismissed with a fine or a bribe. But *murder*? My throat closed. I couldn't make a sound.

Satisfied that he'd knocked the wind out of me, Allenby continued. 'It's all about the incident in Arizona last July, of course. He said you were on that train that was hijacked with his liquor . . . ah, medicine . . . on board.'

'I . . . uh . . . yes. Yes, I was.' The word *murder* had filled my head with visions of a gallows and a hooded hangman, and I struggled to pull my attention back to Allenby. 'But . . . well, it *was* his liquor, wasn't it? So there should be no question of theft, and as for the men who were killed in the gunfight, even the local sheriff agreed that it had been self-defense. They were about to shoot us.'

'We're counting on you to testify accordingly. And we've already talked to that sheriff in Arizona. What's his name? Barnett?'

'Barnes. I can tell you the names of others on that train who could support my story.' I spelled the names of the sisters and the waiter who'd been with me in the dining car when it was hijacked. 'When's the trial?'

'In a few weeks. No date set yet. Considering the gravity of the charges, there's no question of bail. I tried, but the donations weren't greasing the skids like they usually do.' He shook his head. 'I wish to hell I knew why everybody suddenly got religion.'

'When are visiting hours?'

Mr Allenby shook his head. 'These are federal charges. He's been moved to the downtown jail.'

'Where's that?'

'Near the courthouse at Main and Temple. But save yourself the trip. You won't get in.'

'What if I say I'm—'

'Doesn't matter if you're his wife, his sister, or his mother dying of cancer, hon. They aren't letting anybody see him but me, and they're making it damn hard for me.'

But he agreed to take David a letter – one that would probably be read by the guards, he cautioned – so I sat down and began to write.

FIVE

I t was early days for *The Black Pirate*, but we spent the next week filming some of the final scenes with Billie Dove, the actress who played the captive princess. The general public would be surprised to learn – as I had been – that scenes weren't filmed in order from beginning to end; it would have been easier for the actors to work that way but harder for everyone else, however the real reason was cost. Sequential filming took longer, so we skipped around, grouping scenes according to their sets and which extras were involved.

Technicolor brought new challenges. For one thing, it brought a complete change of camera equipment, which cost a king's ransom. Which is why the studio needed David's money. Colors filmed indoors looked different when filmed outdoors, meaning we needed twice the costumes so that the princess's dress wouldn't change shades of blue when she moved from the captain's quarters to the deck, which is why I was dashing back and forth from the set to Wardrobe and Make-up a hundred times a day.

'Jessie, we've got the indoor shawl. Miss Dove thinks she left the other one in Make-up. And tell Roy we'll need him in thirty minutes.'

That's why I was in Make-up on Saturday when Barbara Petrovitch caught sight of me. I hadn't seen her since she'd returned to work.

'Oh, Jessie!' she called. 'Do you have a minute?'

I didn't, but I skidded to a halt. 'Barbara! I'm so glad to see you back at the job! We all missed you on location.'

'Yes, yes. I'm glad to be back. It's so very hard to concentrate . . . but it's worse at home alone. I'm lonesome for Joe.' Her eyes grew misty. I understood. I was lonesome too, but my own situation was nothing compared to hers. David would be back soon; Joe would never come home. Feeling guilty, I gave her a hug.

'Jessie,' she said with a tremor in her voice, 'there's been no news on Joe's killer. The police don't care about finding him any longer.'

'Oh, Barbara, I'm sure that's not the case. These things take time. I know they're doing their best.'

She shook her head. 'I called yesterday and talked to that detective in charge. He sounded impatient, like I was bothering him. Told me he'd call as soon as they knew anything, but I know a cold shoulder when I get one.'

'I'm sure he'll let you know as soon as they have any solid information.'

'They've given up. I could hear it in his voice. I mean, the murderer just vanished into thin air, so what can they do? And so, well, I wondered . . . everyone knows how good you are at solving murders, would you . . . I mean, could you solve this one too?'

'Gosh, I don't think I could do better than the police.' That was false modesty on my part. Truth was, I *did* think I could do better than the police, because I had done just that in the recent past. Why, was anybody's guess – my take was that the honest few on the police force lacked imagination and the dishonest ones were so busy taking bribes from bootleggers, they couldn't be bothered with solving crimes. I didn't have any special talent, but I seemed to notice things others didn't. And my knack for impersonation didn't hurt my ability to collect information.

'That's not so!' Barbara protested. 'Everyone at the studio talks about how you figured out who killed Lila Walker when the police never even investigated her death.' Tears pooled in the corners of her eyes as she fished in her pocket for a handkerchief. 'I know nothing will bring Joe back. I just want justice for him. He was such a good man. It's not right that his killer would get away with murder. Why, he might kill somebody else!'

Tears conquer all. Besides, if truth be known, I'd been burning with curiosity since I'd first heard about the weird circumstances surrounding Joe's murder and the vanishing killer. I pushed any worries about danger to the back of my mind. Think of poor Barbara, I told myself. I'd just dig around a little and see what turned up. This investigation wouldn't be dangerous.

I patted her arm. 'Sure, Barbara, sure. Don't cry. I'll give it a try.'

'Oh, thank you, Jessie!' She grasped my hand and kissed it, embarrassing me so much I looked over my shoulder to make sure no one was watching. 'Thank you, thank you! I know you'll succeed. You're so clever.'

Assuring her I'd do my best, I extricated myself from the awkward scene and fled to the safety of the pirates.

The next day was Sunday, and I figured no harm would come from visiting the scene of the crime to ask a few questions. And the investigation would take my mind off David. Hopping a Red Car downtown, I arrived at the Lyceum Theater on South Spring Street in plenty of time for Sunday afternoon's opening matinee. Back in its heyday, the Lyceum had been a theater for vaudeville and legit, but changing times had caused its owner to embrace the pictures exclusively. As I approached, I saw an old man selling popcorn on the sidewalk. Food was never allowed inside theaters, but it smelled so good that I promised him I'd buy a bag if he were still there when I came out.

The feature film wasn't due to start for half an hour, and I had work to do. I bought a dime ducat for a Buster Keaton picture I'd already seen and explored the lobby and the orchestra floor, noting the position of the exits and the lava-tories before climbing the stairs to the balcony. Halfway up, I reached the unmarked door to the projectionist's booth. It was closed, and my knock was met with silence. I tried the handle. Locked tight.

The theater was large with a balcony that held more than two hundred red-plush seats. One glance over the railing to the floor below was enough to tell me that no man, even an acrobatic wonder like Douglas Fairbanks, could jump down safely since he would have landed on seat backs and not on a flat floor. I thought it unlikely anyone could have survived without a broken leg at the very least. No handholds below the railing would have permitted a man to shorten the drop, no closets or alcoves or water closets offered a hiding place, and the single staircase was the one I'd used coming up, the one that passed the projectionist's booth. The only place a man might have concealed himself was under the seats, and to do that, he would have to have been as small and thin as a child.

The sound of a door closing drew me back down to the projectionist's booth. A boy with thick cheaters and a bad complexion answered my knock. He looked about seventeen.

'Hello,' I said, offering my hand to shake. 'I'm Jessie Beckett, and I'm investigating the Petrovitch murder. I know you're busy getting ready for the 11 o'clock, but I wonder if you could answer a couple of quick questions for me about the day Joe Petrovitch was shot?'

'Well, I don't—'

'Don't worry, I won't hold you up – you can go ahead and load the first reel while we talk.' Taking advantage of his youth, I stepped past him and into the small booth before he could think of a polite way to refuse. 'It must have been shocking for you – how did you react when a stranger burst through the door? Or was that how it happened?'

He removed his cheaters and polished the lenses on his shirttail. 'That's just how it happened, miss. Like I told the police – you're not from the police, are you?'

'No, I work for Douglas Fairbanks and so does Mrs Petrovitch.'

That seemed to be better credentials than the police. 'Oh, I see. Sure, like I told the cops, this man came in without knocking. He wore a red coat. He was holding a gun. He said something I couldn't understand, then he fired three shots right into Joe.' The memory made him wince.

'What else did you notice about him . . . ah, what did you say your name was?'

'Ben Salinas.' He held out his hand. 'Pleased to make your acquaintance, Miss Beckett. And the other thing I noticed was he wore eyeglasses.'

'Like yours?' His had dark, thick rims.

'Rounder than mine, but pretty much the same.'

'I see. Anything else? Was he tall?'

'No, average.'

'Fat?'

'No, average. He had a beard.'

'What color?'

'Dark.'

'Big and bushy? Or cut close to the skin?'

'Not so big. Not like a mountain man or anything like that.'

'A mustache?'

'Yes, a thin mustache. Like Mr Fairbanks has.'

'Did you notice anything else about him? Like was his skin pale or reddish, or were his eyes small or bug-eyed?'

He gave this due consideration before shaking his head. 'No, he was just regular looking.'

'What was he wearing besides the red coat?'

'A cap. I didn't notice his trousers or shoes.'

'Was his hair under the cap dark like his beard?'

'I couldn't say. The cap covered it up, I expect.'

'What did you mean when you said he shouted something you didn't understand?'

'It was some foreign talk.'

'Oh? Did you recognize the language?'

'Naw. It didn't sound like Spanish. I don't know any Spanish, but I hear a lot of it around here, so I kinda know what it sounds like. And it didn't sound like Latin – I go to church every Sunday and the priest talks Latin. But those are the only two languages I ever heard.'

'But Joe seemed to understand it?'

He shrugged. 'I guess so. Maybe it was Joe's language.'

'Joe was foreign?' No one had mentioned that.

'I guess so. He had a funny accent anyway.'

'Where was he from?'

'I don't know. But he was from somewhere else. His English wasn't that good.'

It was an interesting picture I was assembling, a picture of a killer who spoke a mysterious foreign language and sounded suspiciously average. No memorable features except a beard, mustache, and eyeglasses – all of which could be removed in one second flat. I had a strong hunch that these accessories were part of a disguise.

'Did you know anyone who disliked Mr Petrovitch?'

'Not enough to kill him.'

'What did you think of him?'

Ben looked around nervously, as if someone might be standing close enough to overhear us. No one was anywhere near. 'He never said much. He taught me to do this job.'

'That was good of him.'

'Well, yeah. But it was so he could leave during the film.'

'Leave to go where?'

'He never said. He didn't talk much, and I didn't like to ask questions.'

I released Ben Salinas to his film reels and made my way back to the lobby where I waited unobtrusively until the film had begun. Once the lobby cleared, I approached the ushers, who by then had gathered at the open door where a fragrant breeze cooled the air. There were six of them, all young and bored. No doubt they'd seen the film a dozen times. I picked out the oldest-looking one, a freckled lad of about sixteen, and gave him a flirty smile as I held out my hand.

'Hey, boys. I'm Jessie Beckett, and I'm here on behalf of Mrs Petrovitch to ask a few questions about Joe Petrovitch's murder. Were any of you fellas here when he was killed?'

'Sure,' said the target boy, who no doubt pegged me at his own age. 'I was here. I told the cops everything. Sam and Marty were too,' he said, pointing with his thumb to two younger boys. 'Jake wasn't.' He gestured toward Jake, who looked glum to have missed this exciting day in history.

'I was here too,' offered another boy, not to be outdone. 'I helped the cops search the audience as they left. The people didn't know there had been a murder, not then they didn't. No one heard the gunshots over the noise of the music.'

'Tell me what happened after the gunshots.'

Proud to be asked, the boys jockeyed to be first. The oldest lad won out. 'I heard the three shots, but I thought they were just some popping noise from the projector. I didn't think anything about it. Then a minute later, the assistant Ben, he comes running downstairs like he's seen a ghost and he yells,

"Someone shot Joe!" And I thought . . . well, we all laughed 'cause we thought he was joking. Then we knew he wasn't. "Call the cops!" he shouted.'

'Who called the cops?'

'I did,' piped up a younger boy with pride. 'I ran into the street and saw a cop at the corner, so I ran over and got him here right away.'

'And no one left the theater then?'

They shook their heads.

'And what other doors are there in this theater that someone might have used?' The boys pointed to several lobby doors. 'No, I mean, what about doors behind the screen or in the back?'

'No door behind the screen, but there's a door that goes to the back alley. You get there from the side aisle in front of the screen.'

I'd seen that one during my earlier tour of the place. 'So someone could have run downstairs from the balcony and into the orchestra, and then out that side door?' I asked.

'Sure they could of, but one of us would of seen him and people in the audience would have noticed when the door opened and all the light came in, and no one did.'

'Tell me what happened when the police arrived.'

The older boy resumed his tale. 'The first copper went up to the projection booth and saw the mess. He said Joe was dead. All bloody and very dead. He ran to the call box to get help and soon five more coppers showed up. Two went to that side door, the rest stayed right here –' he pointed to the lobby exits – 'and waited for the picture to end. It was Chaplin's *The Gold Rush,* and it didn't have long to go. No one left the theater during that time. Then, when the picture was over, people started coming out. The coppers knew who they were looking for – red coat, beard, specs – and they knew he hadn't left the theater yet, so they waited at each exit and let people leave slowly, one by one. That was a stupid killer, to wear a bright red coat that would be so recognizable. They stopped every man who even came close. No one complained, once they knew a murder had been done.'

'And no red coat or gun was ever found?'

'Nope.'

'Did they search people carefully or just look at them? And what about women's handbags?'

'They searched pretty good. And every handbag too, looking for a gun. I helped with that.'

Either the coat and gun had made it past the cops, which seemed unlikely given their search of the exiting audience, or they'd been abandoned in the theater. The 'stupid killer' seemed fiendishly clever to me. I'd learned enough from my stint with vaudeville magic acts to know that obvious details like a red coat were meant to distract. Could the killer have been a magician? 'Was the theater thoroughly searched afterward?'

'Three times!' declared the shortest boy. 'The cops went over it with whisk brooms and found nothing.'

'Under the seats? Inside the commode tanks?'

They nodded.

I was marshalling my thoughts at this point, wondering if the police had searched the women as closely as the men and thinking that if I were the killer, I'd have positioned a female confederate in the audience who would hide my pistol and red coat beneath her skirt. Then another safe place to stash a gun in a theater occurred to me.

'How much time between the end of this show and the start of the next?' I asked.

'About half an hour.'

'How would you boys like to help me find the murder weapon? If it didn't leave the theater, I bet I know where it is.'

SIX

Barbara Petrovitch was delighted to see me. 'Welcome, Jessie, come in! Can I bring you some lemonade?' The popcorn had made only a dent in my appetite, so I dug into the cake she set in front of me. 'Eat, please. I have so much food . . . people have been so kind. Mr Shala, a friend of Joe's who came to the funeral, brought this walnut cake over just this morning. It's called a *torta*. He said it was made from a traditional Albanian recipe. His wife made it – isn't that dear? Now, tell me, you've been working on the murder already, haven't you? I can tell!'

'I visited Joe's theater a little while ago. And I wanted to ask you some questions, if you don't mind.'

'Ask, ask. I'm ready. But eat up, first, then let's move out onto the front porch. The beautiful day lifts my spirits.'

I soon polished off the delicious *torta*, and we settled into the wicker chairs. 'I only just learned that Joe spoke English with an accent. He wasn't born here?'

'No, but he lived in America for many years. I don't know how many. Maybe ten. Yeah, ten at least. Maybe fifteen. I don't really know. He came from Serbia when he was young and changed his first name to Joe. He said it made him feel more American.'

I had heard of Serbia. I didn't know where it was, but it had something to do with the start of the Great War back in 1914. 'So his native language was Serbian?' She nodded. 'Do you speak Serbian?'

'Gracious, no.'

'Well, it seems the killer did. A few words at least. Did the police know that?'

'I think so . . . I'm not sure.'

'I don't remember meeting any of Joe's relatives at the funeral.'

'He didn't have any. He told me that when he came to America, a distant cousin in New York gave him a job and put him up until he got his feet on the ground, but that's all. He never spoke about any family in Serbia. He didn't talk about the past at all. I think it was too painful. I asked once and it upset him so much, I didn't dare bring it up again.'

'I understand.' And I did. Asking the wrong questions in this house got you a fat lip. I thought of young Salinas back at the theater, also reluctant to question Joe.

'That New York cousin wrote him a letter just a few weeks ago. The only time he ever wrote was whilst we were married. I wanted to write back and tell him about Joe's passing, but

. . .' Her lower lip trembled. 'But I didn't have a return address. The police brought the letter back yesterday.'

I frowned. 'What did the police want with the letter?'

'They wanted to get someone to read it. It was written in Serbian, but I didn't know that for sure then because I'd never seen Serbian written down. They found someone who could read it.'

'What did it say?'

'Nothing much. Do you want to see it?' She rose from the chair before I could respond and disappeared into the house.

I let my eyes wander up and down and across the tree-lined street. It was a friendly neighborhood with small houses neatly painted and yards kept tidy. Children sped past on bicycles, a man was washing a roadster, and barefoot youngsters splashed in and out of a tin tub. Joe Petrovitch was proving stubbornly unknowable. My investigation wasn't going anywhere until I could learn more about him and why someone would want to kill him. A cousin would surely know some history.

Barbara returned in a minute with the letter. A postmark from September 20, four weeks ago, canceled its two-cent stamp. There was no return address.

I removed the single sheet of paper and glanced at the writing. It wasn't like Spanish with letters like ours, nor was it like Chinese with no alphabet a regular person could make out. It was something in between, with some normal letters and some symbols. It looked to be only a few sentences. It was signed with a single, short name, a name that started with what looked like a P. I wondered if it was his first name and whether his last name might be Petrovitch, like Joe's. 'Did the police tell you what it said?'

She nodded. 'They found a man – a policeman, as a matter of fact – right here in Los Angeles, who was born in Greece or Macedonia or somewhere like that and who knew some Serbian. He said the languages were similar and he could make out what it said. The cousin was writing to tell Joe that a friend of his who lived in New York had died. He was a cook in a restaurant.'

'Does it give his name?'

'I think so, but I don't remember.' I examined the letter

again. There seemed to be some words that might have been
a name, but the odd alphabet made it impossible for me to
tell. I handed the letter back to her. 'Joe must have been pretty
upset when he got this.'

'He didn't say anything about it to me, but I never saw him
sad. He kept his feelings locked up tight.'

'Did Joe have a group of friends he liked to go around with?
You know, men who would get together for drinks, cards,
pool, or anything like that?'

'Well, Joe was kind of a loner, but sure, there were some
friends. He used to go downtown on Saturday nights.'

'Were any of them Serbian?'

'Oh, I wouldn't know about that. I never met them. They
didn't come over here. Joe liked to keep his private life private.'

Even from his wife, it seemed. 'Did you see any men at
the funeral who might have been friends of his? Men you
didn't know, but who introduced themselves as Joe's friends?'

'N-no, I don't think so, but I don't remember that day too
well. Maybe my brother Simon could answer you better.'

'It would help to find this cousin and a few of Joe's friends.'

'Why?'

I couldn't say what I was thinking, that it was strange that
no one, including his wife, seemed to know much about this
man's past. Surely there was someone, somewhere, who did.
'I'd like to talk to someone who knew Joe. Outside of the
home, I mean. Maybe then we'd learn if he had any enemies
or was involved in any activities that might have gotten him
killed.'

'Gracious, my Joe would never do anything illegal like
bootlegging or gambling!'

Unless he was like David, using a respectable job to hide
his criminal goings-on. Funny how blind women could be
when it came to their men.

'I'm sure that's true, but it would be good to talk with a
friend or two. I understand your brother didn't get along with
Joe.'

'Oh, no! Where did you hear that? You're mistaken.
Everyone liked Joe. He and Simon were fast friends. Joe was
such a dear. Never touched a drop, not like some I could

name.' Her voice took on a wistful note and a faraway look came into her eyes. I braced for the flood of tears that never came.

'But they fought once.'

She waved her hand as if shooing away flies. 'They were like brothers. Brothers quarrel sometimes. Simon misunderstood some things that he blamed on Joe when they were really my fault.'

'What was that?'

'I don't see that it matters . . .'

'I believe it does, Barbara.'

'Oh, of course, if you say so, of course. Well, I'm ashamed to say that I wasn't always the best of wives,' she said, smoothing her skirt with her hands in a nervous sort of way. 'I'd do things – silly things – that would provoke Joe. Dinner wouldn't be on time, or his shirts wouldn't be ironed properly – things that were easy to do right. He was particular and liked things just so. I'm so stupid sometimes. He had good reason to be angry with me.' She gave a little-girl giggle that grated. 'He only corrected me because he loved me so much and wanted me to be perfect, but sometimes he didn't know his own strength. Some men don't, you know? Afterward, he was very, very sorry and would be so sweet, begging my forgiveness and bringing me flowers to make up for his moment of weakness. He never intended to hurt me. I knew that. Of course, I forgave him. I understood. I'm sure you know how it is with men, they can't always control their passionate natures, and Joe was a passionate man.'

The first time a passionate man knocked me around would be the last time he'd get the chance, but I nodded through clenched teeth and told Barbara I'd see her at the studio tomorrow. As I rode the Red Car home, I wondered if the police had tracked down any of Joe's Los Angeles friends for questioning – if, indeed, there were any. It seemed none had come to his funeral – none that Barbara remembered anyway, and considering the amount of publicity surrounding his death, it was inconceivable that his friends would not be aware of it. I turned my thoughts toward finding the New York cousin.

*   *   *

The sight of Officer Carl Delaney perched on the front porch of our old Fernwood farmhouse brought me up short. He was sitting on a rickety wooden chair with peeling paint and a broken stretcher, his legs extended straight out before him and his face hidden behind the Sunday paper, but I knew who it was. His uniform and his nerve gave him away. No other cop in all of Los Angeles would have made himself as much at home on my front porch. I stopped on the sidewalk, still as a stalking cat, while I tried to figure out what he was up to and how to play it.

'Come join me,' he called, without even rustling the damn newspaper. The man had eyes in the back of his head.

'What laws did I break now?' I groused as I climbed the steps.

He rested the newspaper in his lap. His warm brown eyes smiled at me, and I let down my guard a little. 'None that everybody else isn't breaking, but why don't we talk about crime for a while? Your recent adventures in crime solving, I mean.'

My guard went back up. 'I haven't solved any crimes.'

'Not in the last week or two, I guess – have a seat there, Jessie – but you're off on another murder investigation as sure as I'm sitting here minding my own business, which is what I wish you'd do now and then, for your own good. The Los Angeles city fathers, in their infinite wisdom, have employed hundreds of men to fight crime and investigate murders, and they prefer that pretty young girls not get involved in this dangerous business.'

'Well, bully for the city fathers. I'm not involved in any dangerous activity.' I used my upstage, snooty voice that would cow most people. Not Carl. He merely regarded me as if I were a fourteen-year-old brat in need of reining in.

'Come on, Jessie, sit down. Let's not quarrel. Even if you don't realize it, I'm on your side.'

'Really?'

I glared at him for several moments before I realized it was futile. I was not going to intimidate this man. He already knew he was not going to intimidate me – he'd ceased trying months ago. I gave in and took the other dilapidated wicker chair. 'So,

Carl. It's been a long day. I'd like a drink. Can I get you one?
I've got gin or whiskey – the real McCoy. Or are you going
to arrest me for violations of the Volstead Act?'

'Not if you tell me you've had this liquor since before
Prohibition started.'

'I've had this liquor since before Prohibition started.'

He smiled at the bald-faced lie. 'Then it's legal. I'll have
whiskey with a piece of ice, if you have any. No water.' He
went back to the newspaper as I entered the house.

Myrna heard me come up the stairs to the bathroom and
stuck her head out of her room. 'He's been here over an hour,'
she whispered. 'He asked where you were, but I told him I
didn't know. And it wasn't a lie; I didn't know. Where were
you? He's not going to arrest you again, is he? He's kinda
cute, isn't he?'

'Don't worry. I was investigating that shooting at the Lyceum
Theater downtown, and somehow he found out about it.' I
shook my head in bewilderment. 'The man must be clair-
voyant.' I heard voices coming from the porch.

'Sounds like Helen's home from the market,' said Myrna.
'Melva and Lillian are at the beach with friends.'

'What are *you* doing home alone on a pretty Sunday
afternoon?'

'Rehearsing my part for tomorrow. It's that one I told you
about, for *Caveman*. I'm not sure, but I think if I do a very,
very good job, I'll get my name in the credits this time.'

I squeezed her hand. 'I'd like to see you do your bit, after
Carl's gone home.'

I took my time washing up before taking my bottle of
whiskey down to the kitchen for glasses. Helen Reynolds, a
salesgirl at Robinson's department store who had recently been
promoted from gloves to unmentionables, was there, unloading
a box of groceries. A gawky child stood beside her, arms
dangling at her sides.

If she hadn't been wearing a sailor dress with pleated skirt,
I'm not sure I'd have been able to determine whether she was
male or female, and it took a second hard look to peg her age.
She was about twelve or thirteen, I guessed, and a more unat-
tractive girl would be hard to find. All knees and elbows, she

had a pointed little nose, cheekbones like an Apache Indian, angry eyes hooded by bushy brows, and dark, uneven hair she must have hacked off herself with a dull knife. A battered straw hat and scuffed Oxfords completed the look.

'Hello, Helen,' I said as I fished the ice pick out of the utility drawer. 'Hello,' I added to the young person.

'Oh, Jessie, this is Kit Riley. She's a cousin of mine who's staying with me for a week.'

'Hello, Kit. How nice to have you visit with us.'

Kit's unblinking eyes followed me to the icebox where, pick in hand, I started chipping away at the block of ice in the top compartment. Clearly, the rude little girl was unhappy with the arrangement.

'Um, Kit's deaf, Jessie. She can't hear or speak. Her mother said she can read and write, though, so we need to write things down when we want to talk to her. I've got this notepad to use.'

'I see,' I said, somewhat abashed at having judged her so quickly. I took the pencil and wrote 'Welcome Kit!' on the pad. She glanced at it but made no response. 'I didn't know you had family in Los Angeles, Helen.'

'I didn't either. Rose Ann Riley – that's Kit's mother – is my mother's cousin, so I guess that makes Kit and me second cousins, right? But I didn't know Rose Ann lived in Los Angeles. And I've never met Kit before today.'

I nodded to Helen as I poured three fingers of golden liquid into each glass, added a chunk of ice, and rejoined Carl on the porch. It was top quality hooch, part of the large shipment of legal, 'medicinal' whiskey that David had bought for his drug stores. The best medicine money could buy. Carl probably knew it came from David's stock, but I didn't mention that. I didn't want to talk about David and his arrest, not to Carl. I didn't want to see Carl hide his satisfaction.

'Damnation!' he said, savoring the first sip. 'I haven't tasted whiskey like this in years. Thank you kindly, ma'am.'

The chair swing creaked when I sat, and I caught Carl glancing at the blue ceiling as if to make sure the chains were fastened securely. We shared the silence for a few minutes, each waiting for the other to break it. Finally I did.

'So how did you know I was investigating the Lyceum murder?'

'Well, now, let's see, it was about one minute after you left the theater that those usher boys called down to headquarters all excited, asking for Bruce Vogel, the detective investigating that case, so they could tell him what they'd found. They dropped your name, of course, and he recognized it.' I admit this gave me pause, that police detectives in downtown Los Angeles were recognizing my name when I lived over here in Hollywood, but I shrugged it off, telling myself that I couldn't worry about policemen's gossip. 'Vogel knew I'd had some dealings with you in the past, so he telephoned me.'

'So you could warn me off?'

In no rush, he savored another sip of whiskey. 'I've given up trying to warn you off. You're stubborn as a team of mules and set on getting your own way, and I know when I'm licked. I persuaded Vogel that you could help him. He didn't want to work with a girl, but I said I would.'

'Why?'

'Because I want to solve this murder, and I don't much care how it gets done or who gets the credit. And while you can be a pig-headed young lady, you also have an uncanny knack for reading people, for sensing what they are thinking. I've never known a person to notice things the way you do. It's a shame the department doesn't hire women because you'd peel the paint off most of the detectives on the force.'

I almost thanked him for the compliment, but he had more to say, and I wanted to hear it all before I let praise go to my head.

'Since I know you're going to keep at this with or without my approval, I'd prefer to be working with you, in case you stumble into something dangerous. What do you say?'

Now it was my turn to sip my drink and contemplate our tree-lined street. No question I could use someone on the police force to give me information about what they had discovered and what they were thinking. Carl was honest – probably the only honest cop on the Los Angeles roster – and he caught on fast. I liked Carl okay, and I trusted him as much as I could ever trust a man wearing a police uniform. A lifetime in vaudeville had left me skittish around cops. All vaudeville performers are. We're easy targets. Traveling around like we do from town to town, never staying in one place for longer than a week, we get blamed for lots of things we don't do. People love vaudeville players when they're on stage; off stage we're no better than gypsies or tramps, always on the move. It's simpler to pin crimes on us than to bother finding the real culprit.

I decided to accept, but I kept him waiting a while longer, just as he had. I saw his lips twitch, and I knew he had recognized my payback. 'It's a deal,' I said finally. I held out my hand and we shook.

'So, partner, tell me what you learned at the theater this afternoon.'

Having someone trustworthy to confide in can be a great relief. I knew Carl would understand what was bothering me. He was good at understanding.

'You know what, Carl? It wasn't what I expected. After I talked with the ushers and the projectionist, I started thinking hard about the killer. A stupid man, said one of the ushers, to wear a red coat so easily recognized. But the killer wasn't stupid at all. He was very clever. The coat's color was a distraction, like his disguise. The beard and mustache were designed to be noticed and to come off in a jiffy. He knew he couldn't run downstairs after firing those shots – the ushers would hear the gunfire and try to stop a fleeing man. Much safer to run up the stairs to the balcony and take off the disguise there. Even if they had halted the picture and emptied the theater right away, he'd have had time to change his appearance. It couldn't have taken more than a few seconds.'

'And as it turned out, they let the picture run to the end, giving him plenty of time.'

'Right. No one in the audience would have noticed the gunshots over the music and everyone would have been engrossed in the story – it was a Chaplin picture, after all – so no one in the balcony would have noticed a man entering from the rear door. Standing in the dark behind the last row, he could remove his disguise – the coat, eyeglasses, mustache, cap, and beard – without being seen. But what to do with these things? And more important, the gun? At first I thought he might have had an accomplice, a woman waiting in the balcony who could stash the disguise under a long skirt, maybe wrap the stuff around her thigh. That's always a possibility, but the gun makes for a more difficult problem. He had to assume the police would search the ladies' purses, so that was out. I imagined myself as the killer, standing behind the last row. I asked myself, What would I do with the disguise and the gun? The easiest solution would be to wipe the gun clean of fingerprints and leave everything on the floor under a seat. They would be found as soon as the balcony was searched. But that's not what happened. And I wondered why. Why didn't the killer just abandon the evidence and let the police find it? There would have been no way to link him to the stuff.'

I searched Carl's face, but he made no move to respond. So I answered my own question. 'Because he wanted to keep the disguise or the gun or both. He couldn't count on sneaking them out, and he couldn't leave them where the police would discover them. He needed to leave them hidden in a safe spot until he could return for them.'

'Why would he want to keep them?'

'I'm not sure. Guns are expensive. Or maybe this one had some sentimental value, like it belonged to his father, or something like that. Anyway, I asked myself, Where would I hide these things where they wouldn't be found during the police sweep? I looked around and the answer was easy, because it was the only one possible. Inside the cushion of a seat. There are a couple hundred seats in that balcony, but the one he chose would probably be in the back row, behind the audience. A knife or sharp instrument would cut the upholstery where it attaches to the frame, and he could slip the gun inside with the stuffing. Anyone sitting on that particular seat cushion would feel something lumpy, but he counted on that not happening.'

'What if there were people sitting in the back row? They would see him.'

I hadn't spent a lifetime in vaudeville theaters without

knowing where the best seats were. 'The favorite seats in any balcony are the front rows, so it was unlikely that there would be people in the back unless every seat in the theater was taken—'

'Or if a pair of young lovers was more interested in the dark than *The Gold Rush*.'

That sounded like the voice of experience, but I moved along without comment. 'Whatever the circumstances, there is one seat in this particular theater that I promise you no one ever sits in, and that is the one on the far right facing the stage, partly behind the pillar. You can't see the whole screen from that seat. I know. I tested it. I suspect that seat has never been used. The killer could sit himself in the seat beside that one and lean over to cut the plush upholstery without being noticed. I tried that too. And remember, it's dark while the film is running. He slits the fabric where it meets the frame, slips the gun inside where it's surrounded by the stuffing, and tucks the fabric back in. It won't hold if someone sits on it, but that's about as likely as a lightning strike. When the police search the joint, they don't manhandle each seat, they just look underneath where they see nothing.'

'What about the disguise and the red coat?'

'Those would fit inside a seat cushion too but not the same one. And none of the other cushions were slit, which is why I think the killer must have carried those items out of the theater with him. A theatrical coat like the red one he wore could be made of a thin fabric like silk, and maybe he folded it flat against his chest under his shirt or inside his trouser leg.'

'And the rest of the disguise?'

'The mustache and beard are so small they could have been concealed anywhere on his person. The eyeglasses he may have worn or put in a pocket. Who's suspicious of eyeglasses?'

'And you think he returned for the gun soon after?'

'I know he did, because the upholstery was slit and the gun wasn't there today.'

Carl fell silent as he sipped his whiskey and mulled over what I'd told him. So far, all the sharing had gone one way. It was my turn to ask questions.

'Does your fella Vogel have any suspects?'

He shook his head glumly.

'Does he know that Joe Petrovitch was a wife beater?'

He nodded glumly.

'Does he know that Simon Wallace, Barbara's brother, beat up Joe once and threatened to kill him if he hit Barbara again?'

More nods.

'Simon would seem to be a pretty good candidate for the role of murderer. Does Vogel know where Simon was that afternoon?'

'Simon Wallace is a longshoreman with a tough reputation all right, but he was ringside at the fights that day. With friends who vouch for him.'

'Friends often do that.' I was that kind of friend. I'd already decided I would say whatever I needed to say if it would keep David out of prison, perjury be damned. 'Isn't the new arena located near the Lyceum?'

'You're suggesting Simon Wallace ran four blocks to the theater, shot Joe, waited for the end of the film and the slow exit of all the spectators, and ran back to the arena without being missed?'

'It's probably a coincidence that the arena and the theater are so close together, but you gotta admit, it's one heck of a coincidence. However, I don't think Simon Wallace pulled the trigger. The young projectionist described the killer as an average-sized man. Average height, average weight, average looks. That's not how anyone would describe Wallace. Still, it wouldn't be the first time someone hired a killer to do the job. Did Detective Vogel ever find any of Joe's friends to interview?'

Carl shook his head.

'Didn't any of his friends come to the funeral?'

'Unfortunately, Vogel didn't have the chance to attend or he would have nosed around some.'

What Carl meant was Vogel didn't bother to attend or didn't think it worth his while. My opinion of the ineffectual Detective Vogel sank even lower. 'I talked to Joe's wife Barbara today. I saw the Serbian letter. Did you know about that?'

'Yep. Officer Steve Marks translated it for Vogel. It didn't

say much. Just that some friend of his had died in New York.'
'I'd like to know the name of Joe's cousin who wrote it.
Surely it's in there. I just couldn't read all those funny-looking
letters.'

'Why?' he asked, in an echo of the question Barbara had
posed an hour earlier.

'I thought if I could get his name, I might find out an address
and write him. Maybe learn something about Joe and whether
he had any enemies. For all we know, Joe is a New York
gangster who fled to the other side of the country – that would
explain why he has no past and no friends.'

'Until his past and his "friends" caught up with him, you
mean? I'll admit, Joe's murder does have the flavor of a mob
hit – deadly and efficient. I'll ask Marks if he remembers the
cousin's name; if not, I'll swing by the Petrovitch house and
pick up the letter so he can see it again.' He drained the last
of his whiskey. 'Any chance of another taste of that swell
firewater before I go?'

SEVEN

'Jessie, can I borrow your heavy blanket for a few days to
make a pallet on the floor for Kit?'

Helen had appeared at the kitchen door as I sliced off
two pieces of bread for a toasted cheese sandwich. Carl
had taken himself away, and I was ready for something to eat.
'Sure,' I said, plopping a chunk of butter in the frying pan
and cutting into a hunk of orange cheese. 'You could take my
bedspread too.'

Kit trailed into the kitchen behind Helen, sullen as a wild
animal newly caged, but since she couldn't understand the
conversation, I felt free to say, 'It's nice that she's come to
stay, Helen, but what are you going to do about tomorrow?'

'Tomorrow?' she asked.

Kit slumped into a chair and glared at me.

'Tomorrow. Monday. You, me, and the girls are all going

to work in the morning and Kit will be home alone all day. Or does she go to school?'

'Gosh, I never . . .' Helen reached for the pad of paper and scribbled something. Kit scribbled back. I looked over at the results. She'd written 'No school'.

I took up the pencil. 'Kit, we are afraid you will be lonely tomorrow, all by yourself and nothing to do.'

She'd scrawled 'Book.'

'She likes to read?' I asked Helen.

'I guess so. I'm sorry, Jessie, I really don't know what to do with her. Do you think it's a problem having her here alone all day tomorrow?'

'Certainly not for us, but I'm afraid she'll be bored to death. How old did you say she is?'

'Eleven. Gee, Jessie, what can I do? I need to go to work. You need to go to work. Everyone needs to go to work! Rose Ann should have known that I couldn't stay home with her.' She took the notepad and scribbled, 'I'll be home at 5:30. Will you be all right alone during the day?'

Kit gave the paper a contemptuous glance and, without picking up the pencil, gave a curt nod. Helen sighed. 'I hope I'm not arrested for truancy or something like that.'

'Don't worry, Helen, it's only a few days,' I said, taking a spatula and pressing my sandwich into the frying pan before flipping it over. 'There's plenty of bread and cheese, if you need some supper . . .'

The telephone bell in the back hall gave a harsh ring. Helen was closest. She stepped out of the kitchen and lifted the receiver. 'Jessie, it's for you.'

My heart gave a leap. Maybe it was David's lawyer with some good news.

No such luck. It was my Johnny-on-the-spot policeman.

'I didn't need to go by the Petrovitch home,' Carl said, his voice crackling across the wires. 'Detective Vogel had written out the translation Officer Marks provided. Unfortunately, there was no name for Joe Petrovitch's cousin. He signed the letter "Rodjak" which isn't his name. Turns out that means "cousin" in Serbian. He does tell the name of the cook who died – Jeton Ilitch, for what it's worth.' He spelled it for me. 'I know that isn't what you were looking for, but it's the best I could do. Sorry, kid.' I bristled. Only David could call me kid. My thank-you was frigid.

I finished the sandwich and milk, rinsed the bottle, and set it outside in the box for the milkman. Upstairs in Myrna's room, we played penny poker for an hour. I lost forty-five cents. Tomorrow's lunch would be a banana and coffee.

'Geez Louise, Jessie, you're miles away tonight,' exclaimed Myrna as she scooped up my last seven pennies. 'I know you're worried about David. We all are, but you can't let it consume you.'

Easy for her to say. But she was right.

For the remainder of the evening, I kept my thoughts busy trying to breach the barricades that blocked all progress on the Petrovitch case. It had been only one day, but I was stuck. The no-name cousin was the only link I had to Joe's past, but if I couldn't get to him directly, maybe the dead cook's name would lead me there. Jeton Ilitch, the cook. One of the New York newspapers would surely have printed an obituary and the obituary would surely have listed his surviving relatives. If I could hunt up even one of those relatives, he might lead me to this Rodjak cousin who had sent the bad news to Joe.

I knew from playing New York during my vaudeville days that the city had more newspapers than any city in the world, dailies like Pulitzer's *World* and Hearst's *Journal*, plus dozens more in every foreign language under the sun, but there was no way to search them from the other side of the country. So I stretched back into my own past and pulled forward the name of someone who could.

Grabbing a scrap of paper and a pencil, I began composing a telegram I would send the following morning to the Liberty Theater in New York City to Miss Adele Astaire. She was a vaudeville kid I'd met when I was six and she was eight – I'd adored her ever since.

DEAREST ADELE WISH I COULD HAVE SEEN YOU
AND FREDDIE IN LADY BE GOOD STOP EVERYONE
SO PROUD OF YOUR SUCCESS I LEFT VAUDEVILLE
LAST YEAR NOW WORK PICKFORD FAIRBANKS

STUDIO HOLLYWOOD LOVE JOB FRIENDS &
LIVING IN ONE PLACE STOP KNOW YOURE BUSY
PREPARING UPCOMING LONDON TOUR BUT
NEED HELP WITH MURDER INVESTIGATION
PLEASE VISIT JOURNAL OR WORLD OFFICES
FIND JETON ILITCH OBITUARY WAS COOK WHO
DIED FIRST HALF SEPTEMBER ALL INFORMATION
ABOUT HIM APPRECIATED ESPECIALLY NEXT OF
KIN
LOVE TO YOUR MOTHER AND FREDDIE FROM
BABY PS MY NAME IS JESSIE BECKETT NOW

I was busy scratching out as many unnecessary words as I
could to keep the price down when a knock at the door turned
my head.

'Sorry to interrupt,' said Helen. 'I wonder if I might have
that bedding? Or if you're busy, I can come back later.'

'No, no, I'm done. Just drafting a telegram to an old vaudeville friend.' Dragging my chair to the closet, I reached up to
the top shelf where I stored my extra blanket. It didn't get
much use in this climate.

'I guess you've got a lot of vaudeville friends, traveling
around like you did your whole life.'

'I suppose I do, but this is one I haven't seen in a dozen
years. Not since my mother died. Fortunately vaudeville friends
last forever. Here you go. And did you want my bedspread too?'

'If you can spare it.'

'Of course. It'll make a thicker mattress. Trust me, I'm a
pallet pro. I slept on the floor for much of my childhood. Have
you heard of Adele Astaire?'

Helen shook her head.

'She's the toast of Broadway, but New York's a long way
from here, so I understand why her name isn't familiar. Adele
and her little brother Freddie played the Orpheum circuit when
my mother and I did, and we shared a billing with them many
times over the years. Back then, their name was Austerlitz,
but when the Great War came, everything German sounded
dangerously unpatriotic, so their mother changed it to Astaire.
Our mothers were friends, although I was always proud that

mine was a performer while Mrs Astaire was just her children's manager.'

'So what's their talent? Do they sing and dance, like you?'

'They sing and dance a whole lot better than me! Plus Adele is a fabulous comedienne. She's always been the star of the act. They just wrapped up a long run of 'Lady Be Good', a Gershwin Brothers musical, and they're taking it to London next year. Have you heard of the Gershwin boys?'

'I'm afraid not.'

We girls liked to razz Helen that she was the only person in Hollywood who didn't care a fig about the pictures. That wasn't all – she wasn't interested in vaudeville, legit, or musical entertainments either, or anything that happened indoors. She suffered through her department-store job to pay the bills, but every other minute was spent hiking in the desert or along the seashore, picking up curious bits of nature and pretty rocks and sketching unusual flowers. Blonde and wispy, she was serious about a young man who was keen on wilderness camping – which gave us girls another reason to tease her.

'Well, I haven't seen Adele for years, but I thought she might be able to help me with this Petrovitch murder. Unless she's already left for London. I hope not. Here, this should give you enough to make a pallet for Kit. I think if you fold it this way . . .'

EIGHT

Monday evening, I left the studio through the front gate and climbed onto the Red Car toward downtown Los Angeles a scant five minutes after Director Parker dismissed us. Barbara had telephoned her brother, Simon, earlier in the day, explaining that she'd asked me for help and begging him to make time to answer my questions. He'd agreed, probably only to humor her.

I found the Wallace home with little effort. Simon was waiting on the front porch with his wife, Myrtle.

'Can I get you some lemonade, Jessie?' she asked. Her husband's glass was full of an amber liquid that did not resemble lemonade, and when I noticed a bottle of what looked to be genuine Old Grand-Dad at his feet, I couldn't help but wonder if it had come from one of David's drug stores.

But only lemonade was on offer, so I replied, 'I would love some, thank you.' Removing my hat and gloves, I helped myself to a seat in the shade.

While Myrtle clattered about in the kitchen, Simon glared at the unruly rose bushes creeping up the side of the porch, waiting, it seemed, for his wife to return before he opened the conversation. As soon as she handed me my glass, he began.

'Let me just start out honest, Miss Beckett, and say that I don't hold with females poking their noses into things that don't concern them. But I understand my sister asked you for your help, and I know you're a friend of hers, so I'll keep the rest of my opinions to myself. Why don't you tell me what you want to know, so we can be done with this, and I won't be late to my lodge meeting?'

'Thank you, Mr Wallace. I'm here to learn anything I can about Joe: his background, his friends, his family. Anything that might help me understand why someone would want to kill him.'

'Lotsa guys would want to kill him. Including me. But I didn't. The police know where I was when Joe was gunned down.'

'Do you know anything about his family or friends?'

'I don't know any more than Barbara when it comes to Joe's family. Don't think he had any in this country. He gave the impression that his family in the old country was dead or scattered in the war.'

'What about his friends here in Los Angeles?'

'You know what, it's hard to believe now but me and Joe were friendly back when he was courting Barbara. I even asked if he wanted to join my lodge. He said he didn't go in for that sorta thing. I didn't know any of his friends.'

'I understand you like going to the fights. Did you ever see Joe at the arena?'

He shook his head. 'Ran into him once in a gin joint on a

Saturday night. He was with some toughs. Nodded at me and kept going.'

'Did he drink or gamble?'

'No more or less than any man.'

'Was he involved in anything illegal?'

'Yeah, he drank and gambled. And years ago, right when Prohibition started, he worked someplace making bathtub gin. He gave us a bottle – remember, Myrtle?'

'Awful stuff,' she said. 'We had to mix it with juice to drink it.'

'His assistant at the theater said he'd leave the job for long periods. Any idea what he was doing?'

'Nope.'

'You stood beside your sister at the funeral, shaking hands with everyone who came. I know she appreciated that kindness. I wonder, though, did you meet anyone who said they were Joe's friend?'

'Yeah, a few.'

'Did you know them?'

'Never seen 'em before.'

'Do you remember their names or anything about them?'

He gave this serious thought before answering. 'Not really. I remember a coupla huskies who came in together. And another one who was a puny fella with an accent like Joe's. A nancy-boy.'

'Could you describe any of those men?'

'Just did. And that's all I can do for you, lady – I mean, Miss Beckett. You could help Barbara best by getting her to forget about that no-good bum and put all this behind her. She's a good girl, our Barbara. She'll have another chance, next time with a decent man, or I'll know the reason why.'

He got to his feet, signaling the end of the interview, and walked me to the corner where we waited for our streetcars. His came first. I was headed in the opposite direction, back toward Hollywood, and as I waited for my ride, I realized I was holding only one glove. And wouldn't you know, it was my nicest pair.

Vexed, I retraced my steps to the Wallace house, my eyes on the sidewalk. No glove. As I approached the house, there was Myrtle waiting on the porch, holding it up with a smile.

'Looking for this?' she called to me. 'I just found it underneath the chair where you were sitting.'

'What a relief! It's my favorite pair.'

'That's always the one you lose, isn't it?' She'd said scarcely a word while her husband was there; suddenly she seemed downright gabby. I thought she might want a bit of company, what with her husband going off and leaving her alone like that. When she perched on the step, I took it as an invitation to linger.

'I can see why you and your husband aren't sorry Joe is gone.'

'Well, I wouldn't wish death on anybody, and I'm sorry for poor Barbara, but the world is better off without that one, if you want my opinion.'

I did, very much. 'The police suspected Simon at first, didn't they?'

'Yes, and that was a little scary, I don't mind saying. I knew he couldn't have done it, but lots of people heard him threaten to kill Joe when he found out Joe was knocking Barbara around.'

'And he's a big, strong fella.'

She giggled. 'He is that. He's got a flash temper too, and he's quick with his fists, but my Simon's not a killer.'

'I take it he did beat up Joe once.'

'Twice.' She nodded, reaching into the pocket of her housedress for a cigarette and matches. She lit her own, then held them out to me. I took one. It seemed the sociable thing to do.

'He never hit you, did he?'

She looked shocked. 'Heavens, no! Simon believes only scum would hit a woman. A real gentleman, Simon is.'

'What did you think of Joe? Aside from his hitting your sister-in-law.'

'To my way of thinking, Joe was a good example of why a girl shouldn't marry a foreigner. They are just different. In a bad way.'

'I see.'

'But he was a good provider. He bought her that house.'

'In the time you knew him, was he always a projectionist?'

'That and making the gin Simon told you about. Whew! That stuff was rotgut. We never asked for another bottle, and he never offered.'

'Did Barbara know about that? She never mentioned it.'

'Barbara has a way of overlooking what she doesn't want to know. She probably told you Joe didn't drink, gamble, or hit her either.'

I admitted she had. My thoughts turned back to the Petrovitch house. Small but nice, and in a pretty neighborhood with shady trees and a riot of flowers. Of course, Barbara had a job too, and I guessed she made a bit more each week than my own $60, nonetheless, that house cost some money. Theater owners made a good living, but nobody working the operation did. I figured Joe was probably still working the gin job. Maybe that's what he was doing when he left that teenage boy in charge in the projection booth.

'I guess you don't remember meeting any of Joe's friends at the funeral?'

'Just the ones Simon mentioned. And I don't remember their names either. They weren't from his theater. I do remember that nice theater man, the manager, Mr Thomas or Thompson, I think it was.'

'Maybe that pair of toughs worked with Joe making gin.'

'Could be. If they did, you wouldn't want to go hunting them down, if you get my meaning.'

'I'm sorry . . .?'

'Just that I remember Joe saying, back when he and Barbara were newly married and he was still friendly with us, that the gin operation was run by the Ardizzone gang.'

'The what?'

'How long have you lived here?'

'About a year.'

Evidently that explained my woeful ignorance.

'Joseph Ardizzone is boss of those gangsters who do all the bootlegging in these parts. And most of the other crime that goes with it. You never heard of him?'

'Nope.'

'They call him "Iron Man" Ardizzone.'

That did ring a faint bell. I must have seen some reference

to 'Iron Man' in the newspapers. Had Joe Petrovitch run afoul of the gangsters who paid him? Or had he siphoned off some of the profits and paid the price?

NINE

A Western Union boy delivered Adele Astaire's reply on Wednesday, shortly after I arrived home from the studio. I tipped him a dime and ripped into it.

HOW WONDERFUL TO HEAR FROM YOU HOW EXCITING YOUR NEW LIFE IN HOLLYWOOD SOUNDS I DONT MISS VAUDEVILLES VAGABOND DAYS A BIT STOP MUCH NICER STAYING IN ONE PLACE FOR A WHILE STOP FREDDIE & I DELIGHTED TO HELP INVESTIGATE MURDER WE ARE AT LEISURE NOW PLANNING LONDON SEASON SO WENT AT ONCE TO NEWSPAPER OFFICE WHERE THEY HAVE PLACE CALLED MORGUE TO KEEP OLD NEWSPAPERS STOP ISNT THAT GRUESOME STOP NICE MAN RECOGNIZED US FROM SHOW & REMEMBERED DEATH OF COOK BUT HERES THE KICKER IT WASNT DEATH HIS WAS MURDER TOO STOP SMALL ARTICLE ON PAGE 3 SAID DINERS AT LA TERRASSE RESTAURANT SHOCKED WHEN GUNMAN SHOT COOK IN KITCHEN KILLER RAN OUT BACK DOOR GOT AWAY STOP

NEWSPAPERMAN SAID MURDERS LIKE THIS ARE COMMON STOP HAVE DOUBLED SINCE PROHIBITION BEGAN WITH GANGSTERS SHOOTING PEOPLE EVERY NIGHT STOP ARTICLE SAID POLICE ARE HELPLESS STOP NO NEXT OF KIN OR FUNERAL ARRANGEMENTS MENTIONED SORRY FOR DEAD END

WE ARE IN LONDON ALL NEXT YEAR WOULD

LOVE TO HAVE YOU STAY WITH US IF YOU COME
STOP MAYBE ONE DAY WE WILL COME TO
HOLLYWOOD TO BE IN PICTURES STOP FREDDIE
SAYS DONT MARRY ANYONE BUT HIM FONDLY
ADELE

My delight at hearing from my old friend soured as I realized
her reckoning was correct. A dead end. No next of kin to trace
back to Joe's cousin. The murder part came as a surprise,
though. Until that moment, I'd assumed Jeton Ilitch had died
of a fall down the steps or tuberculosis or perhaps been run
over in the clogged streets of New York City where horse-
drawn wagons jostled for space with gasoline-powered
automobiles and trucks. But Jeton Ilitch had not 'died'. He'd
been murdered. Did two men murdered on opposite sides of
the country merit the word coincidence? I figured it probably
did. These days, anyway.

Gangster killings had become a daily occurrence, although
most of them took place in big cities like New York, Detroit,
or Chicago. The victims were usually other gangsters, except
when the occasional bystander got in the way of the bullets.
The killers never saw the inside of a courtroom. It seemed so
unfair – David was in jail for far less.

I poured myself a glass of David's 'medicine', picked up a
sweater, and went to the patio to ponder my next move. The
flagstones that had soaked up heat during the day were giving
some of it back now that the sun had set, so it was pleasant
even as twilight was fading. I was not alone. At the edge of
the patio with her back against the house sat Kit, so still I
almost didn't notice her, her chin on her knees and her eyes
locked on the pages of a book balanced on her bare feet. I
would have acknowledged her with a smile but she never
looked up, so engrossed was she in her reading. That kid must
have cat's eyes, I thought, to read in such dim light. Then I
looked closer. I recognized the book. It was mine.

Well, it wasn't really *mine*. I'd borrowed it from one of the
switchboard gals. *The Sheik* by E.M. Hull was the scandalous
book that had inspired the Paramount picture of the same
name, the one that transformed Rudolph Valentino from

unknown Italian immigrant to the leading man who caused women all over the world to swoon with desire. Most fathers refused to allow their daughters to watch the film and most husbands forbade their wives, but somehow, it had earned Paramount a fortune, and Valentino-of-the-smoldering-eyes was poised to make a sequel. Clearly, this was not something an eleven-year-old girl ought to be reading, but that wasn't what troubled me. *The Sheik* had been on my bedside table under several magazines and a glass of water. Not only had Kit been in my room, she would have had to rummage around a good deal to have come across it.

I made excuses for her in my head: she was young; she didn't understand the concept of privacy; she'd finished her own book and had nothing else to do; she couldn't be expected to stay in Helen's room and the kitchen all day – but none of those took the sting out of my annoyance. I got the notepad and pencil from the kitchen and scribbled a few lines. When she didn't react when I approached, I tapped her on one knobby knee.

She looked up at me with eyes like the windows of a vacant house. I handed her the notepad. It read: 'Polite people ask before borrowing another person's belongings. In the future, please ask before you take anything from my room.' She gave my message a dismissive sniff and, without wasting a second glance in my direction, turned the page and resumed reading. I could have slapped the little brat.

And I might have too, if Melva hadn't called out to the house just then, 'Anyone who wants boiled potatoes and sliced ham for dinner, speak now or forever hold your peace so I know how many potatoes to peel. And come help me peel them.'

I went inside to take out my hostility on the spuds.

By the end of the meal, I'd cooled off enough to announce to the girls that I was going to walk to the library before it closed. I wrote the message so Kit could read it, and asked if she wanted to come along and choose some books. There may have been a spark of interest in her dull eyes; in any event, she nodded.

The Cahuenga Library on Santa Monica was not far from our house, so Kit, Helen, and I headed that way as soon as we'd washed up the dinner plates. 'I want to look at a map of Europe,' I told Helen, 'before someone finds out that I don't know where Serbia is.'

'Gosh, I don't know where Serbia is either,' she said, 'but I'm terrible with geography.'

'I know where England is,' I said. 'And France and Spain. The rest of Europe is somewhere to the right of those countries, but that's as good as I can do.' Like most vaudeville kids, I hadn't gone to school a single day of my life, and my lack of education embarrassed me sometimes. I'd brought some thin paper with me so I could trace a copy of a map to take home.

'Well, I don't want to look up anything,' said Helen. 'I'm just happy to get outside and walk in this glorious night-time air. Hear that? An owl doing his night-time hunting. I'm sure Kit will be happy to have some new books to read. She sure gobbles up the newspaper I bring home each day.' She heaved a great sigh. 'Work was so tiresome today. I'm sick of selling silk lingerie to haughty WAMPAS Baby Stars . . . Can't wait for Sunday when I can – oh, I wonder if Kit will want to go with me to the beach? Surely she will . . .'

'Maybe her mother will be back by then.'

'I hope so. I hope she'll pay for the cot.'

'Cot?'

'Oh, you didn't see it. I bought a canvas camp bed. Lillian and I carried it upstairs to my room earlier. Kit was afraid to sleep on the floor after she saw a spider last night. She's very afraid of spiders. I mean, none of us likes spiders, but she's *very* afraid of them. Trembling afraid. I killed the spider – it was just a little one – but that didn't console her. She says she can't sleep on the floor with the spiders. We don't have a davenport, so, I went out and bought a cot.'

'Well, it's not a bad thing to have, in case one of us has company.'

'Yeah, I know. I still hope Rose Ann will reimburse me.'

The next morning, I rose early to avoid the rush for the water closet. I flagged down a Red Car before eight o'clock, arriving at the studio minutes before the hour in time to grab some coffee at the canteen before heading to my desk. I had hardly reacquainted myself with my chair when I was called to the pirate set where we launched into the scene where Douglas gets his revenge for his father's death. Morning became afternoon without even a pause for lunch. Finally at three, Director Parker gave us fifteen minutes. Exhausted, I sank to the floor in a quiet corner where I sat Indian-style, balancing a root beer in one hand and a hot dog in the other. Douglas passed by, saw me, and paused just as I took a big bite.

'No, no, don't get up, Jessie,' he said when I started to rise. 'I heard from Mildred that you're investigating Joe's murder.'

I swallowed. 'If you've no objection.'

'Why should I? I hope you can do something. Poor Barbara is beside herself. And speaking selfishly, her mind's not on her work. We need her full attention. I'd rather you didn't take any time off to do it, though. At least, not until we're finished filming. Let me know if I can help with money.'

Not two minutes later, Barbara Petrovitch crept into my solitude.

'Thank goodness you're here! I mean, hello, Jessie. I was hoping you'd be here.' She held out an unopened envelope. 'This was returned in this morning's mail,' she said in a weak voice. 'I was afraid to open it . . .'

I glanced at the envelope. The black-ink address had been overlaid by an official-looking, red-ink stamp that proclaimed in all capitals: 'RETURN TO SENDER: DECEASED.'

'Is this your husband's handwriting?' I asked Barbara.

'It is. And it came back marked like that. Somebody else is dead. The person he wrote to.' She shivered.

The bodies were piling up.

I looked more closely at the address. The dead somebody had lived in St. Louis, Missouri. His name was Aleksandar Jovanovitch. 'Do you know this Jovanovitch person?'

'No. But I guess Joe did.'

'May I open it?'

Barbara cringed. Never mind that Joe had gone to his reward, the poor woman was still terrified of displeasing him. 'I . . . I guess so. I mean, there's nothing wrong with that now, I guess, is there?'

'Not a thing,' I said, slipping my finger carefully under the flap so as not to tear the envelope. I was betting the police would want to see this. I drew out a sheet of cheap paper. The message was in Serbian, although I did recognize two American words: Los Angeles. 'Not much we can do right now, Barbara. Let me give the police a call. We'll ask for that same man, Officer Marks, to come translate this for us. It may be nothing. Then again . . .'

Carl Delaney brought Officer Steve Marks by my house after supper. A burly man of about forty, Marks looked more crook than cop, with a dark countenance, bad teeth, and a frown that persisted even when he smiled. Which was only once. Melva and Lillian were still eating dinner, so I led the men through the house onto the patio for some privacy. 'Sorry we don't have a parlor,' I explained. 'We turned the parlor and the dining room into bedrooms so we could split the rent five ways instead of three.' Kit was there, sitting at the edge of the fishpond dropping crumbs to the goldfish. The newspaper she'd been reading was spread carelessly all over the ground. A flash of curiosity interrupted her stone-faced expression when she spotted us.

'That's Kit,' I said. 'My roommate's cousin. She won't bother us; she's deaf and dumb.'

Carl waved at her and smiled as we sat at the wooden table. 'I saw her last time I was here. She living with you gals now?'

'She's staying with Helen this week while her mother is out of town.' I handed the envelope to Marks and asked how he came to know Serbian.

'I am not Serbian,' he said with enough haste that I gathered it was a nationality he wanted no part of. 'I am Macedonian.' Thank heavens I didn't have to fake that I knew where that country was – I had it on my newly drawn map of Europe. It was above Greece, and the librarian told me it had joined up with some other countries to become Yugoslavia. 'In that part of the world, borders change often, and most people speak several languages.' He opened the envelope and studied the single sheet of paper before saying, 'It's written by Joe Petrovitch, of course. He writes, "Have you heard about the death of our friend in New York?"'

'Jeton Ilitch,' said Carl. 'The cook.'

I interrupted the translation to say, 'I learned something about the cook yesterday from a vaudeville friend in New York. She went to the newspaper office and found the article about his death. It wasn't just death. It was murder. He was shot at the restaurant where he worked. Something to do with gangsters, the police think. What do you make of that? Too much coincidence that two Serbian friends are shot within a few weeks of each other?'

Carl pondered this news for a moment before replying. 'Well, they don't seem to have been in touch with each other, so you can't argue they were working together. Murders in the big cities have doubled or tripled in recent years thanks to the gangsters. And immigrants – especially Irish, Jews, and Italians – make up most of those gangs, so they're the ones getting murdered. So, I guess I'm saying no, I don't think it's too big a coincidence for two immigrants to be murdered three thousand miles apart. Just a regular-size coincidence.' He turned to Officer Marks. 'So what else does Mr Petrovitch have to say?'

Marks cleared his throat. 'He tells the man Jovanovitch that he is well. He is married.'

'It sounds as if Joe has been out-of-touch with this friend for some years too,' said Carl, 'if he is just now mentioning his marriage.'

Marks refolded the paper. 'That's all?' I asked him. 'There's more writing than that.' I'd seen the words Los Angeles.

'The other part is of no interest to the case.' He looked back at the letter. 'It says, "I work as a director for a big moving picture company in Los Angeles and have a big house" – this is not true, we know, but he says it. "I hope you are well". That is all he says.' His translation complete, he set the letter on the table and turned tired eyes toward Kit who was trying to catch a goldfish with her hands.

'A man of few words, our Joe,' said Carl. 'What do you think, Jessie?'

'I think Joe and his friends have had no contact in recent years, not since Joe's marriage to Barbara, anyway, and I understand that was about four years ago, until the death of one caused this exchange of letters to start. I'm wondering when Aleksandar Jovanovitch passed away. A few weeks ago, like the cook in New York? Or a few years ago? How 'bout I check *Variety* and see if I know a vaudeville act playing St. Louis this week? Maybe somebody can find out the date of death for us.'

Carl stood. 'Supposing we find out. What does that tell us?'

'Depends. If it happened a good while ago, it's a vote for coincidence. People die all the time.'

'And if it happened recently?'

'Then I want to know how he died. If it was a heart attack, I'm still a believer in coincidences. If he was murdered, I'm jumping ship.'

TEN

David was never far from my mind. Every day, I pestered Mike Allenby for news. Any progress toward bail? How were David's spirits holding up? Had a court date been scheduled yet? Even bad news would have been better than drifting along without any information whatsoever. By now I had a first-name relationship with Veronica, a tart secretary with a nasal voice who slurped coffee while she talked on the telephone and blocked my every attempt to reach Allenby.

'Oh, you again. Sorry, dearie, we have no information for you today. Mr Allenby will telephone as soon as he has something to report. Bye bye, hon.'

David was no better. He didn't answer my letters, which meant he wasn't getting them. At least, that's what I chose to believe. And after that incident aboard the Catalina steamship, Douglas Fairbanks hadn't mentioned David a single time. Even Kit felt sorry for me. Once when I'd slammed the telephone receiver down after Veronica had given me the sack, I turned to find Kit leaning on the doorjamb staring at me with a concerned frown. Sometimes I had the notion she understood more than we gave her credit for.

That night, as some of us girls were relaxing on the patio, Lillian came outside with a pair of scissors, a mirror, and a comb in her hands. 'Jessie, can I bother you to trim my bangs? Any longer and I'll start tripping over furniture.'

'Sure. Pull up a chair.'

'And I want to look like Louise Brooks when you're done,' she teased.

I have no special talent as a hair stylist, but cutting a straight line ranks up there with my better accomplishments. As I snipped, an idea came to me. I looked at Kit, who had laid aside the newspaper and was watching the operation with unusual interest. Pointing to the scissors and then to her, I mimed the question by raising my eyebrows. To my surprise, she gave an eager nod. As Lillian stood up and brushed herself off, I motioned Kit to the chair.

'Next customer!' I said with a flourish. Suddenly, it was a group effort with Lillian holding the mirror and the others tossing out suggestions as I combed through Kit's tangles. In Hollywood, everyone was a director.

'Just below the earlobe,' said Melva.

'Even it up on the right,' said Lillian.

'Another half inch on the bangs,' said Helen. 'This is wonderful, Jessie. She's starting to look like a girl. Her own mother won't recognize her.'

'She's really not as bad looking as you think, is she?' mused Melva, cocking her head to one side and squinting like a portrait artist evaluating her subject. 'I'd kill for those cheek-bones. You think we can do something about those awful eyebrows?'

'I'll get my tweezers.' Lillian dashed inside.

'Have you heard anything from Rose Ann, Helen?' I asked. 'I hope she's found something. Did she say what sort of job she was looking for?'

'Not in so many words, but she's a singer. Not vaudeville, like you, but cabarets or speakeasies. I've never heard her sing, but Mother says she's always had a lovely, husky voice.'

'Sad, when you think about it,' said Melva. 'Or do I mean ironic? A singer with a child who can never hear her voice. Sorta like an artist with a blind kid.'

Helen continued. 'All Rose Ann told me was that she had some out-of-town leads to pursue. Said she needed to get out of town and find someplace new to live. And when she was settled, she'd send for Kit.'

'Send for Kit?' I said with genuine surprise. 'Not come and get her? Eleven is pretty young to go traveling alone.' And I oughta know. I'd been traveling alone since I was twelve, and there had been some pretty tense times that I wouldn't wish on any young girl.

'Yeah,' said Helen, 'and I doubt she could manage that enormous suitcase she brought. It weighed a ton. The two of us had trouble muscling it up the stairs. I don't really remember what Rose Ann said, Jessie. I expect we'll see her or at least hear from her this weekend.'

The next day, the postman brought a surprise, a letter from New York. Adele had sent me the newspaper clipping telling of Jeton Ilitch's murder.

Dearest Jessie, I thought you would like to read the article in The World *for yourself, so I batted my eyelashes at the newspaperman at the morgue until he cut it out for me which he wasn't supposed to do so I felt quite the vamp! Then Freddie and I had a brainwave. He looked up the address of the restaurant La Terrasse where the cook was killed and what do you think? It was in the theater district not far from our own Liberty Theater. So we decided to eat dinner there and play like real detectives!!! La Terrasse is nothing special as restaurants go but the owner recognized us from the show and came over to say how honored he was, et cetera, et cetera, and would we like a nice bottle of real French wine? So we invited him to sit with us and have a glass, so we could give him the third degree like they do in the pictures.*

I kissed the letter. Dear old Adele – she hadn't changed a bit. Sassy and full of mischief, she'd snatched at my plea for help as if it were an invitation to an exciting adventure with Sherlock Holmes. I could picture her and Freddie going into La Terrasse – wouldn't the owner have been thrilled to have such grand

Broadway stars in his establishment? He'd have been putty in her hands – no man was immune to Adele's charms.

He told us all about the cook's getting shot just <u>six weeks ago</u>. A man had come in and ordered coq au vin and a bottle of wine. He was ordinary looking, with a heavy, dark beard and old-fashioned handlebar mustache. He ate his meal, paid for it (that's the surprising part, I think, don't you?), and went into the kitchen. No one thought anything about it, just that he was going to say something to the cook. Then there were three bangs. Some people screamed. (Here in gangster-land, we know what that means!) The owner came and cautiously crept toward the kitchen where a frightened woman was standing who shouted the man had gone out the back door. So the owner hurried to get a policeman who was at the corner. The policeman ran around back but too late. The shooter had gotten clean away.

The dead man worked there only a year or so. Freddie asked if anyone knew him well. No one did, not very well. They knew he'd come from Serbia about ten years ago. His English was pretty good. One of the waiters said he talked about being in the army during the Great War. Not many people came to his funeral. No wife, no kids. We can go back again if you have something else you want us to ask.

Wasting no time, I telephoned Carl Delaney to read him the letter.

'Are you still thinking coincidence?' he asked.

'Some of the details sound awfully familiar. The shooting happened at work. A man was shot three times. By a man with a beard and mustache. Who disappeared.'

'True. But lots of men wear beards and mustaches, and the descriptions of these were quite different in style. And three thousand miles separated the two. And if you want to kill somebody for certain, three bullets will sure do it. But let's see what we find out about St. Louis before we land on anything definite.'

'I'll check a copy of *Variety* on Monday at the studio.'

Carl's advice was steady. Still . . . the coincidences were beginning to preen themselves like a vain woman before a mirror, and I was not one to shove them aside so easily.

ELEVEN

D irector Parker gave us a full hour for lunch on Monday, so I tucked a copy of *Variety* under my arm and headed to the commissary where fifty cents bought me the lamb chop special and warm apple pie. A meal like that would cost seventy-five cents or a dollar anywhere else, but the studio provided us employees with decent food at good prices, if not always the time to eat it. I spread out alone at a corner table and flipped to the page listing the Big Time acts currently playing St. Louis.

'Excuse me, Jessie. May I join you?' With my nose in the paper, I hadn't been aware of Mildred Young's approach. 'I see you are busy, but there aren't any other tables. I won't bother you with chitchat.'

'Have a seat, Mildred. I'm finished with the newspaper. Unfortunately, I don't see anyone I know on this week's schedule for St. Louis. I'll take a crack at it again next week.'

'Hmm, yes. Barbara told me about Joe's return-to-sender letter.'

'I'm trying to find someone who can help me learn the particulars about that man's death. I know a few of this week's acts but not well enough to ask for a big favor like that. I need someone I've toured with, like the Cat Circus or The Little Darlings.'

She nodded. Before she came to work at Pickford-Fairbanks, Mildred had plied her make-up trade in theater circles. Except for the actors who had started their careers in legit or vaudeville, not many people in Hollywood understood the entertainment world outside of moving pictures . . . it was comfortable not having to explain things.

'The Little Darlings. Wasn't that your last act?'

'I was with them for several years. Longer than any other act. We were like the Seven Little Foys – song and dance, short vignettes. They're still playing Big Time, but with only three kids instead of seven.'

'Do you miss them?'

'Sometimes. They were kinda like family, for a time anyway. Come to think of it, The Little Darlings are the reason I'm sitting here today. If they hadn't let me go last year, I'd probably still be traipsing around the country with my hair in ringlets and a side-lacer flattening my bosom. I admit, I didn't appreciate being fired at the time, but now I'm glad it happened.'

'Funny how things work out, isn't it? You think you're facing tragedy, and it turns out to be a blessing you never imagined.' She paused for a moment of reflection – into her own past, perhaps – and I reflected myself on how much I admired this self-described 'old maid'. An independent woman long before our modern age, Mildred had paid her own way for a good twenty years when most spinsters still clung to a brother or nephew for support. But as I was thinking about her, she was thinking about me. 'Why don't you go to St. Louis yourself? You went East a while back to investigate Ruby Glynn's murder. You could make the round trip in a week.'

I shook my head and swallowed my mouthful of potatoes. 'Back then, Douglas was still writing *The Black Pirate* scenario. Now we're in the thick of filming. I can't get away. Anyway,' I said confidently, 'St. Louis is a big city. Next week there will probably be an act I know. Care for a bite of this pie?'

I was in good humor all day because Mike Allenby was coming to see me after work. Finally, I would learn something about David and what was expected of me at his trial. All thoughts of the Petrovitch murder evaporated into the warm afternoon air as I anticipated the visit and reviewed in my mind the questions I would ask him.

'I'll ask the questions, if you don't mind, hon,' Allenby said as soon as I'd opened my mouth. 'When I'm finished, if there's anything I didn't cover, you can point it out.' I clamped my jaws shut and twisted my lips into something that I hoped look like an agreeable expression. It wouldn't help David for his girl to fight with his lawyer. 'What's the matter with that little kid?' he said, lowering his voice to a whisper. 'She's staring like there were horns growing out of my head.'

We were sitting on the front porch below an overhead light bulb that shone on the papers in his lap. The other girls were in their rooms or in the kitchen, except Kit who was curled up on the chair swing at the other end of the porch, one bare foot tucked under her. With a pad of paper on her lap and a pencil in her hand, she looked like a stenog poised to take notes. She was, indeed, watching us with that unblinking intensity of hers which, if it no longer irked me, would make anyone who didn't know her uneasy. 'The child is visiting her cousin here this week. She likes to draw faces; that's why she's staring. But she's deaf, so you can speak freely.'

'Fine and dandy. So, first things first. We got a court date. Tomorrow.'

'What! Why – What – How am I—'

'I'm ready. And you are too. It's better if you don't have too much time to stew over it.'

My heart raced. He had known about the court date for days, I was sure. Weeks, probably. He could have told me earlier, the miserable bastard. I bit back a sharp retort and put as much sugar as I could into my reply. 'What do you need me to do? Tell me what to say, and I'll say it.'

'I appreciate the offer, Miss Beckett, but I'm going to ask you to do something I seldom ask my witnesses. I'm going to ask you to tell the truth about that train incident. This is one of those rare incidences where the truth can't be improved on, and you'll tell it more convincingly if we don't over-rehearse. Sincerity will be your best weapon. I'm calling you to the stand to address the murder charge.'

'What about—?'

He held up his hand to stop me. 'The other charges are being covered by other people. Trust me, I know what I'm doing. You're going to tell about the hijacked railroad cars and

the shoot-out. Sheriff Barnes comes in from Arizona tomorrow
– he'll go up after you to corroborate your account.'

'What about the other witnesses who were on the train with
me? The colored waiter and the spinster sisters?'

'One of the sisters will be here. Miss Eleanor Vandergrift.
The other . . . uhhh –' he peered down at his notes – 'Miss
Pamela was not well enough to travel but signed an affidavit
to be presented to the court. The waiter couldn't be located.
Evidently he left his railroad job shortly after the incident.'

'Oh dear. I hope it was a new opportunity that took him
away rather than fear after our ordeal.'

Allenby's shoulder shrug told me he had no idea and couldn't
care less. 'To be frank, I'm not worried about the murder
charge. It's just a case of overcharging, to scare us. They do
it all the time.'

'It worked. I'm very scared about a murder charge, considering the consequences.'

'The other charges carry lesser penalties but are harder to
defend. However, I'm confident we'll prevail on all charges.
Now, I'll begin by asking you the usual questions: your name
and address, how you came to know the defendant, and what
your job is. The job will impress the jury.'

'It's hardly an impressive job.'

'True, but it's with Pickford-Fairbanks. That will make an
impact. When I ask you a question, look at me when you
begin your response, then shift to looking at the jury. Try to
look each one in the eyes at some point. A good witness is
likeable. So, now we'll rehearse. How did you come to know
the defendant, Miss Beckett?'

The lies started here. The lawyer didn't know the truth or
he'd never have been so blasé about wanting honesty. I could
only imagine the effect on the court were I to tell how I'd
really met David: in Oregon when I'd been impersonating an
heiress to swindle her family out of her fortune, where David
was Portland's bootleg king, smuggling hooch from Canada
and overseeing speakeasies, brothels, and gambling dens. I
didn't know how much Allenby knew about David's past, but
now was not the time to enlighten him. 'I met Mr Carr here
in Hollywood at a dinner at Pickfair, the home of Douglas

Fairbanks and Mary Pickford. We've been friends for several months.'

'Good. Very good. Be sure to remember that part about Pickfair. That'll slay 'em. You're as good as a film star yourself if you've been to Pickfair. All right, now, tell me, Miss Beckett, in your own words, what happened that day on the train when you were coming home from New Orleans.'

For the next hour, I related what happened on that frightening day last summer when I was returning to Los Angeles and the last two cars on the train were uncoupled at a remote stop in Arizona. Allenby interrupted at regular intervals to clarify something or to improve my testimony in some way, but he never suggested I say anything untrue.

'The whiskey they were after was legal whiskey, isn't that correct, Miss Beckett? Be sure to call it medicinal whiskey each time you say it, hon, and throw in that it was government bonded and how you saw the bottles and knew that to be true.'

I told how the men who were supposed to have been guarding the shipment had conspired with sidekicks to loot the train, how they fell out with one another, murdered the colored cook and the stationmaster, held me and the Vandergrift sisters prisoner, and were fixing to shoot us all when David and his men rode onto the scene. I told about the gunfight that ensued and how David's men killed the last of the thieves just before the sheriff came up with his deputies and federal agents.

'And you killed two of the men yourself, didn't you, Miss Beckett?'

'I wasn't sure you wanted me to say that. Yes, I did – kill two of them, I mean, but it wasn't intentional. I'm not sorry because it was self-defense, as Sheriff Barnes later said. He'll tell them that, won't he? They shot at the waiter and would have killed the three of us women next. We had seen too much to be left alive.' I shuddered at the memory.

'Miss Vandergrift's testimony will support yours. And the sheriff's too, of course. Now, after I'm finished, the judge will allow the fed's district attorney to question you. This will be harder. He's not your friend, although he'll act friendly to try to throw you off. He'll try to make it look like you're telling lies, and he'll try to find holes in your testimony. He'll ask

you if I told you what to say, and you'll say no, that when
we met, *you* told *me* what you were going to say, not the other
way around. Got it?'

I nodded. It wasn't much different from learning lines for
the stage. In fact, it calmed me to think of it as just another
performance before an unusual sort of audience.

'I don't know what this other lawyer will ask you, but you're
safest sticking to the truth. I'm telling Miss Vandergrift that
as well, because we don't want you two giving different
accounts.'

I nodded again. 'Don't worry, I'll pay close attention to the
witnesses that come before me and make sure I don't contradict
them.'

'No, no, no. You aren't allowed in the courtroom except to
testify. You aren't allowed to hear the other witnesses.'

'Oh. Sorry. I've never done this before.'

'Don't be nervous. You'll be fine. Meet me at the federal
courthouse at 8 sharp tomorrow morning. Don't talk to anyone
between now and then. There will probably be newspapermen
lying in wait as you walk up to the courthouse – this case has
received a lot of attention. Just smile and nod at them and
don't open your mouth.'

My expression must have revealed my anxiety, because Mr
Allenby squeezed my knee in an overly familiar way and said,
'Don't worry.'

'I can't help it!' I said, standing up to remove his hand
without actually doing so. 'What if . . . what if the jury doesn't
believe us? What if they—'

'Don't you worry, hon. I'm the best there is in California,
bar none, and if Plan A doesn't work, I have Plan B waiting
in the wings.'

'What's Plan B?'

'Never you mind your pretty little head about that.'

I said good night to Mr Allenby and went indoors. Kit's
perpetual scowl deepened. She unfolded her legs and followed
me inside.

TWELVE

I f I had been on trial for my own life, I do believe I would have felt more composed than I did on that day, Tuesday, November 3, as I climbed the steps and entered the courthouse at Main and Temple. After all, a lifetime spent in front of audiences that jeered as well as cheered should have equipped me with enough poise to soothe any amount of stage fright, and a jury is nothing more than an audience empowered to judge and to determine a performer's fate. I knew my part to perfection. I'd chosen my costume carefully – an ivory tunic dress with its pleated skirt demurely hemmed below the knee – and applied my make-up – a light application of kohl rimming the eyes and subdued lipstick – to emphasize my wide-eyed, ingénue honesty.

So why was I shivering like a dead leaf in a gale? Because it wasn't my life; it was David's. And I owed him a life for what he did for me in Oregon last year.

Hands clasped tight, I sat on a hard oak bench beside Miss Eleanor Vandergrift, not moving, not breathing, as if absolute stillness would let me hear what was going on inside the courtroom. It did not. The trial had begun an hour earlier, and I could not discern a single word. Mike Allenby had told me I'd be among the first called to the stand. *What was taking so long?* It must be bad. As if reading my mind, Miss Vandergrift reached over to pat my wrist.

'It will all be over soon, Jessie.'

I wanted to shush her so I could hear. 'That's what I'm afraid of.'

'Lawyer Allenby seems quite confident.'

'It isn't his neck in the noose.'

It was Eleanor's and my first meeting since our ordeal on the train last summer. Now, as then, she knew when to talk and when to keep still. I watched the clock on the wall as the hands took an hour to move one minute, straining to hear something from the courtroom. Anything. Nothing.

A door opened. A grim-faced man came out. The bailiff.

'Miss Beckett?' He looked uncertainly from Eleanor to me. It felt as if I were watching the scene, not participating in it. The one of us who was Miss Beckett took a deep breath and stood. Willing her weak knees to support her, Miss Beckett followed him into the courtroom with her eyes focused squarely on the man's back.

Another man was waiting beside the witness box, holding a Bible. He stepped forward. 'Raise your right hand. Do you solemnly state that the evidence you shall give in this matter shall be the truth, the whole truth, and nothing but the truth, so help you God?'

'I do.' The sound of my voice, clear and firm, gave me confidence. Raise the curtain. I was on stage. My confidence surged, as it always did.

'Please be seated.'

Only then did I dare look at David. It was a quick glance – I did not want to appear to be looking for encouragement or sending a silent message to a lover, but it was long enough to note that he looked fit, if a bit pale, and very serious. It would take all the acting skill I had to handle my role. 'It won't help David's case if jurors think you are romantically linked. Such an idea might cause them to doubt your testimony,' Allenby had said. So I had resolved to behave in a calm, unemotional manner, as if testifying in court was something I did every Tuesday. Evidently Allenby had given similar instructions to David, for he gave no outward sign of recognition when I entered. Our eyes met for a brief moment as I sat down in the chair beside the judge, and I believe I saw his chin dip in a cautious nod. Words were not necessary between us.

'Good morning, Miss Beckett,' said Allenby. 'Thank you for coming today. Would you begin by stating your name and address, please.'

Preliminaries accomplished, he proceeded exactly as he'd said he would.

'Miss Beckett, please tell the jury how you know Mr Carr.'

I took a deep breath. Luckily, no one could see how hard my heart was pounding. Allenby crafted his questions to produce short, precise answers, and I responded accordingly. *Never elaborate. Never go beyond what is minimally required.* If I failed to give enough detail, he would prompt me. Give less; he would ask for more. Each time, I directed my response to him, then turned my head slightly to address the jury. There were twelve jurors, all men save for three women, none of them young. This was good for me – an older male audience is easier to charm than a female one. Whether it was good for David, I could not say. I did wonder, though, about the three women, because Allenby had told me the jury was entirely male.

'And when, exactly, did you realize your life was in danger from these ruthless gangsters?' he asked.

A courtroom is nothing more than a theater. As if on stage, I played the part of a sincere, modest, and uncomplicated young woman who had been badly frightened during a train robbery some months earlier – a role not far from the truth – relating my story with just the right touch of hesitation and earnest fortitude to sway the jurors to my side.

When Allenby had finished, I braced myself for the onrushing storm. It was exactly as he had predicted – the smarmy U.S. district attorney pretended to be my best friend. I pretended to believe him.

'Miss Beckett, thank you for coming today,' he oozed.

Crossing my ankles and running my fingers through my hair in a casual gesture that indicated I had nothing to hide, I scrutinized this enemy lawyer who would conduct the cross-examination. He was old, fifty at least, and wore a too-dark toupee. He was trying to kill David. I hated him.

So I smiled sweetly as he asked, 'There were seven men killed that night in Arizona, is that correct, Miss Beckett?'

'Yes, sir.'

'And three wounded?'

Don't get trapped into speculating about anything. If you don't know an answer, say so. 'I can't speak to that, sir. I didn't know of any men wounded.'

'Excuse me, I mis-stated the number. There was only one man wounded, isn't that so?'

I saw right away that he was trying to get me to make one

false claim so he could challenge everything else that came out of my mouth. I straightened my shoulders and repeated, 'I can't say. It's possible, but I wasn't aware of any men wounded.'

'You claimed earlier that these men were killed in self-defense, correct?'

'Yes.'

'And you were afraid for your life because several men had already been killed, correct?'

'Yes.'

'When did you learn that the cook and the stationmaster were dead?'

Don't rush. Consider the question carefully before replying.

'Shortly after the sheriff arrived.'

'So you didn't know about their deaths while the gun fighting was going on?'

'I did not.'

'So you didn't actually see them killed, did you?'

'No.'

'So you couldn't have really thought your life was in danger, could you?'

'Yes, sir, I did. I had a gun pointed at me for several hours and saw three of the seven men killed.'

'Who killed those three?'

'The boss gangster shot one of his own men in cold blood on the platform when they argued. We four in the dining car overcame the two who were holding us at gunpoint.'

'You didn't see the other two gangsters killed?'

'No.'

'Why not?'

'It was dark and they were shooting from behind rocks.'

'So it's possible that those men were captured alive and then murdered before the sheriff arrived?'

Don't be trapped into speculation. He'll use it against you.

'I couldn't speak to that. I only know what I saw.'

He posed other questions that seemed designed to poke holes in my contention that the deaths had been self-defense. If that were his tactic, he would find that Eleanor Vandergrift sang the same song. So would Sheriff Barnes, but less effectively because he hadn't been there during the gun battle, only after it was over.

It seemed like I testified for hours. Later I learned it was thirty-two minutes. I ventured a last look at David as I stepped down from the witness chair. Anyone who was watching him might have seen one eye twitch, but I knew it was a wink for me. He was pleased with my performance.

I passed Eleanor Vandergrift coming into the courtroom as I exited, her head high, her rigid posture defined by her old-fashioned corset. That woman was made of iron. She wasn't going to help the government's case against David one bit.

The bailiff said I could leave. 'The trial will go on for hours, miss, you can go home now.'

Nothing doing, I thought, resuming my seat on the hall bench. After Eleanor Vandergrift emerged, she sat with me for a while, urging me to get something to eat or drink. When I refused to budge, she left and came back with some coffee and an apple. 'Drink up. I promised to return the cup and saucer or forfeit my first-born child.' I tried to smile but couldn't. Nor could I eat. The thought of food turned my stomach. I did drink the coffee. 'Put this in your purse for later, then,' she urged.

Eleanor stayed with me for as long as she could, until she had to leave to catch her train home to Arizona. I started to thank her but choked on the words. She squeezed my hand and promised me it would turn out all right. As she made her way down the corridor and vanished through the double doors, I felt very much alone.

Then it was over. At six thirty, the doors of the courtroom burst open and people – newspapermen in the lead – streamed out, their animated voices filling the hall. There was no reading the verdict on their faces. I tried to push my way inside, but it was slow going with the flood against me, like a fish swimming upstream. Finally, I burst through and saw David standing with Allenby and a deputy. In handcuffs.

With an incoherent cry, I threw myself at David, who just in time lifted his cuffed wrists over my head so I was inside the circle of his arms. Allenby pulled out his wallet and handed the deputy a bill. The deputy nodded and backed off.

'You did great, kid,' he said.

'No, no! You're not guilty!' If I held on tight enough, no one could take him away.

'You got me off the murder charge. The rest is penny-ante stuff. I won't be gone long. Mike'll fill you in on the details. Just calm down. I got an appointment with this gentleman here,' he said, nodding toward the deputy waiting to escort him back to jail.

'No!' I held on tighter.

'Go on home. I'll see you soon. Mike, can you . . . uh, please . . .'

Allenby pried my arms from around David's waist and pulled me away. The deputy led David out a side door. He didn't say anything else or even look back at me. The door closed behind them with a dull thud that I felt inside my heart.

Still focused on the door, I said, 'Tell me, quick.'

'They got him on the tax and insurance charges. The judge gave him three and a half years—'

'*What?*'

The room went dark. The floor came up to meet me.

When I opened my eyes, I was lying on a bench in the court-room with Mike Allenby hovering over me, mopping my forehead with a cold, wet handkerchief. Showing unusual – for him – empathy, he propped me into a sitting position and waited until I got my bearings before he tried to explain.

'You okay now? People faint all the time in here. Good thing I caught you going down. Now, I'm gonna walk you to my car – it's parked right out back – and drive you straight home. Then we're going to have a talk. You ready to stand up?'

Still a little dizzy, I nodded. I wanted nothing more than to get out of that horrid room. My knees felt like jelly, but the lawyer held firmly onto my arm and steered me through the hallway and out the rear door of the courthouse. We pulled out of the parking lot in Allenby's fancy emerald-green Packard and headed toward Hollywood in silence.

Less than half an hour later, he pulled up to the curb in front of our house on Fernwood.

'I'm fine now. I don't need any help.' But my words sounded ungrateful, so I added, 'Thank you for bringing me home.'

'Let's get you safe inside before I leave,' he said, walking beside me into the house and through to the kitchen where Helen and Myrna were sharing a pot of tea. They leaped to their feet when they heard the front door open.

'What's the verdict?' both girls called out.

'Good news,' said Allenby with that false, peppy voice people use when they're about to deliver a blow. 'Not guilty on the murder and theft charges. Not-so-good news: guilty on the tax and fraud charges. But we aren't done with that yet. She's had a rough day.' Talking nonstop, he guided me out the back door onto the patio where Melva was pulling clothes off the line, and he deposited me on the lounge chair. 'You girls got any hooch around here? She could sure use a belt. So could I, come to that. Ice, too. And can you cook up something easy she could eat? I'm pretty sure she hasn't had a bite all day.'

I could hear Myrna charging up the staircase for the bottle of David's whiskey – it was about to live up to its claim as medicinal alcohol – and Helen banging pots and running the taps in the kitchen. Only then did I notice Kit crouched beside the fishpond. The commotion brought a spark of life into her empty eyes. I didn't have the energy to write out an explanation for her. Helen could do that later.

The lawyer waited until Myrna brought two glasses of whiskey. 'Here, this'll fix what ails you,' he said, taking a swig from his own glass. I didn't need persuading. He turned to Myrna who was wringing her hands and looking desperate to do something else helpful. 'Ah, you, girl, what's your name?'

'Myrna Loy.'

'Yeah, Myrna. Thanks, sweetheart. Now if you don't mind, I need some privacy here with my client.'

'Oh, gosh, sure. I'll go help Helen in the kitchen.'

He knew enough not to bother about Kit, who had resumed her place in a wicker chair with her sketchbook on her lap.

'Okay. Okay, now, listen up, Jessie, this is what's what. The jury found our friend not guilty of murder or theft – that's good – but guilty of tax evasion and insurance fraud. Which,

just between you and me and the fish here, is a fair verdict.
But we weren't going for fair, we were going for complete
acquittal, so we aren't happy one bit. This is just the beginning. We're going to be fighting back, so don't panic. No way
that sentence will stand. I have Plan B ready to roll out.'

'I thought you were confident about Plan A. What went
wrong?'

'I was never worried about the murder or theft charges. We
had you, Miss Vandergrift, and that squeaky-clean sheriff to
set the jury straight about murder and rock-solid proof that
the whiskey was legal and belonged to Mr Carr all along, so
no theft there. The feds knew that too. They aren't dumb. Well,
they are, mostly, but not these fellas. Bad luck that we got the
only honest feds in the state. This was always about the insurance fraud and the taxes. When I couldn't get them to budge
on bail or buy our way clear of the charges, I knew something
was going on underneath the surface. I looked under a lot of
rocks, you know? And each time I found slime and thought,
aha, that's what's really going on. Then I'd learn something
else, and realize I was wrong. It was something else. Normally,
this sort of thing can be made to disappear with a donation
of cash or hooch to the judge or district attorney or even a
well-placed office clerk can be worth his weight in bottles,
but this time, nothing was greasing the skids. Nothing! Finally,
though, I had everything lined up perfect. I bribed the jury.'

I gasped.

'Not personally, of course, I'm no moron. Someone handles
these things for me. Unfortunately, the judge got tipped off
and brought in the alternate jurors this morning. I was shocked,
mind you, *shocked* this morning when I learned about the
bribery attempt!'

'But three and a half years!'

He shook his head impatiently. 'You can't think like that.
Trust me, it'll never happen. First of all, I'll be filing an appeal
tomorrow.'

'On what grounds?'

'Geez, there's lots of grounds. Starting with a challenge to
the judge's dismissal of the first jury after they'd been legally
impaneled.'

'Because he learned they were bought off.'

'But was it a rumor? Who told him? Did he have proof? You don't just dismiss a jury over some vague suspicion. Anyway, there are plenty of other things I can cite in his instructions to the jury. He gave them almost fifty instructions before they retired, and I can find flaws in most of them. And even the flimsiest grounds give us the chance to pay off some judges higher up the ladder. Or buy a parole. If it comes down to Plan C, we buy Carr a pardon from the governor. Expensive, but foolproof. The moral of the story is: don't worry – everything's gonna be just fine.'

The screen door banged behind Helen as she emerged from the kitchen carrying a tray. 'Here, Jessie, try to eat some of this oatmeal. I put lots of brown sugar on it. And milk. You'll feel better with some food inside you. There's more, Mr Allenby, if you'd like some . . .?'

The dismay on his face suggested he fancied a bowl of oatmeal about as much as a supper of warm gruel. 'Uh, no thanks, sweetheart. I'm more a steak-and-potatoes kinda guy. Jessie, you call my secretary if you have any more questions.' Myrna escorted him out through the house as Helen and Kit kept me company. I could tell the girls were afraid to leave me alone.

'Don't worry, Helen, I'm not going to drown myself in the fishpond.'

'I know, Jessie. We're all so very sorry about David. But honestly, I know it'll all turn out fine in the end. Look here!' she said, in a patent attempt to distract me from my problems. 'Look what Kit's been drawing!' She took the sketchbook out of Kit's hands and held it up so I could see the drawing of me, sitting on the lounge chair, which she'd not finished. I reached out for a closer look.

It wasn't a good likeness. The child really didn't have much artistic talent, poor kid, but drawing portraits seemed to amuse her, and she had little enough to occupy her hours. I gave her an encouraging smile and feigned an interest in her work, flipping back a few pages to see some of her previous drawings.

'Kit's going to stay with us another week,' said Helen. 'I

got a telegram from Rose Ann yesterday asking if she could impose a little while longer. She was up north in San Francisco and hadn't found a place to live yet. I hope you don't mind.'

I assured her I did not. 'Kit is no trouble. I'm only sorry the child has so little to do during the daytime.' I came to the picture she had drawn on Monday night when Allenby and I had been meeting on the porch. She'd exaggerated all his features, much like caricature artists do, making his ears bigger than they were, his hair thinner, and his stomach fatter. Atop his head she'd drawn two black horns, giving him a sinister appearance. I scribbled on the bottom of the picture, 'Sprinkle salt on him and he'd shrivel up like a grub. But I'm trying to be nice because he's helping David,' and returned it to her with a smile.

I only hoped he was as good as David seemed to think he was.

THIRTEEN

Pickford-Fairbanks was not one of Hollywood's larger studios. Squeezed onto eighteen acres behind Santa Monica Boulevard at Formosa, it opened in 1922, and in the three years since, buildings had sprouted like mushrooms after a cool rain. Most offices were located in the low stucco building that fronted Santa Monica, but my workspace was in a bungalow toward the back. Every day we passed through the front gate where a security guard kept a keen eye out to make sure no tourists, salesmen, or nosy children slipped inside. The entrance was narrow, just wide enough to admit an automobile, and it was topped by a painted arch that read Pickford-Fairbanks Studios.

Usually I grabbed a cup of coffee at the canteen and headed straight to my desk or the set, but today I arrived early – at seven thirty – for a breakfast of eggs, bacon, and warm cinnamon bread. David's lawyer was right: life looked better on a full stomach. And keeping my mind on my work while

Allenby spun his spider's web of legal intrigue would distract me from brooding about David.

Once when I was young and my mother and I were playing in Atlanta, I went exploring on my own and was lost for most of a day. When a kindly gentleman returned me to my mother, she hugged me tight, cried, shouted, and spanked the daylights out of me. The next time I saw David, I didn't know which I'd do first: throw myself in his arms or slap him. I was furious that he'd become involved in another shady scheme, especially when he kept swearing he'd left his old life behind, and worried sick that a long prison sentence would smother all his good qualities, leaving only bitter dregs. David was . . . well, David. He really was a good person – although how someone could be a bootlegger and gangster and killer and still be a good person, I couldn't explain to anyone, not even myself. But I cared for him. I don't know if it was love, but I cared. A lot.

After breakfast, I made my way to the set for the ship's deck, which was wedged in between two old sets that had not seen action since the filming of *Don Q: Son of Zorro*. Although we had not yet reached the halfway point in *The Black Pirate*, we were, that morning, preparing to shoot the final scenes. This was not one that involved acrobatics or explosions or technical wizardry; it was the simple, romantic climax that comes when the princess, having learned that the pirate chief is really a duke, falls into his arms for a happily-ever-after embrace. Something I wasn't going to experience for a long, long while.

There is a secret to this scene that very few people know: Billie Dove, the actress who played the princess, was not in it. On an impulse, Mary Pickford donned Billie's blue gown and wig that day and stepped into the part for a joke, thus adding another chapter to the legend of her love for Douglas Fairbanks. So Douglas is really kissing his wife in that last moment of the picture, a fact made all the more emotional for me, missing David as I did.

Miss Pickford laughingly insisted on several takes. Finished at last, she reached up on tiptoes and whispered something into Douglas's ear that brought his eyes straight to me. An earnest conversation ensued. Then she left the set. But when

Douglas made no move to beckon me over and we had moved on to another scene on the poop deck, I figured I had misread the situation. It was not until Director Parker called for a short break an hour later that Douglas approached me, still dressed in his raggedy pirate garb.

'Jessie,' he began, draping one muscular arm around my shoulders and guiding me to a quiet corner. 'A problem has come up. I've just learned that a gaggle of newspapermen is milling about the front gate asking for you.'

'Me? Oh, dear. Why?'

'Hmmm, yes. Looks like your testimony at yesterday's trial has made you popular with that highly unsavory crowd. I can only imagine what they want to ask you. I've sent an extra guard to the gate. That will keep them out of the studio, of course, and Mary has notified the police chief that we will not tolerate this sort of harassment.'

'Thank you.' I thought he would ask me about my testimony and what had happened in court yesterday, but he did not. I suppose he didn't need to – it was in this morning's paper – but I wanted him to ask. I wanted him to care about David.

'Hmmm, yes. I expect some officers will arrive shortly and will run off these troublemakers. But they can't prevent them from congregating on the public sidewalks, so I'm afraid they are going to hang around across the street until you come out. Sort of like vultures waiting for their prey to give up the ghost.'

Me and dead game. Some analogy.

'I can manage them.'

'No,' he said firmly, 'we'll manage this together. Nobody threatens my employees. There's a way to get off the property from the back street that few know about. I've sent someone to see if there are any newspapermen there. If the coast is clear, you can give them the slip and be back at your house before they're any the wiser.'

'You want me to leave now?'

'Listen, I have a long-term plan to deal with these bums. It's brilliant. Remember a few days ago when you asked me about going to St. Louis, and I said to wait until we were finished filming? Well, I've changed my mind. Your investigation into Joe Petrovitch's murder really should take precedence

over everything else, and this is the opportune moment for
you to make the trip. Two birds, one stone. And it would serve
those vultures right.'

Director Parker approached but Douglas waved him away
with a do-not-disturb flick of the wrist.

'Go to my secretary first and get some money. Whatever
you want. For Barbara's sake, we want to pay all your expenses,
and don't argue with me, I insist you travel first class. Wait
in my office until Blinky Jakes comes for you – he'll show
you where to slip through the back lot fence and make your
getaway. Be on the next train to St. Louis. When you've
finished your investigation and come home in a week or two,
all this unpleasantness will have blown over. What's wrong?'

'I . . . uh . . . you don't need me here?'

'Of course, we need you! But I'll talk to Julia Girone and
get her to pull someone from one of Mary's crews to pinch
hit while you're gone. Never worry about that.'

I did worry. People in film production liked to bandy about
that joke warning you not to go to the lavatory or you'd find
someone else in your chair when you got back. So much talent
chasing so few jobs let studio bosses demand sixteen-hour
days, seven-day weeks, and no vacations. Being so easy to
replace concerned me more than I cared to admit at that
moment, so I resolved to brood later. For now, Douglas was
enjoying himself immensely, always the adventurous boy on
a lark, full of plans to spirit me out of his studio right under
the noses of the bloodhound press. Another triumph for the
Black Pirate! I could do nothing but join the intrigue.

I ran to Make-up to tell Barbara Petrovitch where I was
going and get her to fit me with a dark wig before I sneaked
out of the studio. Blinky Jakes found me in the main office,
my wallet full of cash, and led me through the maze of sets
to a corner of the back lot I had never visited before. There,
hidden behind stacks of wood, ladders, buckets, barrels, and
cans of paint, was a padlocked gate. Blinky took a key from
his pocket and wrenched the gate open. I squeezed through
the narrow opening, emerging onto Poinsettia Street, and
headed home by a different route. Luck was with me: no
reporters were lurking about my house.

'Hello . . . I'm home early!' I called out as I entered the house. No one answered. I looked around for Kit, who could not, obviously, have heard me shout, but I found no trace of the child, indoors or out. Just yesterday's newspaper scattered about the kitchen, proving she'd been there earlier. If she was leaving the house during the day, none of us was aware of it. A cautionary voice in my head told me that Kit was Helen's cousin and none of my concern, but I was uneasy. An unchaperoned child should, by definition, be everyone's responsibility. I left a note for Helen to let her know what was going on and went upstairs to pack for a week's trip.

I had no sooner finished choosing the most practical clothes and packing them in my largest valise than there came a knock at the front door. To my great surprise, it was Officer Delaney. Kit was standing behind him.

'Why, Carl, what's happened? Is Kit all right?'

Kit sidled past him into the house, her head down.

'Sure she is. I passed her on the street about ten blocks away, recognized her, and asked if she wanted a ride home.' He grinned. 'Well, I didn't actually ask, I pointed to the back of my motorcycle, and she hopped on. Judging by her big smile, it was her first time.'

'Well, thank you very much. I'm sorry to have troubled you . . .'

'No trouble. I was coming to see you anyway. Can I come in?'

I tried to mask my reluctance as I showed him into the kitchen where Kit was rooting around for something to eat.

'The station got a complaint about some reporters blocking the entrance at Pickford-Fairbanks, so they sent me and Brickles over to clean it up. They were waiting for you. After we shooed 'em to the other side of the street, I went inside to speak to you. Someone confessed you'd snuck out the back. So I came here to warn you. Brickles told the boys you'd be out at lunch-time, but as soon as they figure out that's a lie, they'll be heading this way. They know your address from yesterday's trial.'

'I didn't want to give it out.'

'But you had to, I know. They always ask a witness for

name and address. I was going to suggest you go to a hotel for a few days, or move in with a friend. Just until this blows over.'

'I'm leaving town.'

'Well, now, I don't think you need to go that far . . .'

'Mr Fairbanks told me to stay clear of the studio for a week or two. He suggested I use the time to follow up on that Petrovitch letter, the one from St. Louis, to see if it leads to any information about Joe and who would want to kill him. I did try to find some Big Time vaudeville friends playing St. Louis this week or next, but there were none, so I may as well go there myself. I have the time now.' I spoke that last line a little bitterly.

Carl had this way of looking hard into a person's eyes and reading what was written on their brain. 'You worried about losing your job?'

I sighed. 'Maybe a little. If this dies down quickly, then no, it won't cost me my job. By the time I return, this will be old news. I hope.' I didn't want to talk to Carl about David and the trial; I didn't want to see him gloat. I knew he didn't like David. David didn't like him. I fancy I had something to do with that.

'The newspapers want to turn that trial into a bigger scandal than it is,' said Carl. 'There are plenty who would love to link it to Pickford and Fairbanks. Drag them down a notch. Even film stars with millions of fans have enemies. And a lot of people are jealous of their success. Nothing sells papers like scandal.'

No one knew that better than I did.

Having gobbled up her bread and butter, Kit crunched into an apple with gusto. Before she could disappear outdoors, I motioned for her to clean up her plate. 'Thank you for bringing Kit home. I don't know where she gets to when we're all away.'

'You're welcome. She's a good kid.'

I wasn't too sure about that, but I let the comment slide.

'I'd better go finish packing—'

Before I could stand, he said, 'I'd offer you a ride to the station but we'd never manage it on the motorcycle with your suitcase.' The image made me smile. 'When does your train leave?'

'The next one pulls out at around 3.'

'When does it get to St. Louis?'

'In the wee hours of Saturday morning.'

He grimaced. 'You got a place to stay?'

I couldn't help but be touched by his concern. 'Yes, Dad,' I teased.

'It's just that I know a decent hotel that isn't too expensive.'

'You know St. Louis?'

I could feel him pull back. He had blundered into his private past – a place he clearly did not want to be. Which only made me want to hear about it even more. I glanced at Kit who was watching us intently as she nibbled her apple to the core.

'Only a little.'

His reluctance to elaborate stemmed from shyness, not deviousness. Some people just don't like talking about themselves, and Carl was one of those. But I had been curious about his background for some time now, and this was the best chance I'd had to understand him a little better. So I pressed ahead, as gently as I could. 'How do you know St. Louis?'

'I grew up not far from there.'

'Really? Where?'

Long pause. 'Belleville, Illinois. No one's heard of it.'

'A big town?'

'Small town.'

'Did you live in town?'

'No, outside town.'

This was like pulling teeth. 'In another small town outside that town?'

'My family had a farm east of Belleville.'

Everybody's family had a farm. Unless you were in vaudeville. Farmers, I'd heard, went into town on Saturdays to shop and socialize. 'So you went into St. Louis on Saturdays?'

He shook his head. 'We went into Belleville on Saturdays. We went to St. Louis once or twice a year. Have you been there before?'

Oh, no, he wasn't turning the spotlight on me! 'A few times, but only to the theater district. Did you ever see a vaudeville show in St. Louis?'

'No.'

'In Belleville?'

'No.'

'Why not?'

'My father didn't hold with such things.'

'Because we're all immoral people going straight to Hell?'

'Because we didn't have the money.' He looked around the kitchen, as if planning an escape route. 'I better let you go pack . . .'

'Your family lost the farm?'

'No, they're still there.'

'Who's there? Your parents?'

He gave a sigh of resignation. 'My father died ten years ago. We struggled to keep the farm going. I'm not a farmer, never was any good at it. When my sister got married, it was my chance to leave. As soon as Betty's husband moved in with Mom – he's as good a farmer as God ever made – I joined the army to see the world.'

'That's how you got to France.'

Kit picked up her sketchpad and started drawing Carl's face. I could feel him relax a little. This conversation stuff wasn't as painful as he'd expected.

'Soon as America got into the war, I was on the transport to France. Spent a year there. Not all of it in the trenches. Twice I got a pass to Paris. The only city this rube had ever seen before that was St. Louis. When I saw Paris . . . well, nothing compares to Paris.' His expression softened as he gazed into the space above Kit's head, into the past.

'If you liked it so much, why didn't you stay there?'

He blinked back to the present and smiled at me. 'When you're in the army, you don't tell them where you're going; they tell you. The war ended. They shipped us home. I liked the army. I wanted to stay in, but they didn't need all of us soldiers any more, so they demobbed us at Fort Sam Houston, gave us a train ticket to wherever we wanted to go. I didn't want to return to the farm, didn't like Texas, and trains don't run to Paris. So I thought, "go west, young man" and went to

Los Angeles where I figured the police would be kinda like the army.'

'Is it?'

'Kinda.'

'And do you like Los Angeles?'

The wistful expression returned. 'It's nice here. But nothing's like Paris. One day, I'm going back.'

'To live?'

He shrugged his shoulders. 'When I have enough money saved up, I'll go back and see if it measures up to my memories. Maybe get a job there.'

'You speak French?'

'No, but I got a French grammar book. I can read it pretty good. I'm like Kit here, we can read the language but can't speak it, isn't that so, Kitty Kat?' He leaned over and chucked Kit under the chin as he stood up from the table. Her poker face didn't crack. He reached for her pencil and below his portrait scrawled, 'I didn't know I was such a handsome fella,' which succeeded in making her lips twitch. 'You'd better get packing if you're going to make the three o'clock train. Remember, we're partners on this case, so keep me posted if you learn anything about Jovanovitch and how he died.'

'I promise. And I thought of something you might do while I'm gone. Put Joe Petrovitch's obituary in the New York newspapers, English and Serbian. There must be a Serbian newspaper in that city – every immigrant group seems to have its own native-language newspaper.'

'What do you hope to learn?'

'Probably nothing, but maybe someone will see it and remember Joe and want to send a nice note to his widow – be sure to include her name and address. Maybe we'll learn something about him, about why anyone would want to kill him.'

'While I'm at it, I'll run the same thing in Serbian newspapers in Chicago and Detroit and some other big cities.'

'Good idea. Who knows what might turn up?'

I made it to La Grande depot with half an hour to spare before my train pulled out. I stood in line at the ticket office, booked first-class passage to St. Louis with Fairbanks money, then studied the fluttering numbers on the departures and arrivals board before signaling for a redcap to wheel my valise to track 2. Shoeshine boys vied with newsboys for my attention; a dog protested at being stuffed into a cage; travelers hollered to each other; babies wailed bloody murder. La Grande was one of the largest depots of the Atchison, Topeka, and the Santa Fe line, a great cavern of a place where the footsteps and shouts of a thousand rushing people echoed from the polished floor to the ceiling before being drowned out by the snakelike hiss of steam and the ear-splitting squeal of brakes as the monstrous engines pulled into their tracks.

I've heard people say that the aroma of fresh-baked bread or some other delicious cookery scent reminded them of home. Growing up in hotels and boarding houses as I did and spending every weekend in transit – jumping, as they say in vaudeville parlance, to the next stop on the route – I found the acrid scent of burning coal smelled more like home to me. Second-class passenger cars evoked a similar feeling. Very few vaudeville players could afford the luxury of first-class accommodations, with Pullman berths and elegant dining cars, which is why I have always been able to sleep as soundly sitting up as lying down. But today I was traveling like rich folks, and the Queen of England could not have felt as pampered as I did when the colored porter showed me to my seat with its pull-down berth above.

'My name is Jackson, miss, and I'll be your porter. May I make a dinner reservation for you? Service begins at 6.'

Settling into the spacious, leather seat, I stretched my legs out on the footrest, removed my hat and gloves, and began reading the newspaper in the hope that it would steer my thoughts away from David. Where was he now? Eating horrid prison fare while I dined à la Fred Harvey? Sleeping in a stuffy cell with murderers bunked above and below him? Leaving town felt like desertion, but staying away from Pickford-Fairbanks Studios and the ensuing bad press was really the only thing I could do to help. I had to trust that Mike Allenby would handle everything else.

As the train sped through Arizona, disturbing dreams about ventriloquism seeped into my unconscious mind, robbing me of sleep. Ventriloquist dummies with wide leers climbed off their masters' knees and menaced the audience where I was sitting, unable to move from my seat. Their lips moved, not in the way of puppet's lips, up and down, but like human lips. I arched backward but their heads came closer to mine, their red-painted lips moving in raucous lyrics to music I could feel but not hear.

Where had these sinister thoughts come from? I had never worked in a ventriloquist act. I hadn't even seen one in ages. Naturally, during twenty-four years in vaudeville, I had been acquainted with several ventriloquists, so I knew how hard they practiced to perfect their speech without lip movement, I knew their tricks to throw their voices, I knew the sleight of hand they used to draw the audience's attention to their dummies and away from their own mouths. I couldn't imagine what had brought these images into my head at this particular time, but something about ventriloquism – lips and mouths and hidden speech – continued to devil me throughout the night.

FOURTEEN

The Chase Hotel staff was accustomed to guests showing up in the middle of the night off the train, and in no time, a bellboy had whisked my valise upstairs and I had collapsed into a lovely bed with paper-crisp sheets. I slept late into Saturday morning, soaked in the biggest bathtub I'd ever seen, and enjoyed a light breakfast before heading out to track down the last known address of the late Aleksandar Jovanovitch.

The taxi driver never asked me to show him my money, something I often hear since I don't look rich and do look sixteen. I figured he waived the requirement seeing as how I'd walked out of this swank, new hotel guarded by two doormen wearing uniforms a French general would envy. My beige wool dress with its crocheted neckline and jabot in rose-colored yarn helped with the mature look I was aiming for. The driver gave a smart salute as I climbed into the back seat and told him the address that had been on the return-to-sender envelope Barbara Petrovitch had shown me. As we drove along, I saw in the distance an enormous industrial complex with half a dozen smokestacks puffing away.

'What's that big factory over there?' I asked.

'That'd be Anheuser-Busch, miss.'

'But I . . . I thought they had closed five years ago.'

'Most of the breweries did close back then. Threw thousands of men out of work, my brother among them. But Mr Busch, he's the biggest brewer in the country, and he's determined to stay in business no matter what. They had to let go most of their men, but they've kept going.'

'What do they make nowadays?'

'Oh, lots of things. Ice cream for one. And Bevo.'

'Bevo?'

'You never heard of Bevo? That's one of them beers without alcohol. Busch tried it for a few years but I ask you, who's gonna pay a dime for a bottle of Bevo? Nobody, that's who. I think they quit making it, now that they hit on syrup.'

I was out of my depth here. 'Syrup?'

'You a teetotaler, miss?'

'No, sir, I'm not.'

'Well, you don't know much, do you? Beggin' your pardon, miss. Here's how it is: syrup is malt extract. You buy it in cans from the grocer and make your beer at home. Me and the missus do it every month. You add water and yeast and wait a while and it turns into real beer, not Bevo. Of course it isn't as good as the breweries used to make, but it wets your whistle. And it's legal.'

'That sounds like the grape bricks we have in California. They're dehydrated blocks of grape pulp and skins that people use to make wine at home. My friend Melva tried it last month in our kitchen.'

'How did it come out?'

'Not so good.'

'Gussie Busch Jr. runs the Budweiser Syrup operation. My

cousin works there and he said they made six million pounds of the stuff last year. Six million! You like beer?'

'Sure.'

'You should try making it some time.'

'Maybe I will.'

The driver found the building I was looking for – a sagging, three-story tenement – in a German/Irish section of the city where the dirt streets were clogged with refuse and sewage. When I exclaimed at the poverty, he said we could thank the teetotalers for all the immigrants thrown out of work. I stepped across the matted fur of a dead cat as I got out of the taxi, shuddered, and said, 'Please wait for me. I won't be long.'

The address indicated an apartment on the second floor, so I climbed the stairs, passing two bedraggled urchins huddled barefoot on the landing. The place stank of urine.

No one answered my knock, so I moved to the adjacent door. No one home there either, but the third time's the charm. An unshaven man in long johns appeared. He could have been a casting director from the look he gave me, sweeping me from head to toe with bleary eyes before demanding, 'Wha?'

'Good morning. My name is Sarah Stanley and I'm looking for someone who knew Mr Aleksandar Jovanovitch, the man who lived, until recently, at the apartment two down.' I gestured with one hand and passed him a fiver with the other. He closed his fingers around the bill, leaned out to see where I pointed, then spat on the floor.

'I been here six years, doll, and I never heard of such a fella. Two down's Mabel and some man and a passel of kids.'

'Have they lived there long?'

He scratched his head. 'Not long.'

'Before them. Do you remember a man who lived there before they did?'

'Some fella named Al.'

I was about to shake my head when I realized Al must be Aleksandar. Immigrants often Americanized their names, and Aleksandar seems to have been cut from the same mold. 'Yes, that would be the man. Al Jovanovitch. Do you remember him?'

'Yeah, sure. Uh, no. Not really.'

'Thanks anyway.'

The next woman I found had come to live with her sister just a month earlier. After that, I moved across the hall and got lucky. As soon as the door opened, odors of boiling cabbage wafted toward me. A fleshy woman with fat blond braids and a wailing baby on her hip looked me over with eyes like slits until my five-dollar bill rounded them out and jogged her memory. She remembered Al Jovanovitch.

'He left in September. I remember because this one was newly born and I was up all hours with him,' she said, bouncing the baby to hush him.

'Tell me what you know about Al. I'm a relative of his and my mother's looking for him,' I added so she would know I was on the up and up. The money meant she didn't care. 'What do you mean he left? Moved away?'

'Left. One day he was here, the next, someone else moved in. I don't know where he went. I mind my own business.'

'Was he living alone?'

'So far as I know.'

'What did he look like?'

She put the tip of her little finger in the baby's mouth to stop his crying. 'Big, strong. Dark hair and heavy beard that he didn't shave but every week or so. Talked with an accent.'

'Where was he from?'

She gave me a funny look, like I should know these things if I were really a relative, but the money meant she didn't challenge me. 'I don't know. He wasn't German. That's the only accent I know.'

'Do you remember anything else about him?'

She searched her memory for a moment, then said, 'He worked at one of them automobile factories downtown. Moon, I think it was.'

'Anything else?'

'No, nothing else, except I didn't like him.'

'Why not?'

'Just didn't like the way he looked at me. Made my skin crawl.'

'You've been very helpful,' I said, slipping her another Fairbanks fiver and praying she wouldn't turn it over to her husband to drink up.

Thankfully, my driver was a man who understood the value of a bird in hand.

'Thanks for waiting. Do you know of an automobile factory named Moon?'

'Sure do, miss. It's one of the biggest in the city. Moon Motor Cars. Makes trucks too. You wanna go there now?'

'Do they work Saturday afternoons?'

'Some of the production lines go all day, every day, but by now, the offices are closed.'

'I need to see someone at the office. They're closed Sunday, I'm sure. I'd like to hire you again on Monday, if you could be at the hotel by nine.' I would use Sunday, the day of rest, to work out my strategy for Monday's visit to the moon.

Meanwhile, it was fair on toward Saturday night, and the prospect of an evening moping about the hotel lounge depressed me. I needed something light, something like the witty dialogue of a Shaw or Wilde play or the antics of an animal act. Going home to vaudeville had never before failed to lift my spirits. And my spirits were in great need of lifting that night.

'I'd like to go to the theater tonight,' I said to the desk clerk. 'Could you please recommend the best vaudeville in town?'

'The American is an Orpheum theater,' he said, pulling a copy of *Billboard* out from behind the desk for me to see. 'And a beauty she is, too.' It was the last night of the week's run, but Saturday was also the biggest night of the week. I had already seen the week's schedule before I'd left Los Angeles. I recognized a few of the acts, but knew none of the performers very well. It would be a perfect evening.

Shortly thereafter, I presented myself to the dining room maitre d' dressed in a plaid wool frock, part of the wardrobe I'd bought last year when I'd impersonated the heiress in Oregon, and tucked into an early meal of lobster à la Newberg, potatoes Lyonnaise, and French peas, with Lady Baltimore Cake for dessert. I had brought nothing more suitable to wear to an elegant evening at the theater, but vaudeville was decidedly less ambitious than legit, and my ensemble, when topped by my wraparound coat with its lavish badger-fur collar and cuffs, turned heads.

The American Theater had a familiar feel. The moment I saw the stage, I recognized the unusual drape of its curtain and realized I'd performed here at some point in my murky past, probably during the early years with The Little Darlings. The soaring arches and broad aisle seemed like old friends welcoming me home. Comforted, I found my seat in the second tier, stage left, and settled in with rising anticipation.

It was the usual commotion as ushers hurried to seat people. By curtain time, the orchestra level was nearly full, the balcony and boxes less so. I nodded to the older couple on my left as they were seated and hoped the empty chair to my right would stay that way. Promptly at eight the orchestra struck up the first of four lively pieces – slow, ponderous music was never part of the opening numbers; it would dampen the excitement level. The Holman Brothers: European Comedy Bar Artists came next. Theater managers always slot a 'dumb act' – one without dialogue – in the first position while latecomers were being seated and the audience was settling in. The Sisters McConnell: Eccentric Grotesque Singing and Dancing Comediennes followed with fourteen minutes of talent that left me breathless just watching them. They had three curtain calls. A play came next: *Her Guardian*, a character comedy about a precocious flapper ward and her befuddled uncle.

I knew the fifth act, Those Deere Girls in *Vocal Versatility*. Marjorie and Mildred Deere had shared a billing with The Little Darlings for a few weeks in Virginia and Pennsylvania several years ago. Their choice of songs had changed, naturally, but they brought the same energy to the stage as they had back then. Theirs was the act before the intermission, a spot usually given to the act ranked second best on the program, and they lived up to their billing.

At the intermission I bought a glass of apple juice and chatted with a young couple on their honeymoon to the big city from their family farm. Made me think of Carl Delaney and his own family's farm across the river in Illinois. I wondered about Carl. He was an odd sort. Coming out of Illinois and moving to California, I understood, but Paris? No one else would I take seriously about such a thing, but Carl . . . Carl I took seriously.

The show resumed with Lambert's Dogs: the Most Amazing Animal Act in the Varieties. It was, the program stated, their first time in St. Louis and, I suspected, their first gig in Big Time. They flopped. The audience sat on their hands. The dogs weren't to blame; it was Lambert who lacked any sense of showmanship. If he didn't liven up his routine soon, I suspected the manager would be handing him his pictures and bidding him farewell.

Slotted seventh was Lester, the World's Foremost Ventriloquist. No sooner had the curtains parted than the dream that had plagued me on the train that first night burst into my head again like a Roman candle. I'd forgotten the dream until Lester began his conversation with not one but two dummies on his knees. The act disturbed me in some way I couldn't explain. Something was wrong. Not with Lester – he impressed the audience with his back-and-forth patter, somehow managing to give each puppet a different voice. Mesmerized, I watched and listened as he manipulated the setup to distract the spectators from his lips, riveting their attention on the dummies and their antics. I hardly noticed the next act – and it was the headliner, Ralph Campbell, a stuck-up tenor who had shared a billing with me many years ago. He had a great set of pipes, but that night, I couldn't have told you a single thing about his performance. The finale was, as usual, another dumb act, the Novelle Brothers: Melodious Tumbling Clowns Introducing their Famous Two Loving Nightingales. In a daze, I made my way to the entrance where a line of taxis was lined up bumper to bumper waiting for fares.

Back at the hotel, I asked one of the desk clerks if I could order a bottle of beer.

'Certainly, miss. Would you like it here in the lounge or in your room?'

'My room, please.'

'I'll send it right up.'

'Make it two.'

The beer – genuine Budweiser so they must have come from the hotel's pre-Prohibition stash – and a hot bath soothed my spirits and let me fall asleep without thinking about David, Carl, or ventriloquists. It occurred to me that the list of things

I was trying not to think about at night kept getting longer and longer.

I jolted awake in the wee hours, my head throbbing with images of lips moving without sound, then still lips spewing forth words. I pictured Kit staring at Allenby and me that night on the porch while she drew his ugly portrait. The one where she put black horns on his head. *After* he had said to me, 'She's staring at me like horns were growing out of my head.' That was it. That was what had been bothering me. How had she, a deaf girl, come up with that precise detail? Was she really deaf? Had her mother lied about that? Or could she read lips? And why the charade?

FIFTEEN

Sunday wasn't a good day to investigate the Jovanovitch death, since St. Louis was a church-going city and most everything was closed tighter than a fist. A thick canopy of pewter clouds smothered the treetops, and the wind blew down the wide Mississippi River like it was a funnel, kicking up little whitecaps and filling my nostrils with the moist scent of decay. I spent the day at the river anyway, taking a boat ride and wandering the docks where several barges had tied up and one enormous riverboat was taking on passengers. The powerful current swept along branches, limbs, and whole trees ripped from river banks far upstream, its dirty brown water concealing the submerged danger much like the dark ocean hid the iceberg from the *Titanic*. That evening I took the recommendation of a waiter at the hotel and found my way to a basement speakeasy where a trio of Negro musicians off one of the riverboats were playing jazz, a new sound that I'd heard only a few times. I liked it, sometimes. It was different. Sensual. Unpredictable in a good way. As far as I could tell, it had not caught on in vaudeville, but maybe the colored musicians who moved up from TOBA, the black circuit, to Big Time circuits would bring it along with them.

By Monday, I was ready to perform my role as next of kin to the late Mr Jovanovitch.

To play up my maturity, I wore my below-the-knee wool suit the color of the muddy Mississippi, and the cunning cloche hat and gloves that matched it. My Bevo-hating driver was waiting for me as promised, leaning on his taxi and smoking a Camel when I walked out of the Chase Hotel at nine o'clock.

'Where to today, miss? Moon Motors?' he asked, giving the car door handle a yank.

'The *Post-Dispatch* offices first, please.'

We chatted like old friends about the weather, and he pointed out certain sights as we passed by. St. Louis had once been a fur trading post owned by France, he told me; then it was Spanish, then French when Napoleon took over Spain, until he sold the city and all the Louisiana Territory to the United States.

'That was more than a hundred years ago,' he said, pulling up to the curb. We'd reached a boxy building on Olive Street that was topped by a sign proclaiming it to be St. Louis's newspaper office. 'Now, you take your time, miss. I'll wait right here.'

A young woman greeted me from behind a desk as I entered the lobby.

'I'd like to visit your archives, if you please. Do you call it a morgue?' I asked, remembering Adele Astaire's experience in New York.

She directed me to a Miss Grimsley and pointed to an elevator. 'Basement, please,' I told the boy. With arms that looked too skinny to operate the accordion gate, he wrenched it closed with a fierce clang and turned the crank. The car eased down in a smooth descent.

'Third door on your left,' he said as we touched bottom.

I exited into a narrow hallway where the scuffed walls looked like they hadn't seen a paintbrush since the Great War. The third door was open, and I could hear sharp tension in a conversation as I approached. Two men, one young, one older, were ahead of me at the counter, both of them glaring down at a tiny woman whose face had more wrinkles than those ancient Indian medicine men they always cast in the westerns.

Her hair was pulled up in a bird's-nest bun, probably to give her an extra couple inches, and four yellow pencils protruded from it like knitting needles. An old newspaper lay on the counter between them.

Miss Grimsley could have been sixty or eighty or a hundred; it was impossible to judge, and I suspected no one at the newspaper dared ask. The men towered over her, but she didn't so much as blink at their attempts to bully her. Wearing a severe, steel-gray dress the same color as her hair, she put me in mind of a she-wolf guarding her lair.

'But it's for Mr Pulitzer himself,' protested the younger man, pounding the countertop with his fist to accent the boss's name. 'He ordered me to bring it up!'

'I don't care if it's for the King of Siam,' she snapped, 'you aren't leaving this room with this newspaper.' Pulling a sharp pencil out of her bun, she poked it in his direction as if it were a weapon. 'Sit,' she commanded, nodding toward the wooden library table pushed up against one wall. She turned her attention to the older man, effectively dismissing the other who accepted the pencil with a meek sigh and shuffled to the table to begin copying the necessary portions by hand.

'Article on Mayor Kiel and the North Market Street Dock, please, Miss Grimsley.' She disappeared without comment, returning minutes later with three newspapers. Retrieving another pencil from her bun, she motioned him to the library table, then turned on me with a fierce scowl.

'How do you do, Miss Grimsley. I am Jane Darling from Toronto. I've come to St. Louis to learn as much as I can about my uncle's death this past September and hope you can supply me with his obituary, if indeed there is one. His name was Aleksandar Jovanovitch, but he went by Al.'

She gave me a measured stare that suggested she entertained some doubts about my story, but evidently she concluded there was no danger to the newspaper in handling my request. Turning to the J drawer in a filing cabinet, she flipped through some cards, then disappeared into the labyrinth of shelves before reappearing seconds later.

'There are two relevant papers: this about the death in the local news section and this one the next day with the obituary.'

She placed them on the counter without removing her hands and looked me straight in the eye. 'It says he had no family.'

I'd been up against far worse than Miss Grimsley. 'No *known* family, I suppose they meant,' I replied evenly, putting my hands on the papers and easing them out from under hers. 'He had a sister, my mother, in Toronto. We only just learned of his death last week, I'm sad to say.'

She let me slide the newspapers off the counter and pulled a pencil out of her bun. Following the example of the two men, I accepted the proffered pencil and parked myself at the table.

It was as Carl Delaney and I had suspected: Al Jovanovitch did not die in some machinery accident or from a heart attack. He'd been murdered.

The obituary said Jovanovitch would be buried after a service at Holy Trinity Church, so my driver and I motored over there to see if I could learn anything from its priest. It was a small church and Father Jokovic hadn't actually known Al Jovanovitch, but he'd been willing to conduct services and bury the man. And he was willing to talk to me in my guise as Jovanovitch's niece from Toronto.

'I didn't know him either,' I confessed in my most touchingly sincere manner, 'and I regret that he and my mother fell out some years ago, but she cared about him and was sorry to hear through a friend that he had died. She's unwell, so she sent me south to learn what I could.'

The priest was not old enough to have such a white beard and mustache, I thought. The beard grew all the way down to the middle of his chest, with only a small opening for his mouth. I was glad to see his broad, toothy smile. 'I fear I can tell you little,' he said in English that bore more than a trace of his Old World origins. 'I perform service, pray with mourners, bury the dead. You like to see grave?'

'I would. Tell me, were there many people at the service?'

'Ah, no. Seven or eight men from factory. It was said to me that he come here after war is over and work at Moon Motors. Not so many people know him. No wife, no children, no family. Only your mother. It is often so with immigrants.'

'All the people who came to the service were men?'

'Yes. No women, no children.'

'Who paid for the burial?'

'One man say he was distant cousin. He pay for coffin and donate to church for prayers. If he cannot pay, we still . . .' He waved his hand to show that lack of money would not have prevented the funeral from taking place. I understood – vaudeville has more immigrants than native-born performers. Far from home, immigrants from the same country stick together for comfort, especially in death.

'Do you remember the cousin's name? I'd like to find him and talk to him.'

'His name also is Jovanovitch. Victor, I think. Kind man, brown hair, brown eyes, looks like Jovanovitch, but younger. Perhaps cousin, perhaps same name but not very related. Jovanovitch is common name in Serbia, you know this? Perhaps your mother will know who is young man.'

'Perhaps.'

I was piling up information, but none of it seemed unusual or particularly revealing. A shadowy immigrant community that looked after its own. A lone male who had lived in St. Louis since the end of the war. A young man who paid out of his own pocket for the funeral. The priest walked me out behind the church to the small graveyard where I learned nothing more. I thanked him, returned to the taxi, and set off toward Moon Motors, where Al Jovanovitch had met his maker.

We pulled up to the five-story, red-brick building that housed the main factory, a factory, said my driver, where the Moon brothers had churned out carriages not so many years ago. He let me off at the entrance with a cheerful, 'Take your time, miss. I'll be here when you come out.'

I replaced my cheery smile with a somber expression befitting my mission and greeted the middle-aged secretary at the front desk. 'Hello, Miss Schmidt,' I said with a glance at her name plate, 'I'm Miss Jane Darling, come all this way from Toronto on behalf of my mother to learn about her brother's death here last September. He was Al Jovanovitch.'

Her brown eyes got big as plates. 'Oh, gosh! That was an awful day! I remember!' After dithering about her desk for a minute, she made a telephone call and moments later, another secretary came out of the elevator in a breathless flurry.

'How do you do, Miss Darling. Mr Edward Nestor, our vice-president, would like to see you in his office, if you'll follow me.'

I expected to have to prove myself to someone at some point during this process, but everyone at Moon Motors seemed trusting to the point of naïveté. I gathered not many workers were murdered at the factory and the event had been distressing, not to mention embarrassing. Mr Nestor had been one of the men at the funeral. He was bent on describing the service in detail, and I let him.

'Father Jokovic told me a young man paid for the coffin,' I said, when I could get a word in edgewise. 'Another man who was also named Jovanovitch. Was he employed here too?'

'No, but I remember that man, only because he was the one person at the graveside who did *not* work for me.'

'I'd like to find him. I know Jovanovitch is a common name in Serbia, but he may indeed be a relative, and my mother would appreciate it if I could talk with him.'

Mr Nestor put on a pained expression. 'I'm very sorry, Miss Darling. I had never seen this man before. The others at your uncle's funeral I knew – they came from the factory – but this man was unfamiliar to me.'

'I've been to my uncle's apartment, which of course has been let to another family, but I was wondering what had become of his personal effects. Did anyone you know collect his belongings?'

Now Mr Nestor's eyes narrowed, and I fancied he wondered for the first time about my motives. To put his mind at rest, I hastened to add, 'I'm sure he didn't have much of value, a few dollars, perhaps, and some clothing, and it doesn't matter where those things went, but I was hoping to come home with some family items that would comfort my mother. Photographs or letters or some family keepsakes.'

His brow cleared. 'I never gave a thought to his personal belongings. This other Jovanovitch must have taken care of that.'

'Might I speak with the men from the factory who attended the funeral with you?'

'One was our president. He's in Chicago, but he didn't know your uncle personally, so I don't believe he would have anything to add. The other men worked on the floor with him.' He rose to signal my dismissal. 'I'd take you there myself, but I have a meeting in a few minutes, so if you don't mind, I'll get my assistant to escort you to the floor.' He pressed a button on his desk. The buzzer brought an earnest young man into the office. Thin and shy, with an Adam's apple the size of a golf ball, he looked like someone I could manipulate to my advantage.

'This is Raymond Fletcher. Raymond, Miss Darling here is the niece of Al Jovanovitch, the man who was killed in September. Please escort her to the factory floor and introduce her to anyone who knew her uncle, especially to those who attended his funeral.'

'Yes, sir.' He nodded at me and swallowed hard, as if gathering courage for the ordeal ahead. 'This way, Miss Darling.'

Into the bowels of the beast we went, assailed by fumes, sparks, and a deafening din. It was different only in degree from a film studio back lot, with workers hauling equipment to and fro, lifting large pieces of metal with ceiling pulleys, soldering, hammering, banging metal onto metal, shouting, and swearing. Dodging sparks and covering my ears, I threaded my way through the stations in Raymond Fletcher's wake, removing my hands each time he stopped to comment. Even so, I could barely make out his words above the noise, and I soon realized I was watching his lips to get the gist of his remarks – something about Lockheed hydraulic brakes and six cylinders. '. . . seven thousand vehicles last year . . . on target for ten thousand this year . . .' I pretended to care.

Finally, we reached the far side of the floor where Fletcher motioned for two men to leave off what they were doing and follow us to a sheltered, slightly quieter spot against a brick wall where he made introductions. The men worked in grease-stained undershirts that left their powerful arms and shoulders bare. One pulled a soiled handkerchief out of his pocket and wiped his face and blackened hands. Cleaned up and dressed in colorful tights, either one could have been the Strong Man at the circus. If Al Jovanovitch had been this muscular, he would not have been easy to kill with fists or knives. It would take a gun.

'Finney here worked with your uncle, Miss Darling, and went to his funeral. So did Schwartz.' The two men gave me solemn nods.

I gave them my spiel about Toronto. 'I'm hoping you can tell me what happened that day, the day he was killed.'

The two exchanged glances that seemed to ask who would speak first. Finney won. 'It happened right over there,' he said, pointing to a line of automobile bodies, each one with three men working on it. 'Schwartz and me were there, working with your uncle. With Al. We weren't paying attention to nothing but the cars. Then there was this man beside us. Don't know where he come from. Outta thin air. He looked at Al and shouted something foreign that only Al understood.'

'Serbian,' said Schwartz.

'Yeah, Serbian. Then he was holding a gun. I didn't see him take it out; it was just there in his hand. He shot Al three times in the chest, bang, bang, bang. No one looked over at us because the noise drowned out the shots. We was both so shocked, we didn't move quick enough to grab him, and he got away.'

'I was on the other side of the car,' said Schwartz. He seemed embarrassed that he'd been so ineffectual.

I looked at the place where Jovanovitch had died, almost expecting to see some remnant of the violence. But any blood on the floor was long gone.

'What did the shooter look like?' I asked.

'Nothing special,' said Finney. 'Shorter than me, not a big guy.'

'The police asked us that question later on, and all I could remember was he wore a cap,' said Schwartz, 'and had a mustache and beard.'

'No, no beard,' corrected Finney, 'just a mustache.'

'I say he had a beard,' insisted Schwartz. Finney shook his head.

'Did my uncle recognize him?'

'Didn't seem to. He understood the words the fella shouted, though. The words made him look sick. Afraid. Like he knew the man was gonna kill him even before he saw the gun.'

'Who else saw him? Did the woman at the front desk notice anything when he came in?'

'She told the police he didn't come in that way.'

'How did he get inside then?'

Schwartz shrugged. 'There's other doors. Like over there.' He pointed across the room. 'Then he ran off. He ran that way and went into the johnny. Me and Finney followed, careful-like because he's got a gun. We thought we'd trap him in the johnny until the police came. But just after he ran in, the cleaning woman ran out. She was in there cleaning. She tripped over her bucket and mop, screaming like the devil was after her, saying a man with a gun was climbing out the window. We went in then, careful-like, and the window was wide open. He was gone.'

We walked to the men's lavatory to have a look. Fletcher made sure no one was inside before he held the door open for me. The small room held two water closets on one side and a white enamel trough with spigots on the other. A double sash window opened onto an outdoor alley. An average-size man could have put his knee on the sill and jumped outside in a matter of seconds. We returned to the quiet spot against the wall.

'I was hoping to learn a little about Uncle Al's life here in St. Louis to tell my mother. Did he have any lady friend? Did you know him very well outside of work?'

Finney said, 'Him and me went drinking on Saturdays with some of the boys. We'd go to the fights. He liked the girls but he didn't have no particular one. Never said anything about any family, except that he'd left all that behind in Serbia. He'd been in the war there.'

'Was he new to St. Louis?'

'Not so new. I think he been living here eight or ten years, he said.'

'He worked at Moon Motors all that time?'

'No, he worked here about . . . what, maybe five or six years? Before here he worked at another car factory. I don't know which one; there's lots in this city. And once he mentioned New York. But most foreigners come through New York, so that don't mean nothing.'

'Did he make any enemies? Was there some reason someone would want to kill him?'

Finney shrugged his shoulders. 'I didn't know anybody who had a grudge against him. He was a good man to have at your back in a dustup, though, that I can say for sure!'

'Did he have any debts?'

'Not that he talked about. He played the ponies some, like everybody. Bet at the fights. Didn't go in for cards much.'

'Do you know what happened to his things? He must have had personal belongings at his apartment. I'm sure my mother would like to have any photographs or keepsakes.'

The men shook their heads. 'Never thought to ask,' said Schwartz.

'So you don't know who got his things?'

Finney turned to Schwartz and said, 'You think it coulda been that man at the funeral, the one that didn't work here?'

'Maybe.'

'Who was that?' I asked.

'Dunno his name, just that he didn't work here.'

'Someone must have paid for the coffin. Do you know who?'

'Dunno. The priest, I think.'

I turned to Fletcher, who had remained silent throughout most of this exchange. 'I wonder if I might talk with the woman who was cleaning that day.'

Fletcher shook his head. 'She doesn't work here anymore. She stayed long enough to give the police her story, then she quit, so afraid she was.'

'Do you know where I might find her?'

If he thought it curious that Al's niece wanted to question the cleaning woman, he didn't say so. 'No'm I don't. Her name was Hilda Something-or-other, but she hadn't worked here long. A couple of weeks. The police said they didn't need her any more, so she picked up what was owed her and never came back. Can't say as I blame her for being scared, but nothing like this ever happened before at Moon Motors.'

Pressed, Fletcher checked with a secretary about any employment records for Hilda, but she told us she threw out the file after a person had left. She remembered Hilda as 'a quiet woman and a good worker. I tried to persuade her to stay, but she was that frightened, she couldn't.'

My driver took me next to the public library where I paged through a copy of the most recent city directory, looking for the cousin, Victor Jovanovitch. No such person was listed. It was possible, even likely, that he didn't live in St. Louis but had come in for the funeral, in which case I'd have not the slightest chance of tracking him down this way. Another dead end.

SIXTEEN

So what was I supposed to make of all this? As I boarded the late afternoon train to begin the three-day trip home, I looked forward to sinking into the gentle rhythm of the rails and sifting through my thoughts to discover a nugget among the sludge in the prospector's pan. I was determined to avoid thinking about David and the last time I'd traveled on this train. With him. But the monotonous clickety-clack of the wheels and the endless scenery blowing past the other side of the window turned my thoughts loose and I couldn't help but slide back in time.

A greeting from a porter as he passed me pulled my thoughts back to the present. What would I tell Carl Delaney when I got home? I needed time to wander behind the facts to find the hidden truths.

Carl would surely agree with me that these three murders were related, even though they had occurred hundreds or thousands of miles apart. The three men killed were Serbian immigrants of similar age. They were acquainted. Whether you could call them friends depended upon your definition of that word, but they hadn't been in touch with one another for many years. The death of one had sparked a reconnection. Each was shot three times with a handgun. Each was killed at his work place, not at home or in the street, which would have been safer for the killer. In fact, it seemed to me that the

killer wanted an audience or he'd have chosen to waylay his
victim in a dark alley.

The New York cook, Jeton Ilitch, and the St. Louis factory
worker, Al Jovanovitch, had been in the army. As soon as I
got home, I would ask Barbara Petrovitch if her husband Joe
had served in the army too, but I was pretty sure her answer
would be yes. The question was, which army? While many
immigrants served in the American army during the Great
War, it didn't seem possible that Al Jovanovitch had been
among them – his friends said he'd been living in St. Louis
for about ten years and before that, in New York for an unspeci-
fied length of time. Even counting his time in New York as
only one year, that made eleven, and counting back eleven
years put us at 1913. America hadn't joined the Great War
until 1917. I wasn't likely to get any more information about
the New York cook's death, but I could see what Barbara had
to say about Joe and when he arrived in this country. If she
knew the answers. Maybe he had some immigration papers
from Ellis Island stashed in a drawer somewhere.

Al Jovanovitch and Jeton Ilitch could have served in a
European army before they came to America. A Serbian one,
perhaps? Everyone knew a Serb named Princip had pulled the
trigger in Sarajevo that started the Great War in 1914, but I
wasn't sure which side Serbia had taken in that fight, the Allies
or Central Powers? According to his friends, Al Jovanovitch
was in America by then. Of course, there was always the
possibility that he had lied about his military service when he
came to America. He wouldn't be the first man to claim wartime
experience that he'd never had.

I wondered how the three men knew each other. Had they
met in New York in the Serbian community, or had they been
friends back in the old country? Were they distantly related?
Had they come to America together, or had one come first and
sponsored the others? I'd heard you needed an American
sponsor and the promise of a job before authorities would let
you off the boat at Ellis Island.

Something else was picking at me. The killings had a theatrical quality to them. In each case, the killer – who was surely
the same average-looking person – had walked onto the scene

in a crowded place, shot his victim, and slipped away. There was nothing impulsive about these killings. They were not the passionate actions of a cuckolded husband or a jealous lover. They were meticulously planned. The murderer must have scouted the places in advance; otherwise he would not have known how to make his getaway through a bathroom window, out the back door of a kitchen, or into the balcony. He knew where his victims worked and he had visited the places at least once to learn the lay of the land. Perhaps he'd even passed by his victims in the process. That required cold-blooded nerve.

I was pondering the killer's motive when it hit me – what if he had no motive? No personal motive, that is. What if the three Serbs had been involved in bootlegging, helped themselves to some of the boss's profits, and done a flit? Big city gangsters made it a point of pride to avenge disloyalty in highly public and vicious ways in order to intimidate others. The average-looking murderer who bumped off the three Serbs could have been a button man sent to kill them in a showy way that would make the newspapers and reverberate back home in New York or Chicago or Detroit. What would Carl say to that idea? It made a lot of sense. If true, there would be no chance to bring the killer to justice. Gangs always protected their killers with rock-solid alibis, threats to witnesses, or payoffs.

Passengers bound for California changed trains in Kansas City where we joined up with the westbound Atchison, Topeka and Santa Fe train. Lady Luck brought us a brand-new Pullman car with shiny brass handles and upholstery so spanking fresh it looked like it had been cut from the bolt hours ago. The luxury of first-class travel was spoiling me forever. I settled back into the privacy of my compartment and looked forward to the next meal in the dining car. Fred Harvey food was always reliable. When night fell, my colored porter made up my berth and did everything but sing me a lullaby. And I'm sure he'd have done that if I'd asked.

I lay awake for some time thinking about Kit and devising a way to test my theory that her deafness was a pose, then, should that prove wrong, another way to test whether she could read lips. No way could I just ask . . . she'd fix me with that vacant stare that made people think she had nothing inside her head. It was not until the next morning that I realized I was unlikely to get the chance to put either scheme into play. By the time I got home on Thursday night, the Rileys would be long gone. Rose Ann would surely have come to pick her up by then. I hoped the singer had found a decent-paying job in San Francisco.

I couldn't be too hard on Kit or Rose Ann, knowing, as I did, how hard it was for a mother in show business to raise her daughter alone, without a husband or any relatives to help. Many a time, my mother had left me alone in our hotel room for long hours, and I hadn't always obeyed her orders to stay put. How much more miserable had it been for Kit, being deaf and dumb – for by now I was regretting my suspicions and concluded the lawyer's black horns were a coincidence. After all, what reason would Rose Ann have to mislead Helen about her daughter's deafness?

As our train sped west, each stop brought me closer to Navajo Springs and Holbrook, Arizona, where the awful events of last summer had taken place, and soon I wasn't remembering so much as reliving those terrifying hours when I'd been prisoner of the bootleg thieves.

In Holbrook, our porter said the train would stop for longer than the usual ten minutes, so I climbed down to take a short walk. It was much cooler than it had been last summer, when David and I had walked this street and boarded the train for home. I had changed so much since then, I expected the town to have changed with me, and it had not. There was the ladies' fashion store where David had bought my new clothes; there was the corner hotel with the sky blue ceiling where we had slept. Hurting, I turned back to board the train, pausing only to buy a Los Angeles newspaper to read on the way home. It was two days old, but it was new to me, and reading it would take my mind off David.

No sooner had I resumed my seat and flopped open the paper than my eyes fell on the story in the lower right corner of the local news page. 'Pickford-Fairbanks not tied to felon,' read the headlines. My heart stopped.

'A press release from Pickford-Fairbanks Studios has denied any connection to convicted felon David Carr,' read the article. The statement claimed 'Carr was a minor investor in an earlier film, but Mr Fairbanks and Miss Pickford are not well acquainted with the man and have had no contact with him for many months.' I skimmed to the bottom paragraph where the last sentence kicked me in the gut.

'Miss Jessie Beckett, who testified at the trial on behalf of Mr Carr in relation to his murder charge, worked briefly at the studio in a minor capacity. She is no longer employed at the studio, having left California for parts unknown.'

It's hard reading in the newspaper about being fired.

The only drawback to first-class travel is its lack of vaudeville performers. No one, save the occasional uppity headliner, bought first-class tickets, which meant traveling like this cut me off from other people like me. And the loss of the job I had loved so much made me crave familiar company. So each time I went to the dining car, I asked the waiter to seat me at a table with theater people, if he knew any were there. It really wasn't that hard to tell.

I was pleased that my very next meal found me seated across from Madge and Nalla Frisco, a sister act on their way to Phoenix. We quickly discovered a few friends in common and stretched our meal to a pleasant two hours, during which time I could avoid thinking about David and my troubles. The sisters had brought their own flask of gin, which they generously offered to share. I asked the waiter for three glasses of ice and some sliced limes, sugar, and a little fizzy water and we made cheerful gin rickeys at the table . . . carefully so other diners wouldn't notice and complain. It paid to be cautious: you never knew if you were sitting next to someone from the Anti-Saloon League who would have a heart attack and turn you over to the nearest lawman.

The Frisco girls began telling me all about their brother, who was – I should have seen this coming – a ventriloquist new to Big Time on the Orpheum circuit. I hadn't thought about ventriloquists in ages, and now they were following me around, plotting to keep me awake at night. In self-defense, I turned the conversation to some of the odder novelty acts we'd known.

'Olga Myra was the most amazing act I ever saw,' said Nalla Frisco, shaking her head in wonder. 'She was a violinist who did acrobatics while she played – and played very well, mind you. She billed herself as a "vio-tortionist" and did backwards walkovers like she was made of rubber, touching her head to the floor, never using hands to balance because they were playing the violin.'

'Remember that strong man act in Atlanta?' said Madge. 'They harnessed two teams of horses out in front of the theater to pull in opposite directions against the strong man – I forget his name, Bernard or Bernardo maybe. It seemed a miracle that he wasn't torn in two. Of course, the teams were actually pulling against each other, due to some gimmick I never quite figured out . . .'

'I have a friend,' I said, 'Les Hope, a hoofer, who used to do a dance act where he and his partner danced with the Siamese twins, Daisy and Violet Hilton. I never saw 'em but I can imagine that was a real draw.'

'That doesn't count, Jessie. You have to have seen the act. What's the strangest act *you've seen yourself?*'

I thought a bit. 'Well, the most unusual was probably Helen Keller when she played Big Time for a year or two. It was an act that wasn't an act.'

'We know about her,' said Madge, mixing another gin rickey.

'But we never saw her on stage,' said Nalla.

'I did. She gave a talk with her teacher beside her. She talked, but it was hard to make out what she was saying. Her teacher said that when you can't hear, it's next to impossible to learn to speak.' Suddenly I was thinking of Kit again. 'She would touch people's lips to "hear" what they were saying. It was astonishing. Like a magic act but the magic was real.'

'Last year,' Madge recalled, 'we shared a billing with Birdie Reeves. She can type three hundred words a minute. Not a mistake on the page. And it was no gimmick, I can tell you. She typed one speech while she recited a completely different speech out loud. The kid was only about sixteen years old. I wonder what happened to her . . .'

Nalla spoke up, 'I know the funniest act we ever played with – it was that Tarzan act, remember Madge? Tarzan and another fella who dressed up like an ape. It was a really good costume, and some people thought he really was an ape. So when he broke away and started rampaging down the aisles and over the seats, the audience went all hysterical. Then he took off his mask.'

I chuckled. It was all so familiar. Like reliving my childhood.

Later, back in my seat and feeling drowsy from the gin, I fell to thinking about my mother and some of the acts that had performed alongside hers in the early years of the century. As a child, I remembered her entertaining me with stories about some of the really strange novelty acts she knew: the Indian opera singers, the candle jumper, the snowshoe dancers. And Fulgora. Robert Fulgora, the transfigurator, a friend of hers when I was too young to take notice of such things. I had never known him myself, but when he popped into my head, I had the sense that he'd been there all along, waiting for me to welcome him like an old friend.

Suddenly, a spotlight blazed on the Serbian murders. I didn't know *who* had killed the men. I didn't know *why*. I had only recently learned *how*. But now I knew *what*.

The killer was a transfigurator.

SEVENTEEN

'A trans-a- . . . what?'

'A transfigurator.'

Carl Delaney had met my train at La Grande depot that evening in a police car and driven me home. I hadn't expected to see him there, but Myrna had tipped him off as to my arrival. It was late. Myrna was still awake, but the other girls had gone to bed, so Carl and I sat on the patio in the cool night air, talking in hushed tones while I spilled everything I'd learned in St. Louis.

'Transfigurators are rare in vaudeville. I don't think I've ever seen one on stage. Some people call them quick-change artists, others call them proteans, but proteans are not really the same thing. Proteans perform a sketch with a plot where one person plays all the characters. Transfigurators make quick changes with maybe a word or two of patter, but the gimmick is their speed. Some do it in front of the audience, others during a stroll behind a curtain or a folding screen.'

'Why do you say rare?'

'Probably just out of fashion. Or maybe because it's such a tough act to create. My mother had a transfigurator friend, the Great Fulgora, when I was very young. I don't remember him, but I do remember her telling me about him. He used to take months just to break in a coat, taking it off and putting it on a hundred times a day. Whenever Mother wanted me to get dressed or undressed quickly, she'd say, "Hurry now, fast as the Great Fulgora!"'

I was bone-cracking stiff from three days on the train but could not have slept a wink until I spilled everything to Carl. My thoughts raced like electric current through the wires. 'Fulgora would open his act in street clothes and make ten or twelve changes in front of the audience. Then at the end, he'd walk off stage in woman's clothes and in four seconds flat, he'd stroll back on dressed in full evening clothes. Some people thought it was a trick, that he had a twin brother, but Mother swore he didn't.'

'So you think the killer was one of these transfera . . . quick-change artists, and that the same man shot all three.'

'That or gangster executions. Maybe the killer was a professional button man hired to dispose of each Serb for some reason having to do with bootleg hooch. Like, maybe they stiffed their boss, and he was getting revenge in the showiest way possible to intimidate anyone considering future larceny.'

Carl was never one to waste a word when a look would do. His eyebrows arched in silent skepticism. No matter; I'd only begun.

'But – oh, I just realized how unlikely that is. If those three men were on the run from a gangster boss, the first thing they'd do is change their names. And none of them did. I mean, they changed or shortened their first names, but they made no effort to hide behind a new last name. They were all working and living openly, and for a year or longer, so they couldn't have been worried about someone coming after them.'

'And gangsters looking for revenge don't wait around for four or five years before sending out a killer. Jovanovitch and Petrovitch had worked in their jobs for at least that long.'

He was right. I returned to my original idea about the transfigurator.

'You know, there was something about these murders that struck me from the start as excessively theatrical. Remember the red coat and the mustache and beard? Details people would notice and remember, sure, but also a way to point suspicion away from himself when he appeared *without* those items. Like a magician's use of misdirection, he was forever making you look over there while the trick was happening over here. I never heard of a hired killer doing anything quite that showy.'

'Me neither.'

'Didn't you wonder why the killer didn't just shoot his victims in some deserted street? I'll tell you why: because no one would see. He was a performer. He needed an audience. That's why each man was killed at his work place, not at his home or in the streets. A button man shoots and scrams. He doesn't want to attract notice. This fella stuck around to enjoy the audience's reaction.'

'So he pulled the trigger and then changed clothes to escape?'

'Exactly. He shot Joe Petrovitch in the projection booth, then walked up to the balcony, stashed the gun, whipped off his outer layer of clothes, and strolled out of the theater as a different person. But the other two murders were even bolder than that. Genuine Big Time performances. They had me fooled completely, until tonight. Remember the cook in New York?'

'Jeton Ilitch.'

'Yes. He was shot in the restaurant kitchen by a patron. A man who calmly ate his dinner, paid the bill, then walked into the kitchen and shot the cook.'

'He didn't change clothes. He escaped out the back door into an alley.'

I shook my head. 'That was the misdirection. He whisked off his top layer and had female clothes underneath. Then he stood by the door to the kitchen and screamed that someone had shot the cook and run out the back. It might have looked suspicious if the woman who witnessed the crime had disappeared minutes later, so, with amazing sang-froid, he waited around for the police, gave his statement – or "her" statement – and then waltzed out the front door. Once I figured out what happened at Moon Motors in St. Louis, I looked back at the murders in New York and Hollywood and saw his actions as performances.'

I told Carl about my visit to the newspaper office, the church, and the automobile factory. 'When the killer shot Jovanovitch in the factory, he ran into the WC and opened the window. Then he whisked off his top layer and transformed himself into the cleaning woman. It wouldn't have taken him three seconds to stuff the discarded clothing into his pail of water and exit the WC screaming in falsetto that a man with a gun had jumped out the window.'

'But they knew the cleaning woman.'

'They said she'd been employed there for a couple of weeks. Long enough to figure out the lay of the land and to learn which man was Jovanovitch. Like at the New York restaurant, "she" stuck around long enough to give the police the details, then "she" quit the job, pretending to be afraid. I tried to track down an address, but the office had none. Even if they had, I'm sure it would have proved a fake. He took that job only to learn how best to kill Jovanovitch. The same reason he ate at the restaurant several times before he killed the cook. And no doubt, he'd been to the theater several times to check out the exits, the balcony, and the water closets. Any money says he sashayed out in woman's garb, right under the policemen's noses.'

Carl was nodding now. I knew I had him. Still, doubt shaded his voice when he asked, 'He could masquerade as a woman?'

'Remember, Carl, he wasn't a big he-man sort of fella. Everyone described him as average in size. No distinguishing features – at least, none that couldn't easily be removed like the mustache. Who looks twice at an immigrant cleaning woman in baggy clothing? Or a middle-age matron in a restaurant? People see what they expect to see. Magicians use that to their advantage.'

I snapped my fingers. 'Which reminds me – I realized something else, something that should have hit me sooner. Whenever spectators described the killer, they all used the same words. Like "he vanished", or "he disappeared into thin air", or "he appeared out of nowhere", giving the killer an aura of magic. Well, transfigurators are not unlike magicians in the way they perform.'

I stretched my arms high over my head until my joints popped. Now that I'd delivered my report, I wanted nothing more than to collapse onto my bed like a marionette with its strings snipped.

'You look beat.'

'Gee, thanks.'

He grinned and stood. 'You know I didn't mean it that way. So what now?'

'So now I find the transfigurator.'

I led him through the house and out the front door.

'How?'

'I write some vaudeville friends and ask if anyone knows any transfigurators who have performed in the last few years, but who have *not* performed in the last few months. Someone will know something.'

'Sounds good,' he said, ambling down the short sidewalk to the curb where his police car was parked.

I followed him halfway and called softly to his back, 'Tell your Detective Vogel it may take a while.'

'Won't need to,' he said without turning.

'Huh?'

'He's off the case. It's my case now. Got promoted to detective last week. Goodbye, uniform.'

I don't think it was my imagination, but he seemed to walk taller after he said those words.

First thing the next morning, I called Mike Allenby's law office to ask about his progress in David's appeal. The coffee-slurping secretary hadn't yet mounted her guard; she sent my call through to her boss without any attempt to ward off my advance. Not that it did me any good. The lawyer had nothing to say.

'Appeals take time. This isn't something that happens in a week. Believe me, hon, you'll be the first to know when there's a break in the case.'

'I want to see David. I know prisoners get to have visitors, so don't tell me they can't. And it's Miss Beckett, if you please.'

He heaved a sigh so deep it sounded like God had inflicted no greater trial on his life than my presence. 'Miss Beckett . . .' he began wearily.

I snapped, 'No, don't hand me any excuses. Other people visit prisoners – I can too. I want to see David, and you can fix it. I know you can.'

'Yes, ma'am, I'll have my secretary call you as soon as I learn when you can visit the prison.'

I know a brush-off when I hear one. He would not find it that easy to ignore me. 'I'll call you tomorrow and see what you've arranged.'

I made myself some toast and jam and spread out yesterday's newspaper. I went straight to the listings for 'Help Wanted – Women' to see what jobs were on offer for the fairer sex. There were some secretarial positions, but I didn't type, and some telephone operator jobs, but I hadn't a clue how to work a switchboard. The motion picture industry had brought such an overabundance of talent to Hollywood that someone like me, with a singing voice only marginally better than average, would never find work in a speakeasy or cabaret. I'd never been to school, so female jobs like teacher or nurse were out of my league. If I changed my name, I could apply for jobs in other studios, but the only chance of getting one of those was to use my past connection to Pickford-Fairbanks, which meant I couldn't change my name . . . which meant they'd never hire someone implicated in the trial of a well-known felon like David Carr. The 'Girl Friday' listings were so vague and general that they seemed my best bet.

Meanwhile, I had about fifty dollars in a sock upstairs. I also had a small velvet bag of jewelry that once belonged to my aunt Blanche, a gift from my grandmother last year. The bag held some genuine matched pearls and a variety of precious stones set in rings and necklaces, a bounty that would fetch a pretty penny at some pawnshop or jewelers. But I was holding back from cashing them out until I was desperate for money. Not from sentimentality, no. They were my rainy-day last resort. Some people had insurance policies; I had Aunt Blanche's jewels. I'd not consider selling them before I'd even tried to find work.

Helen came downstairs, looking ready for the department store sales counter in a grass-green wool dress with a plaid collar and cuffs. 'You were quiet last night,' she said. 'I heard you come in with your policeman friend, but we were already dressed for bed, so I didn't come downstairs.'

The 'we' did not go unnoticed.

'Kit's still here, then?'

'Um-hm.' She fussed about the kitchen, scrambling some eggs and slicing some bread.

'Oven's still hot,' I said, 'if you want to toast some bread.'

'Jessie, how many's a few?'

I knew where she was going, but I asked anyway. 'A few what?'

'A few days.'

'Well, a couple of days would be two. A few could be three or four, maybe five. If someone meant six, they'd probably say a week. She's no trouble, Helen, if that's what's worrying you. None of us minds having her here.'

'Thanks, Jessie, I know. I just didn't think she'd be here this long.'

At that, Kit appeared in the doorway, still wearing her pajamas, having descended the stairs so silently neither of us heard the slightest creak. Her hair stuck up in all directions. She yawned and flopped into a chair and glared at the world. If she were waiting for me to fix her breakfast, she would go hungry.

'Haven't you heard from Rose Ann?'

'Not since last week when she sent the telegram from San Francisco.'

'What did she say?'

'Just that she'd be a few more days. She'll probably be back tomorrow, so I shouldn't worry. I just wish she'd telephone.'

'Does Kit seem concerned?'

'Who knows what that odd child is thinking?'

There was one way to find out. 'Kit?' I raised my voice. 'Kit?' She met my eyes with an unflinching gaze that seemed vaguely hostile. 'Would you please write your address?'

Her unfocused eyes stared through me as if I were a pane of clear glass. I asked again, louder. Nothing. I fished in my purse for a pencil and a scrap of paper. 'Would you please write your address?' I scribbled, holding them out toward her.

She looked at the paper, looked at me, and slumped forward onto the table with her head on her arms.

'She probably doesn't know it,' said Helen. 'She's not very bright. Why do you want her address?'

'I thought one of us could go to the house or apartment and knock on some doors. See if any neighbors know how to get in touch with Rose Ann.'

Helen divided the eggs and toast onto two plates, placed one beside Kit's head, and ate her own share hurriedly. 'Good idea. I've got to run, or I'll be late. Have a nice day, Kit,' she said, ruffling the girl's hair before dashing down the walk to catch the Red Car. Kit remained slumped on the table, as lifeless as a dishrag.

I went to the hall telephone and called Barbara Petrovitch, hoping to catch her at home before she left for the studio. And hoping she wouldn't mention my job.

'Good morning, Barbara. This is Jessie Beckett. I've returned from St. Louis.'

'Jessie! How good to hear from you. Did you learn anything about Joe's friend?'

'I think so. Do you have time to talk?'

'Gee, I was just running out the door – we have early call today. But I really want to hear about it . . . can we talk this evening?'

I assured her I'd telephone her later and hung up. Returning to the kitchen, I found Kit in the same position at the table. Her breakfast, however, had vanished from its plate, proving she was alive. I decided it was time to conduct a test.

Standing behind her, I spoke in a voice that was loud and clear, but not a shout. 'Don't move, Kit. There's a spider on your arm. Don't move; I'll get it off.'

I waited for a reaction.

Nothing.

I took a seat in the chair across from her and drummed my fingers on the table. As I hoped, the vibrations brought her head up. With the pencil, I began writing a message, speaking the words as I wrote them. 'I need to write some letters today. I wonder if you might help me? If your penmanship is very good, I will pay you five cents for—'

I stopped mid-sentence. My eyes grew round with horror as I fixed my gaze on her upper arm. In a panicked voice I said, 'Oh dear! A spider's on your arm! Don't move! I'll get it!'

The girl froze. Her face turned white as paste, but she didn't move a muscle as I brushed my hand hard along her arm as if to knock the spider to the ground. As she launched herself in the opposite direction, I made to stomp on the bug, and before she could see that there was nothing there, I had whipped out a piece of scratch paper and pretended to carry the mess to the garbage can.

Trembling like a leaf in a gale, she looked anxiously around the room as if searching for the spider's brothers and sisters. Finally, she inched back to the table where I had resumed my writing.

'There, he's dead and gone and won't bother us any more.' I smiled to reassure her. And I smiled because I had reassured myself that the child was indeed deaf, but that she could read lips. Whenever she appeared to be busy sketching heads, she was also following the conversation, which was how she had come to draw Allenby's black horns right after he'd made that comment. For now, I thought it wise to keep this information to myself. Why, I wasn't quite sure.

'Now,' I said, picking up the pencil and continuing the sentence, 'a nickel for each letter you write. Will you?'

She gave a curt nod. Whether from gratitude or greed, she would help me write a dozen letters to vaudeville friends, asking if they knew of anyone who had performed as a trans-figurator or quick-change artist in the past year. Tomorrow I

would buy copies of *Variety* and *Billboard* and learn which
cities my friends were playing. The entertainment weeklies
listed Big Time acts by city and by theater. A letter addressed
to the theater would find them, as long as it was mailed early
in the week to give it enough time to be delivered before the
act jumped to the next town. The soonest I could expect a
reply would be four days, unless someone sprung for a telegram. Not likely.

That evening, when I figured she'd be home from the studio,
I telephoned Barbara again to give her the news of my trip.
'I have a few questions to ask you, as well,' I added.

'Oh, my, Jessie, I've just walked through the front door and
was about to make dinner. Could you join me here? I'd love
the company. And by the time you arrived, everything would
be ready and you could tell me all about what you
discovered.'

I didn't want to make the effort, but the loneliness in her
voice persuaded me. 'Of course, Barbara, I'd love to come.
I'll be there in about forty minutes,' I said, calculating the
length of the trip and the transfer between streetcar lines.

Thirty-five minutes later, I rapped the Petrovitches' brass
doorknocker.

'Welcome, Jessie,' gushed Barbara when she opened the
door. 'It's so nice to see you! And look who else is here!' she
chirped as she led the way into her parlor where two women
were sitting. Sounds of a symphony poured from a large radio
sitting on the floor between the front windows. 'Did you meet
my sister, Bunny, at Joe's funeral?' she asked.

'Yes, I did,' I said, hiding my dismay. I hadn't bargained
on a hen party. 'Hello, Bunny.'

'Good to see you again, Jessie.'

Barbara continued with her introductions. 'And this is Julia
Shala. Her husband was at the funeral . . . did you meet him?'

'I – I don't think so . . .'

Mrs Shala spoke up in a voice colored with a throaty accent,
'Hello, Miss Beckett. I don't think my husband mentioned
meeting you. Sadly I wasn't able to attend the funeral, but it's
nice to meet you now.'

'Well, then,' Barbara took up the reins of hostess again, 'Miss Jessie Beckett is a dear friend from the studio where we both work.' Obviously Barbara hadn't heard that the studio and I had parted ways. I wondered what people thought – if, indeed, they knew. Perhaps they were told that I had gone out of town, which was true, and assumed I'd be back when the investigation was over. Which was not.

'How do you do, Miss Beckett.'

'Please, call me Jessie,' I said, taking a seat beside her on the sofa. When she did not reciprocate, I chalked it up to old-fashioned manners rather than rudeness.

'Julia is proof that every cloud has a silver lining. She's been such a dear, coming to visit several times since Joe's death and sending lovely food on two occasions. In fact, she baked the cookies we'll have for dessert tonight.'

Now I remembered. 'Oh, was it you who made the delicious walnut *torta* I had on my last visit?' I asked, thinking that it must be cooking, and not her appearance, that gave her pleasure. In no sense a modern woman, Mrs Shala wore her long brown hair wrapped in a nest and pinned against the back of her head, like every pioneer woman for the past century had done. In fact, everything about her was the drab brown of prairie dirt. Her severe, chocolate-colored dress lacked ornamentation, but its cut and quality suggested a professional tailor of some ability, preventing the conclusion that modest circumstances were holding her back. Even her eyes were brown, although sitting as close to her as I was, I noticed the irises were flecked with gold like rays of the sun. Like Bunny, she wore no make-up. I pegged her age at about thirty.

Julia Shala dipped her head modestly. 'I enjoy cooking,' she said with a slight accent. 'It is just my husband and me at home, so it is a pleasure for me to make food for my friends.'

'I've been looking forward to this all day,' said Barbara. 'I'm eager to hear what you learned in St. Louis, Jessie.'

She was obviously not concerned that the other two women would hear my report, so I gave her a shortened version of what I'd shared with Carl the night before, explaining that Al

Jovanovitch had been shot three times at his workplace, just
as Jeton Ilitch and Joe had been. 'And possibly by the same
person,' I added. 'I'm trying to figure out what the three men
had in common that made someone want to kill them. They
were Serbian, of course, we know that, but can you tell me if
they were friends from the Old Country, or had they met in
New York?'

'I'm afraid I don't know,' said Barbara.

The other two women followed our conversation with their
eyes.

'When did Joe come to America?' I asked.

'I'm not sure . . .'

'Would you have any papers that would give a date? Some
immigration papers or maybe a ticket on the boat that brought
him here?'

There was a long pause, and finally Barbara said, 'I'm not
sure, but I know where to look. Before you leave, I'll search
the desk in the bedroom. That would be the only possible
place.'

'Excellent. And one more question: did Joe ever mention
service in the army?'

'Not in America, but when he was younger, he was in the
army back home.'

'Do you remember any details about that? Anything at all?'
Another pause followed, until I said, 'Think that over, and let
me know if you recall anything.'

'Is it important?'

'It might be.'

'Well, then, I'll think hard. But Joe didn't like to talk about
his past. It made him upset.'

'Do you know why?'

'My, no!'

'Would he have talked about his past to anyone other than
you? A priest maybe?' That brought a snort from Bunny.

'Oh, my, no. Joe didn't hold with priests or religion.'

'A friend, then?'

'I'll think on it.'

EIGHTEEN

When there was no word from Rose Ann Riley the next day, I called Metropolitan-6100 and left a message for Carl to telephone me at home. Not ten minutes passed before our telephone bell rang.

'I have a little more information about the Serbs,' I told him. 'I was so tired Thursday night, I forgot to mention that both Jovanovitch and Ilitch had been soldiers. I wondered if Joe Petrovitch had been a soldier too, and if so, which army, so I asked Barbara about it last night. She was sure he'd been in somebody's army, but couldn't tell me much more than that without searching a few drawers. After dinner she found some papers that pointed to his arrival in New York in 1913. Nothing about army service though.'

'So he was in America before the Great War broke out,' said Carl. 'He could have been drafted and shipped back to Europe in 1917. Lots of immigrants were. We had a Greek and a couple of Micks in our unit in France.'

'It's possible. Barbara says Joe mentioned once or twice something about fighting, but she had the sense it was before he came over here. And the men at Moon Motors told me Al had been in St. Louis about ten years, and in New York before that, which would put his arrival roughly in 1913 or 1914 too. Maybe he and Joe came over together. Maybe all three of them came together. Maybe they served in the Serbian army before they came over. This army business is confusing me. I'm heading over to the library this afternoon and see what I can find out.'

'Good idea.'

'Why do you think all these men have similar names? They all end with "-itch".'

'I asked Marks about that the other day. He said it was like in English where lots of names end in "-son" or Scottish where they start with "Mac".'

I grunted. It made sense. But it was hard for me to keep those unfamiliar names straight.

'Another thing, Carl. Could you do me a favor? It's for Kit and Helen, really. Kit's mother hasn't come back for her yet and, well, I don't like to think the worst, but she should have been back by now. According to Helen, she sent a telegram over a week ago from San Francisco, saying it would be just a few more days. She's looking for work and couldn't do it with a kid trailing along. Now that you're a detective, can you check to see if something's happened to her?'

'You think she dumped the kid on Helen and isn't coming back?'

'I hope not.'

'It wouldn't be the first time.'

'More likely she's had an accident or is having a good time with a new friend.'

'Sure, I'll nose around the hospitals, and see if the police in San Francisco have any information on her. What's her name?'

'Rose Ann Riley.'

'What's she look like?'

'I've not met her, but she'd be about thirty or a little older, with dark hair and eyes. According to Helen, she's a talented singer with a husky voice and quite pretty. She's looking for work in speakeasies or on the stage.'

Carl promised to look into it.

After lunch, I told Kit I was going to the library. She wanted to come along.

Libraries were new to me, something I'd discovered only after I'd settled in Hollywood. I'd known about libraries, of course, but I'd never been inside one until last year. When you travel to a new city every week and have no permanent address, it's impossible to get a library card or check out books. All my life, I'd been able to read only the books or newspapers I could beg from other vaudeville performers traveling the same route as ours. Nowadays, my Fernwood address entitled me to all the books I could carry, books of my own choosing. The miracle was, they were free.

Right away, I'd learned that libraries had encyclopedias

where someone had written down everything anyone would ever want to know. You couldn't take those home but you could read them there, which is what I did that afternoon. I read about how the Great War started in 1914 and how Serbia had been on the Allied side against its old enemy, Austria-Hungary. I read about the history of Serbia before that war and since. It wasn't a pretty story. What knocked me back, though, was discovering that Serbia had fought two wars *before* the Great War, one in 1912 and another in 1913. And before that, there had been other wars with Turkey and Bulgaria. For Serbs, the Great War was just a continuation of an unbroken series of battles and bloodshed. I wondered whether they even noticed the end of one war and the start of the next.

It seemed possible that Ilitch, Jovanovitch, and Petrovitch had fought in the Serbian army and immigrated to the United States before the Great War ever started. Did that have any bearing on their murders?

No sooner had we returned home than the telephone jangled off the wall.

'Why, hello again, Carl. We girls are certainly getting our five dollars worth this month,' I said, referring to the service charge. 'Don't tell me you've learned something already.'

'Maybe, maybe not. There's an unidentified body in the San Diego morgue that matches your description of Rose Ann Riley.'

Instinctively I looked around for Kit, but she had gone out back. 'No, that's not Rose Ann. She's in San Francisco.'

'When you last heard from her, she was in San Francisco,' he corrected me gently. 'You said she was looking for work. Isn't it possible she went to San Diego?'

'No . . . I, well . . .' I felt sick. Of course it was possible. I just didn't want to consider it. Speechless, I clutched the receiver and listened as Carl continued.

'I checked the hospitals in 'Frisco and the police there. No score. So I nosed around Los Angeles. Nothing. I checked with a couple other cities. When I reached San Diego, bingo. A woman's body. Found five days ago. No purse. Dark hair, estimated age, thirty-five.'

He paused, and when I said nothing, went on. 'Someone is

going to have to go to San Diego and see if this is Rose Ann Riley. Definitely not Kit. And you don't know her. So that leaves Helen. Or is there anyone else?'

Finding my voice, I replied, 'Helen's mother knows Rose Ann. I'll talk to Helen when she gets home from work.'

'I hope this isn't Kit's mother, Jessie, but it's possible. We need to find out.'

'I understand. I'll talk with Helen.'

'Someone needs to go with her.'

'She has a beau . . . maybe he'll go along.'

'If he won't, I will. The sooner, the better.'

The moment Helen got home from Robinson's, I hurried her into my room, closed the door, and revealed what Carl had discovered. Visibly shaken, she straightened her shoulders and said, 'Mother's not well. Larry's gone to Yosemite Park to see about a wilderness job. It'll have to be me. Will you come with me, Jessie?'

NINETEEN

The three-hour train ride to San Diego seemed to take longer than my three-day trip to St. Louis. I sat in a window seat across from Helen, my face turned toward the sunny California landscape and my hands clasped tightly in my lap as I reviewed all the excellent reasons why this dead woman was not Rose Ann Riley. Helen's head rested back against the seat, her eyes closed. I could tell by her clenched jaw that she was not asleep. Carl Delaney sat beside Helen, reading a newspaper. I'll say this for the man, he knew when to fade into the background.

Traveling with a detective had benefits I did not suspect. A police car met us at the station and drove us directly to the morgue. Being with Carl meant we didn't have to wait for the coroner to work us into his busy schedule; he was waiting for us as if he had nothing better to do that day. In a matter of minutes, we'd signed papers that admitted us to the building and descended into a cool basement that smelled like pickles, only worse. Helen took her handkerchief out of her purse and held it to her nose. A number of gurneys – empty – were lined against one wall. Someone had rolled one of them into the middle of the room. That one was not empty. There was a body on it, covered by a white sheet.

Carl moved close to Helen, positioning himself almost directly behind her.

'Don't worry, I'm not as fragile as I look,' she said with a wry twist to her lips. 'I've seen dead bodies before. My father, for one. I won't swoon.'

The coroner stood beside the gurney, his hands poised over the sheet. There was a silent exchange as he lifted his eyebrows to ask Helen if she were ready. Helen pressed her lips tight and replied with a nod. He lifted the sheet to reveal the head of the unknown woman.

The dead woman's face showed signs of a beating, with cuts on the lip and eyebrow and dark bruises on her jaw. There may have been similar marks or even wounds on other parts of her body, but identification didn't require viewing the entire corpse.

Helen looked, closed her eyes against the sight, then looked again as if making sure. I could tell by her expression that it was Rose Ann.

'To make it official, I have to ask if you know the identity of this woman,' said the coroner.

'I do. That is my mother's cousin.'

'And her name?'

'Rose Ann Riley.'

'Thank you. Now, if you'll follow me, I have some more papers for you to sign.' He covered the battered face that was once Rose Ann and led us up the stairs, back to his spartan office.

After Helen had made arrangements to claim the body and have an undertaker remove it to Los Angeles for a funeral, Carl began his quiet questions.

'How was the body discovered?'

The coroner handed him a police report while answering, 'She was found on the waterfront by some sailors. Naturally,

at first we wondered if they were responsible, thinking she
was a prostitute – begging your pardon, miss, no disrespect
intended, but we have a lot of marines and military here, and
this is a busy port. But there was no evidence of sexual assault,
the sailors had just come off duty, and she'd been dead for
several hours when they found her.'

'No suspects, then?'

The coroner shook his head.

'What was the cause of death?' Carl continued.

'The medical examiner first thought it was internal injuries
from a severe beating, but he soon determined her wounds
were relatively superficial. She'd been knocked around, yes,
but not enough to kill her. So he did an autopsy and discovered
she'd consumed a lethal quantity of methyl alcohol. Wood
alcohol. The stuff's deadly. One teaspoon is enough to kill a
child or blind an adult. A quarter cup'll kill a man. No telling
how much she swallowed.'

Carl nodded his understanding. 'How long does it take?'

'Works different on different people. Usually you don't
know you're poisoned for a coupla hours, then your vision
gets blurry, then you go blind, then a coma, then death.'

'How do you know it was methyl alcohol?'

The coroner sent a worried look in Helen's direction.

'It's all right,' she said gamely. I squeezed her hand. Helen
may have been a wisp of a thing, but she was one tough wisp.
'Well then, wood alcohol autopsies reveal damage in the eyes,
the brain, and the lungs. Tissues are swollen and bloody.
Spongy. If you know what you're looking for, it's pretty hard
to miss.'

'So what do you think happened?' Carl asked.

'There are a lot of gin joints around the docks. Could be
she drank "smoke" at one of them, got roughed up afterwards,
and collapsed when she tried to walk home. Or to wherever
she was staying. Could be she got roughed up first, then drank
the "smoke".'

'Did you see any other wood alcohol cases that night?'

'Nope. Which is why I'm not too keen on those theories.
If some speakeasy was ladling out "smoke", we'd have had
bodies piled high that night. And we didn't. Trouble is, my

only other theory is suicide.' And he looked pointedly at Helen. She shook her head. 'Not Rose Ann. She had a daughter who needed her. She would never have killed herself. And she wasn't down and out, or facing financial ruin, or anything like that.'

'How well did you know her?'

'Not very well,' Helen admitted.

'Was she pregnant?' asked Carl. That was something I would not have considered.

'No.'

'Well, then, we won't take up any more of your time,' Carl said. Turning to Helen, he asked, 'Do you have any other questions, Miss Reynolds?' When she shook her head, he thanked the coroner and escorted Helen and me back out to the street where the automobile was waiting. The entire ordeal had taken less than an hour.

'Would you ladies care to step into a hotel for tea or something to eat before we head back?'

I motioned for Helen to decide.

'That's very kind of you, Mr Delaney, but I'd like to get home as soon as I can. I have a difficult job ahead of me and putting it off only makes it harder.'

I didn't envy Helen. Telling a child that her mother was dead must rank among the more difficult tasks the world has to offer, one made worse by the absence of a father, sister, or brother to share Kit's grief. I was prepared for a silent ride back to Los Angeles, but with the identification of the body behind us and the worries ahead of us, Helen was inclined to talk. I mostly listened.

'How'm I going to tell Kit her mother's dead?' she began, more thinking out loud than launching a discussion. 'How do you tell someone they're an orphan?'

With that question, I was twelve years old again, climbing the worn-carpet steps toward our hotel room, the cloying scent of mothballs seeping into my skin. Mrs Reimschneider, the matron who managed all us children in Kid Kabaret, met me in the hallway in front of the door to our room. The last act of Thursday night was done, and we kids were straggling back to the hotel to have our dinner and fall into our beds.

'Don't go in,' she said, not unkindly. Her double chin and round cheeks with two large moles were as clear in my memory as if I had seen her yesterday. 'Your dear mother has passed. It is very sad, but we've expected it now these few days, haven't we?'

I had nothing to say.

'The undertaker is taking care of her now. You'll sleep in the girls' room tonight. Go get something to eat. We'll look after you from now on.'

Mrs Reimschneider's motto was that a kid could do anything an adult could do, so there was no cosseting of children in Kid Kabaret. Perhaps she was right that staying busy distracted you from grief. Whatever her intention, I never missed a performance. The next day, Saturday, the undertaker buried my mother during our matinee show. Mrs Reimschneider took me to her grave early Sunday morning before the act jumped to the next city. We put a flower on the mound of dirt. I don't know who paid for the funeral or whether there was ever a headstone. I never went back. My mother wasn't there. I knew where she was. She had told me she would be watching me every day from heaven.

'Kit has family,' I told Helen. 'She has you and your mother.' Blood relatives were nothing to scoff at – decent ones fed you and gave you a place to sleep. It was more than I had had. 'You'll want to ask your mother what other relatives there are who might be able to help her. Financially, if they're not able to take her in.'

'I need financial help too. I just arranged for a funeral I can't afford.' She bit her cuticles. 'I'll ask Mother if she can spare a little. But she doesn't have much either. Now that I think of it, she does have a brother in Baltimore. Maybe she can ask him to pitch in. Rose Ann was his cousin too. Jesus, how'm I going to tell Kit her mother's dead? I guess I'll have to write it out when I get home. Can I use the desk in your room?'

'Of course.'

'That'll give me some privacy to think. What'll I say? Someone beat up your mother and she drank poison? I can't say that. I can't say suicide. I'll leave out the beating up part and say she got some bad hooch. An accident. That's probably what it was, anyway, don't you figure? An accident. How's that sound?'

'I think you're on the right track.'

'What about her things? Her clothes and her personal effects. I don't even know where they lived. An apartment, a hotel, a boarding house? She might have had some money that Kit could use. Or I could use for her funeral. Or some things I could sell. Do you think I'm awful to worry about the money?'

'Not at all. You're being realistic. Kit will know where they lived.'

'I don't think she does. She isn't very . . . she's not normal.'

Privately, I thought Kit was a good deal more normal than she let on, but I didn't feel this was the moment to voice my suspicions about lip reading. It would complicate everything at a time when everything was complicated enough. 'You said Larry was out of town?'

She nodded. 'He's gone to Yosemite about a job. He'll be back in a day or two. What'm I going to do about tomorrow? I've gotta go to work. I already lost today's pay and my boss'll be furious if I don't show tomorrow. I could get fired. But I should stay home with Kit.'

'I'll be home tomorrow.' I didn't say: and every day until I can find work. 'Kit won't be alone.'

'Thanks, Jessie.' She leaned over and gave me an awkward hug. 'You're a brick. Thanks for coming with me today. And you too, Mr Delaney. I don't think I could have done it alone.'

In the end, Helen did it alone, breaking the news to Kit as gently as she could. As soon as we got home, she disappeared into my room where she spent half an hour composing her letter for Kit to read. Then I saw her take Kit into their bedroom and hand her the paper. She closed the door. I heard nothing more from them until Helen came downstairs the next morning.

TWENTY

I ought to have been looking for a new job, and I meant to start that very day, but Mike Allenby's unexpected, mid-morning visit drove the subject clean out of my head. None of the girls had mentioned seeing the newspapers that said I'd left Hollywood for parts unknown, which was fine with me – their sympathy would only make me feel worse. But Mr Allenby read the newspapers. He must have seen the studio's press release because he knew he would find me at home.

'I've brought you a letter from David Carr,' he said, tendering an envelope. Someone had already opened it.

'What's the latest?' I asked, inviting him into the kitchen for coffee. The house was empty but for me and Kit, who had not yet come downstairs. The others had gone to work. I poured him a cup and refreshed my own. 'When can I visit the prison?'

'You can't.' He sighed and held up his hands as if to ward off a blow. 'C'mon, lady, don't shoot the messenger!'

His attention shifted to a spot behind me, and I turned to see Kit enter the kitchen on silent bare feet. 'Good morning, Kit,' I said, knowing she would help herself to bread and jam if she were hungry. Did her eyes seem a little red? I might be imagining it. She gave no other outward appearance of grief.

There was room at the kitchen table, but she settled instead on a stool by the icebox, near the back door. A vantage point, I noted, that gave her a clear shot of both our lips without having to turn her head from one to the other. I pulled David's letter out of the envelope and started to read.

Very dear Jessie,
Allenby is confident I'll be out soon but appeals take a long time, months probably. I don't want you to worry about me.
I'm finding the food lousy but the company is

swell. Meanwhile you could really help me and earn my
everlasting gratitude if you would move into the house
and take
care of things there til I get back.
All day long I think of you and at night you're in my
dreams.
Several times a day I think how lucky I am to
have you for my girl.
   David

'Oh my,' was all I could say. I met Allenby's eyes.

'He wants me to persuade you to move into his house. Says it's half yours. That's why I'm here.'

'But . . .' I let the sentence hang, unfinished, while I puzzled out David's motives. 'Does he expect to be released soon?' It would be just like David to play on my sympathies for his current predicament to get me to move into the house right before he was released.

The lawyer heaved a great sigh. 'Nothing is happening on that front. Nothing. It's like there's a logjam in the river holding back the flood, but I can't break it. I've done everything and then some. I can usually find a cooperative judge to consider my appeals. I submitted two dozen – and two or three were even legitimate. All denied. Never happened before. I've even put feelers out to the governor's office, but I can't get anyone to return my telephone calls.'

'What are you saying? That you're finished? That there's nothing else to be done?' The panic welled up inside my throat.

'Hell, no. Mike Allenby never gives up the fight. I'm thinking about laying low for a while and letting this die down, then trying again next year—'

'*Next year?*'

'Early next year. Hell, this is November! It's almost next year now! And next year's an election year. Everyone's more receptive in an election year.'

'I can't believe this, after you said—'

'Look, I know what I said, and I was right when I said it. I don't know what's gone wrong. But things aren't as bad as all that. Worst case is, he gets out early for good behavior.'

'How early?'

He shrugged. 'No telling. Two years maybe—'

I gaped. Two years? How was I to get along without seeing David for two years? And what if he didn't get out for good behavior? What if he had to serve the entire three-and-a-half-year sentence?

'Listen, Miss Beckett, there isn't much you can do to help him at this point. Hell, there isn't much *I* can do to help him, and I'm the best. But this is something. It meant a lot to him that I bring you this letter and urge you to move into the house without delay. Take care of his things. An empty house goes downhill fast. No one's watching out for it – it could get broken into. And think of it, you'd not have to pay rent since he owns it free and clear. No mortgage, right? And you without a job – yeah, I read it in the paper. Sorry, hon. All you'd need is a couple bucks a month for electricity and a few more for property taxes. Whatever the expenses are, they're less than you're paying to live in this . . . ah . . . place. And his house is damn nice, or so I'm told.'

It was at that. I must have looked like I was weakening.

'Here's the key,' he said, handing me three keys tied together with a leather thong. 'I don't know which one is for the house but you'll figure it out. Look, anyone with a grain of sense would jump at this offer. All I'm asking is that you sleep on it a few days. Don't make me go back to that prison cell and disappoint the guy. This is something he really wants. Something you can do to help.'

He paused long enough to drain his cup and refuse my offer for seconds. 'No thanks. That's all I got to say. Let me know what you decide.' And he took his leave. I poured myself the last of the coffee.

Kit hadn't moved from her stool. She sat, drinking a glass of milk and eating her usual bread and jam, watching me with big eyes. Yes, David and I had troubles. But she had worse. I made a snap decision.

'Good morning, Kit,' I began, looking directly into her face and enunciating my words clearly. 'There are no words to tell you how sorry I was to learn that your mother is dead. I know how you are feeling: sad and frightened and empty and angry

– yes, angry, because your mother left you all alone, even though you know very well she didn't want to. I know this because I lost my mother when I was about your age. Like you, I had no father and no sisters or brothers. But you have something I never had. You have family. You have Helen and her mother, and maybe others. I know what you're thinking: where will I go? Who will take care of me? They will step up. That's what family does.'

Her eyes welled up, but no tears fell. She sniffed, rubbed her nose with the back of her hand, and continued to fix me with that vacant, unblinking stare I'd come to despise. I delivered the coup de grâce.

'I also know you can understand me. I know you can read lips.'

From her perch on the high stool, she glared down her nose at me for what seemed like several minutes. Then she sniffed and trumped my card with hers.

'I can talk too,' she said.

I nearly spilled my coffee.

TWENTY-ONE

The twitch at the corner of Kit's lips hinted at her satisfaction at having gotten the best of me. It was a you-think-you're-so smart smirk, and it came packaged with a glint of superiority in her eyes.

'Oh!' was my clever retort. A hundred questions jostled in my head. As soon as I'd recovered my wits, I started with the most obvious.

'Are you really deaf?'

The single nod of her head had me worried that Kit's brief foray into speech had ended as abruptly as it had begun. Determined to keep the conversation going, I asked a question that could not be answered with gestures.

'I thought deaf people couldn't speak?'

She looked for her pencil, and I could see her indecision.

Write or talk? Finally she spoke. 'People born deaf can't speak.'

In my mind, I saw Helen Keller as she had looked that day on the vaudeville stage. Her almost unintelligible speech had to be translated by her helper for us in the audience to understand her words. She had not been born deaf either, but lost her hearing at a very young age, and therefore could learn how to make sounds. But although Miss Keller tried hard for years, she confessed that she was never able to reach the point where average people could understand her. Kit was easy enough to understand, although her voice had an off-key, monotonic quality about it.

'So you were not born deaf?'

'I was five. Meningitis. I was in the hospital for a year. I can still hear some things. Trains and thunder. And drums.'

I suspected she wasn't hearing those sounds as much as she was feeling the vibrations, but I didn't say so.

'How did you learn to read lips?'

'Everyone reads lips, a little. Deaf school taught me some. Mostly I taught myself.'

'I thought you didn't go to school.'

'I don't. They won't let deaf kids go to regular school. They think we're all simps.'

'What about the deaf school?'

'They were mean. I ran away. I told Ma if she sent me back, I'd run away again. Who did you live with when your mother died? And you can stop exaggerating your lips. It makes it harder, not easier.'

'Oh. Well, then.' It was my turn to speak. I steeled myself before stepping back into the unhappy aspects of my past. 'My mother knew she was dying, and she set me up with Kid Kabaret, a flash act where the kids sing and dance and put on two-minute plays.'

'What's that?'

'What's what?'

'A flat act?'

'Flash act,' I corrected her. 'That's a showy act with a lot of performers that brings its own scenery.'

She nodded and I went on. 'My mother's stage name was

Chloë Randall, and she was a singer – a headliner.' I can always hear the dreamy note in my voice when I say those words. My mother was a genuine headliner in her day, what they call a 'star' in the pictures, and I was very proud of her. 'Most of the time, we both worked, but when she got sick – it was cancer that killed her – I was the only one bringing in money for more than a year. And let me tell you, kids in vaudeville don't make a tenth of what adults make. That was a tough year.' That was when I'd started stealing, but Kit didn't need to know about that.

And all of a sudden, I *was* telling her about those days, and the telling was painfully honest. 'That last year, I started stealing. Mother never knew. She'd have been so disappointed. At first it was food. After paying train fares and hotels, there just wasn't enough money to feed us. Then it was aspirin and other medicines from the drug store. Soon, it was whatever I wanted.'

Kit's eyes got wide.

'I'm not proud of that, but I don't see as I had much choice. After my mother died, I stuck with Kid Kabaret for a year or so; then they traded me to an acrobatic act because I was light and limber and could do the really high stunts. After that, I learned to fend for myself and found work with any act that would have me: magicians, song-and-dance, Shakespeare. Sometimes I worked a week or two with an act; other times a whole season. I was small and kept my child-like appearance even as I grew older, so I fit into lots of acts that needed a kid. My last gig was with a family song-and-dance troupe called The Little Darlings. I was with them for several years. I really liked that gig. It was almost like having a real family. I wish it had lasted, but nothing lasts forever, I've learned that lesson all too well. Then I washed up, as they say, in vaudeville.'

Kit scowled me the question.

'It means failed. No one wanted me for kiddie roles any longer, not when they could hire a real kid for a fraction of what they would pay an adult. And I was good at singing, dancing, acting, comedy, acrobatics, magic – just about anything on stage – but I wasn't exceptional at anything. Have you heard the old saying, "jack of all trades, master of none"? That's me. I couldn't find honest work, so I took some jobs that were not so honest. Afterwards, I moved here. A vaudeville friend knew of a job coming open at Pickford-Fairbanks Studios, and he put in a good word for me.' I skipped over the part where I should have admitted I no longer had that job. 'I like it here just fine. In my whole life, I've never lived in one place longer than a week, so this seems like paradise to me. Some things in vaudeville I miss a lot. But not enough to leave what I have here.'

I waited for Kit to digest this large helping of information, and when she didn't speak, I went on. 'So . . . your mother was like mine, I guess. A singer. What kinda of music did she sing?'

'Current songs. Gershwin. Porter. Jazz. She liked jazz. Everyone said she could sing anything and make it sound good.'

'What did you do while she was working?'

She looked up, startled, and I thought for a moment she wasn't going to answer.

'She didn't usually start 'til ten o'clock. Mostly, I went with her to the club or speakeasy or cabaret, wherever she was singing. Usually they had food and someone would give me something to eat for free. I'd watch people. I'd stay up 'til I fell asleep on a table, or if there were booths, I could lie on a bench.'

'Why the charade? Surely your mother knew you could read lips.'

She gave a careless shrug. 'I can read half what people are saying by their lips; the rest I figure out. Ma usually wrote down things to make sure I understood everything.'

'And what about talking?'

The child pulled her knees up to her chin and picked at her bare toes. 'When I talk, people make fun of me. Ma's voice was so beautiful, it hurt her to hear me talk, like singing out of tune, she said. So I stopped. Except with animals and fish. After a while, Ma probably forgot I could talk.'

Kit had lost her hearing relatively late, so, unlike Helen Keller, she had several years of speaking to fall back on. Yet

I understood what she meant about others making fun of her – her speech did not sound natural, and she mixed up certain sounds, like *sh* and *ch*. Anyone could understand her if they tried, but she would have to risk their laughter. It was a lot to ask of a child. Too much for this one.

'Tell me about when you saw my mother.'

'I'm sure Helen told you everything.'

'You tell.'

The kid was checking my story against Helen's. I had to be careful not to contradict whatever Helen had told her last night.

'Well, then, Officer Delaney went with us. When your mother didn't show up, I asked him to check the hospitals in San Francisco, where she had been when she sent us the last telegram. When he turned up nothing there, he contacted police headquarters throughout the state, and that's when he learned there was an unidentified woman in the San Diego morgue. He wanted Helen to see if it was your mother. Helen wanted me to come along for moral support. The medical examiner said she had died several days earlier from alcohol poisoning.' Then, because I didn't know if Rose Ann's funeral would have an open casket or not, I laid the groundwork for her battered face. 'Her face was scraped up, from a fall, the doctor said, but Helen could tell for certain it was your mother.'

Kit disappeared inside herself for long minutes. I cleaned up the coffee cups and then made a proposal.

'How about we cook dinner for everyone tonight?'

She shook her head.

'I don't know how to cook either,' I said, reaching on a shelf for the Fanny Farmer cookbook. 'But Melva has this swell cookbook, and we both know how to read, so let's choose what we want to eat and get started.'

I pulled the reluctant child into the selection process and after much deliberation, we settled on meatloaf and scalloped potatoes with glazed carrots for vegetables. And sugar cookies for dessert. After Kit had made a list of the ingredients we needed, we walked to the butcher's for chunks of beef and pork, and then to the market for the rest. Taking turns at the meat grinder, we ground the beef and pork into mush and mixed it with breadcrumbs, beaten eggs, celery, onion, ketchup, and the spices called for in the recipe, then pressed the whole unappealing glop into a loaf pan. I hoped it tasted better than it looked. It was too early to light the oven, so we covered the pan with a clean dishrag, set it in the icebox, and turned our attention to cookies.

By the time the others got home that evening, Kit and I were relaxing on the patio, our stomachs full of tea and sugar cookies.

'Well, well. I can see what you two have been doing today,' said Helen, throwing me an appreciative smile. 'You'll turn into wife material any day now, Jessie. A good home-cooked dinner is the path to any man's heart. And cookies! I can't wait. You girls have been busy.'

'And we've got good news,' I said, giving Kit a verbal nudge.

'So have I,' said Helen. The words came out in a rush. 'I just heard from Mother who just heard from her brother who sent word that he would not be able to come all the way from Baltimore for Rose Ann's funeral, but he would be happy to cover all of her final expenses himself, and I was so relieved, as you can imagine, and he said some nice things about Rose Ann, too; memories from when they were young, which he had more of than Mother since he was closer to her age than Mother was, and he's promised to send some money for Kit.'

'That's wonderful, Helen,' I said, inserting myself into the conversation when she finally came up for air. Now that I knew Kit could read lips, I didn't want Helen saying anything indiscreet. 'We have good news, too, don't we, Kit?'

Kit scowled and stared into the fishpond.

To get her started, I announced in a chipper voice, 'Kit can read lips.'

'Oh, my,' said Helen, sounding slightly confused. 'How wonderful! When did she learn that? Does that mean we don't have to write things down any longer?'

If Kit thought I was going to pull the entire load, she was mistaken. The news would go over better coming from her. Helen looked from me to Kit and back again, waiting for enlightenment, until finally Kit spoke up.

'I can talk too.'

Helen's jaw dropped.

I took over from there, smoothing the way. 'Since Kit didn't lose her hearing until she was five, she already knew how to talk. Most deaf people are born deaf and can't learn to talk, you know.'

'I, uh, geez, no, I didn't know any deaf people could talk. Deaf and dumb, you know, they go together, I thought.'

'Great news, huh?' I said cheerily, giving Helen an I'll-talk-with-you-later look. Fortunately, she caught my meaning. 'Why don't you light the oven, Helen, so we can get that meatloaf started. I'll boil the water for the carrots.' Once in the kitchen and out of sight, I filled her in on Kit's transformation.

Dinner started awkwardly, since the girls all felt they'd been conned by a kid. Which was true. I knew they were trying to think back, wondering if they had said anything in Kit's presence that they hadn't meant for her to hear. I know I had done that. But everyone's concern for Kit's loss soon took the edge off any hard feelings.

Only later that night, when I'd retired to my room to reread David's letter did I notice its peculiarities. It sounded stilted, not like David at all. 'Very dear Jessie?' He usually called me 'kid' never 'my girl'. And 'everlasting gratitude' sounded like a syrupy film title. I figured some prison guard standing over him while he wrote it must have rattled him.

I lay in bed thinking about how the lines were aligned on the left but uneven on the right. People didn't write sentences like that; they wrote to the right-hand edge of the line before they moved down to the next. Was there some hidden message that I'd missed? Something he didn't want the guards to see? I dismissed that idea. If that were the case, he could have told Mike Allenby and had him relay the message to me.

Unless he didn't trust Allenby any more than he trusted the guards.

I sat up in bed, switched on the lamp, and took another, longer look.

TWENTY-TWO

D awn had just painted pink and blue stripes on the eastern sky when I hopped an early-morning Red Car heading east on Hollywood Boulevard. Half the sun had risen by the time I stepped down at the corner nearest Whitley Heights. I had to restrain myself from breaking into a gallop, so eager was I to reach David's house and search for the cash. For there *had* been a hidden message in the note he'd sent me. The first letter on the left-hand edge of each line, when read vertically, spelled out V-A-L-I-S-E-C-A-S-H. I should have spotted it sooner, but Kit's confession had temporarily blinded me to the peculiarities of David's note.

House key in hand, I approached the front door, fretting every step of the way that someone else had beaten me to it. A month had passed since David's unexpected arrest, a whole month when the house had been empty. Anyone could have come in and ransacked the place, and no one would have known.

As secret messages went, David's wasn't all that hard to crack, but I reasoned that he'd been forced to write in haste, without time to develop some unbreakable spymaster's code – and even if he had, I wouldn't have known to look for it or how to decipher it. The guards routinely read outgoing mail, and I knew Allenby had read it as well. If David had trusted Allenby, he'd have given him the message verbally, but he obviously did not. He trusted no one but me, and I'd not let him down. All I could do was hope no one else had caught his meaning and cleaned out the hidden cash last night.

The modest – for that neighborhood – three-level house with its red tile roof clung to the hillside like a white stucco waterfall. I let myself in the front door. It had always seemed so cheerful when David was there; now my footsteps echoed eerily on the polished wood floor. The rooms had that empty, stale smell that signaled abandonment, and a layer of dust covered the polished furniture. David had been arrested without warning, meaning he hadn't had the chance to close up the house properly. Someone – Allenby's secretary, presumably – had removed the food from the icebox and emptied the drip pan, so no odor of rotting meat assaulted me as I entered.

Where would a man stash his luggage? I opened the small closet by the front door first, but it held nothing but a few coats. I climbed the stairs to the top story and looked in the closets in each of the three bedrooms. No results. In David's room, the unmade bed with its tangled snow-white sheets conjured up vivid images of frolic and laughter from the last night I'd slept there. A whole month ago! Distracted by the memories, I backed out of the bedroom and went down to the lowest level, where I had been but once, to search the maid's room closet and the storage room beside it. David had no live-in servant, but fancy houses like this one were built with such expectations.

Eureka! A trunk, two suitcases, and a grip. One by one, I pulled them out and opened the clasps. I made sure to root around in the linings, in case he'd stuck some hundred-dollar bills beneath the fabric, but there was nothing. I rapped my knuckles on every inside surface in case there was a false wall built into the case. The largest valise felt heavier than the rest. It was locked, which gave me hope that I'd hit pay dirt. It took me some minutes to find a suitable tool in a kitchen drawer and another few minutes to pick the cheap lock. Heart pounding, I opened the lid, only to find some old clothes. Thinking he might have stashed a roll of bills inside a pocket, I turned every one inside out. Empty.

Undaunted, I ransacked every nook and cranny of the lower level. It didn't take long. There was no more luggage or bags of any description to be found. I returned to the main level and conducted a thorough search of kitchen cabinets, a narrow broom closet, and the cupboard in the den, to no avail. David had lived here only a few months, and he wasn't a pack rat. A typical man – he needed very little, and he owned very little. There were not that many places one could hide something as large as a valise.

I had already examined the bedroom closets, but it now

occurred to me there might be an attic with a ceiling opening. I went back upstairs and looked up at every hall and room ceiling. I spied cobwebs but no attic door. Nor did the house have any storage closets tucked into the eaves. There was no garage and no outdoor shed. And two of the bedrooms were entirely empty of furniture. I checked their closets. Nothing.

Utterly frustrated, I stood in David's bedroom with my hands on my hips, thinking hard. Could I have misunderstood the message? Had I overlooked another part of the secret wording? Perhaps the valise was small, and I'd missed it. Perhaps it was inside something else, a drawer maybe. Where would I put a valise?

In a place so obvious, I'd overlooked it entirely. Under the bed. I dropped to my knees beside David's bed and peered under it.

There it was.

I pulled it out, flipped open the lid, and gasped. There was no roll of bills stashed in the lining. There was no wad of cash tucked inside a pocket. There were stacks and stacks upon stacks of well-worn, green bills, each bound with a rubber band, completely filling the valise. Most of the visible bills were twenties; some were tens and hundreds. Grabbing one of the bundles with a shaky hand, I determined that the top bill indicated the ones beneath it. Five rows of hundreds, twenty-five rows of twenties, five rows of tens. I had no earthly idea how to estimate the amount of money that I was looking at – thousands of dollars, surely. No, tens of thousands. Maybe hundreds of thousands?

With a pounding heart and damp palms, I rocked back on my heels, pondering my predicament. I couldn't drag a heavy suitcase full of cash home on the streetcar. Or, perhaps I could, but I'd look so nervous and guilty that someone would snatch it out of my hands. And what would I do with it back at the house on Fernwood? I had no place to put it except under my bed. We didn't even lock our doors. What did David mean for me to do with his cash?

I needed to put it someplace safe. A bank was safe, but I could just imagine the reaction of a pot-bellied, balding banker when a young woman handed him a suitcase full of cash and said, 'I'd like to open an account.' He'd call the cops for sure.

Try as I might, I couldn't think of a safer place than where it was now: under the bed. I closed the case – after removing five bills from the ten-dollar bundle – and shoved it back beneath the bed. I'd write David a carefully worded letter asking him what I was to do with his surprise.

Before I left, I checked every door and window, making certain each was locked tight. Then I circled the house, looking for anything odd or out of place. As I backed through the garden gate and bent to secure the latch, I heard a click and a voice behind me.

'Hands up, lady, or I'll shoot.'

When my heart started beating again, I smiled, raised my hands, and turned slowly.

'Don't shoot, sheriff,' I said to the pint-sized desperado in the neighboring yard. He must have been about seven.

'Are you a burglar? Mama says there might be burglars.'

'No, siree bob, I'm no burglar. I'm a friend of Mr Carr who lives here. He had to go away for a while, so I'm looking after his house while he's gone. Can I put my hands down now?'

The lad holstered his gun and pushed his cowboy hat back from his forehead. His knee socks were streaked with mud, his shoes scuffed, and one of the suspenders holding up his knickers had come unhooked, indicating a vigorous morning chasing crooks.

'Do you know Mr Carr?' I asked.

'Sure I do. He used to let me come over and play with his Rin Tin Tin dog,' he said solemnly, reminding me of David's German shepherd, Rip. 'I was sad when he died.'

'I was sad too. Rip was very brave. But he was very old.' I doubted David had shared the circumstances of Rip's death with the youngster, so I glossed over the details.

'We buried him over here,' the boy said. 'Come look.' And he led me to a shady corner of the walled garden where there was a wooden marker with 'R.I.P. Rip' on it. 'Get it? Mr Carr said R.I.P. means Rest In Peace and that spells Rip too. Get it?' I nodded my understanding. 'Mama said he was in heaven now, chasing squirrels. What's your name?'

'Jessie. What's yours?'

'Billy.'

'Well, Billy, I need to go home now, but I'll be back soon.
Tell your mother not to worry about burglars any more. I'm
going to be living here until Mr Carr gets back, so the house
won't be empty. I'll be taking care of the place. With your
help, of course, we'll keep the burglars away.'

TWENTY-THREE

Another funeral. It seemed like yesterday I was strug-
gling with the back buttons of my dark purple mourning
dress, getting ready for Joe Petrovitch's funeral, and
here came another one, this time for Rose Ann Riley. Old
people dying is sad, but not tragic. Funerals for murdered
people, though – especially innocent victims like Rose Ann
– offend every sense of fairness and decency and left me
feeling outraged. At least this funeral had nothing to do with
the Serbian murders I was trying to solve.

We were a small group gathered together that Friday
morning. Rose Ann's death had not been reported in any of
the Los Angeles papers, so there were no newspapermen at
the gravesite. Of course, Melva, Lillian, Myrna, and I were
there, and Carl Delaney came. Helen's beau, Larry, home at
last from his job-seeking venture into Yosemite National Park,
drove over to Riverside to pick up Mrs Reynolds, Helen's
mother, and bring her to us. When Helen asked Kit if there
was anyone she wanted to notify – Rose Ann's former
employer, perhaps, or some friends or neighbors – Kit reprised
her sullen silence for an answer. The child had nothing suitable to wear, so Helen bought a simple black dress in children's
ready-to-wear at Robinson's. It was too big, but there wasn't
time to have it altered. In the ill-fitting black dress, black hat,
and black stockings, she looked like an inmate out of Jane
Eyre's bleak orphanage.

It was unfortunate, I thought, that mourners were able to
view Rose Ann's body as it lay in the casket. The funeral
parlor's make-up man had done his level best to color over

the bruises on her face and mask the cuts, but it wasn't convincing. And it didn't look like scrapes from a stumble, not to me, anyway. Luckily, Kit was too young to come to that conclusion, for she simply stared intently at her mother for the last time and made no sound when they closed the lid.

Mrs Reynolds was sweet in that vague, helpless way so many older women assume, purposefully or not, as they age. I pegged her at about fifty. Halfway through the service at the gravesite, the minister paused and, looking directly at her, said, 'I'm afraid I never had the pleasure of knowing Rose Ann Riley, so I wonder if anyone here would like to say a few words in tribute to her.'

Mrs Reynolds gave a quiet nod that suggested she was prepared to play her part. 'Of all of us present today, except for Kit, of course, I believe I knew Rose Ann best, so perhaps it's for me to speak on her behalf. We were first cousins,' she explained to any of us who were unaware of the relationship, 'but as sometimes happens in families, there was a great distance between us in age. Almost twenty years. So I remember little Rose Ann when she was a baby, and when she was a youngster who came to visit. From the time she could talk, she was singing, and such a pretty voice she had! Mother would play the piano and little Rose Ann would sing – why, I remember one time when . . .' And for about ten minutes, she related some mundane stories about Rose Ann, finishing with a story about Kit's birth and how Rose Ann doted on her new baby girl. It was a good performance, and we were all touched.

We all – except Carl, who had to return to work – went back to our house for lunch, where Mrs Reynolds sat beside Kit and made a special effort to communicate with the child. I had to admire her resolve – it was a trying task in the best of circumstances, and today was assuredly not that. An uncanny quiet shrouded the girl. She sat motionless, lost inside herself, oblivious to everyone and everything. Having refused to speak for so many years, she clung to her practice of staring through people and ignoring them until they gave up trying to coax a response out of her. Old habits would not, or could not, change overnight, but Mrs Reynolds had the patience and gentle persistence to persuade her to eat a few bites and react with an occasional gesture.

In the midst of all this, the mailman brought a stack of letters, among them the first responses to my request for information about transfigurators that had gone out a week ago. I had three replies: two had no knowledge of any recent transfigurators. The other remembered a man from about five years back who went by the name of Bombolini. His uninspiring protean act hadn't lasted long, my friend said, but I made a mental note of the name.

The following day, five more letters arrived: two that regretted being unable to help me and three that put forth possible names. The cast of suspects was starting to file past me like actors auditioning for a play. One was The Great Rudolpho, known to his mother as Rudolph Schreckheise, who advertised himself as a magician and worked the Orpheum circuit, but he performed one trick that included a quick-change component. Another – this one from my old friend Angie with the Cat Circus – told of a performer named Seb Yancey, a Negro protean who worked the TOBA circuit. Since none of the eyewitnesses had seen a colored killer, I dismissed this nomination out of hand. A third letter, this one from a juggler I had known a dozen years ago, told me he had shared a billing last year with a transfigurator named Vesa Leka. 'A foreigner who did a good act,' the juggler wrote. 'Audiences didn't sit on their hands. But he left vaudeville about six months ago, and I'm thinking he may have died, because no one leaves during the applause.' This sounded promising since the man was a foreigner and had quit around the time the killings had started, although I would have been happier if his name had ended in '–itch', like all the dead Serbian men.

That evening after supper, when all of us girls except Kit were sitting outside, Helen came out with a tray of pretty drinks and a plate of store-bought chocolates.

'Ladies,' she began. 'I have an after-dinner treat and something to celebrate. Help me pass these, Melva.'

'What are they?' asked Myrna breathlessly.

'A drink Larry and I learned about in Mexico last month. It's orange juice, lime juice, and tequila, called a Tequila

Sunrise. I couldn't make the exact recipe, but this is close. The tequila is the real McCoy. We brought it back with us.' She'd gone to a good deal of trouble to decorate each drink with a wooden skewer that pierced a thin slice of lime and a small strawberry. 'It's delicious, Helen,' I said, 'and we're dying of curiosity, so spill the news!'

'Well, then.' She raised her voice in the manner of a vaudeville emcee and cleared her throat. 'Ahem . . . Ladies and ladies! I'd like to announce, drum roll please, that Mr Lawrence Evans has asked Miss Helen Reynolds to marry him and –' here we all began squealing with delight '– and Miss Helen Reynolds has accepted!'

Our hoots and hollers probably disturbed neighbors a mile away, but we didn't care. The announcement was hardly a shock – Helen had been seeing Larry for some months, and we knew they were madly in love. All us girls liked Larry, an earnest young man who shared Helen's passion for the outdoors. It was a perfect match.

'You gals know he was in Yosemite last week about a job, right? Well, he was offered that job, and he starts as a park ranger in two weeks. He was waiting to see about it before he asked me to marry him, and, well, he asked me right when he got home with the good news, but I, well, I wanted to tell you sooner, but I couldn't be making happy announcements when we were burying Kit's poor mother. The thing is, I couldn't hold back any longer because we're getting married next weekend –' she paused as we all gasped '– yes, next weekend, and then moving to Yosemite right away before his job starts. I've already given notice at Robinson's.'

Everyone talked at once, offering help with the wedding dinner, the ceremony, the packing up, and the move.

'There won't be much to plan,' Helen said. 'You know me, I'm not the white-dress-and-train kind of gal. I've got a new green dress to wear, and we'll say our vows to the Justice of the Peace.'

'We'll have a reception right here afterwards!' Myrna said. 'I'll organize it.'

'We'll all make some of the food,' said Lillian.

'Hold on, there, girls,' I said, laughing. 'I don't think you want me cooking my famous cowboy sandwiches, so maybe I'd better provide the beverages.' I suffered a sharp pang, thinking of David and how he'd've enjoyed the celebration. And how he'd've contributed some of his genuine Old Grand-Dad, too.

'What will you do out there, Helen?' asked Myrna. 'Won't you be awfully lonely?'

'Oh, Myrna, me? Lonely? With all those thousands of acres of wilderness and all the animals and waterfalls and hiking trails? I'll be in heaven. Larry says they're building a new museum and after that, a big hotel for all the tourists who want to come, so I'm sure I can get paid work whenever I want it. And I'll be making a home for Larry in a ranger's cabin, so I'll have plenty to do.'

After a few moments, I found myself next to Helen and took the opportunity to pose a quiet question. 'What about Kit?'

'I was just coming to that. That's the other good news. My mother really warmed to Kit yesterday and said she wanted to give her a home in Riverside.' She frowned. 'I know it isn't perfect, but Kit can't come with us to Yosemite. There aren't any schools or libraries or stores – heck, there are hardly any people! It's real wilderness living. My mother offered to clear out the spare bedroom, the one that used to be mine, and with us so far away, Kit will be company for her – you know, Larry said it was three hundred miles from here to Yosemite. We just can't take her with us. I told Kit a little while ago.'

'What did she say?'

'The same thing she always says: nothing. I couldn't get so much as a blink out of her. I don't know what else I can do, Jessie. This really is for the best. Mother is a very good person, I promise. She goes to a big church and has lots of friends and says some of them have children or grandchildren Kit's age. I know she'll take good care of Kit, and Larry and I will be visiting at least once a year.'

'You've done a lot for her, Helen. As much as anyone could have done. It's been hard on you these past weeks, I know. Congratulations on your engagement. I think everything is going to work out just fine. Kit's a lucky girl to have such a wonderful family.'

I meant every word. Kit was lucky indeed. I would have killed to have had some dear person like Mrs Reynolds waiting in the wings when my own mother died.

TWENTY-FOUR

Mildred Young, my hair-stylist friend, rang me up the next morning to see if I could join her for lunch. She named a place on Sunset Boulevard near the studio where we had eaten before, a place that was open on Sundays, and I agreed to meet her at one o'clock.

'Of course you heard about me losing my job,' I said as I slid into the small booth in the corner where she was waiting. Might as well not beat around the bush.

She pressed her lips together in a tight line and looked down at her menu. Then she reached across the table and clasped my hands in hers. 'That was a beastly thing for him to do, Jessie,' she said.

'It must be the talk of the studio.'

'No.' She squeezed my hands. 'No one at the studio is saying much at all. Most don't even know you're gone. They don't read the papers, and there was no announcement at work. They probably just figure you're still on one of your investigations for Mr Fairbanks. But those of us who do know about it think you've been treated quite shabbily.'

We all had such strong loyalties to Mary Pickford and Douglas Fairbanks that it seemed treasonous to criticize either one. Even now, I made excuses for them.

'Douglas didn't have much choice, Mildred. I'm sure it was a last resort. The thing he cares for most in this world, besides Miss Pickford, is their studio. Their association with a convicted criminal like David was dangerous publicity.'

'But you? You couldn't help that you had to testify. And after all you've done for Mr Fairbanks in the past with your investigations!'

How good it was to have a friend and supporter! Her spirited

defense brought tears to my eyes. I blinked them back and
took a few sips of water to swallow the burning in my throat.
The waiter came up at that moment and we ordered.

'What are you planning to do?' she asked when he moved
to the next table.

I shrugged. 'What else? Get another job.'

She took out a scrap of newspaper and passed it to me. 'I
thought as much. This was in today's paper. Paramount is
advertising for a script girl; so is Celestial Studios and a couple
more, but I've never heard of them.'

Shaking my head, I sighed. 'Don't you see, Mildred? The
only chance I have of getting another job like the one I had
is my experience at Pickford-Fairbanks. And the reason no
other studio would hire me is my experience at Pickford-
Fairbanks. Whether I use my real name or not, I'm finished
with the picture business. No, don't worry about me, I'll find
another line of work.'

'Like what?'

'I'm not qualified for much. I was thinking about trying for
one of those Girl Friday positions.'

'There are a million girls in Hollywood looking for work
until they get discovered,' she said with a frown. 'You'd make
no more than about twenty-five dollars a week.' We both knew
that wasn't enough to live on unless I shared a cheap board-
inghouse room with another girl. But Mildred didn't know
about David's valise under the bed, and I didn't know, yet,
what he expected me to do with the money. The truth was, I
probably didn't need a job, not for the paycheck anyway. But
I was a working girl. I'd never *not* had a job in my life. What
would I do with myself without a job? Sit alone all day in
David's living room drinking coffee? Without the self-respect
and discipline that comes with honest work, I was afraid I
might slide back into – well, dishonest work.

'You can come stay with me,' she said. 'That's what I wanted
to tell you. You've seen my little house. It isn't much, I know,
and it isn't located too close to the streetcar lines, but it's all
mine. You can have that spare room upstairs for as long as
you care to stay, and you don't have to pay rent.'

That did make me cry. I blinked hard and dabbed my eyes with the napkin. Right on cue, the waiter interrupted with our soup and pimento sandwiches, allowing me to regain my composure. 'Mildred, you are the dearest person on earth! You'll never know how much I appreciate that offer. But I'm going to be fine.' I told her about David's house, where I planned to live for the next couple of years, and reassured her that I would have enough money to get by. In her blunt, pragmatic way, she gave a nod of acceptance and changed the subject.

'Barbara Petrovitch tells me you are still working on the investigation. She's been keeping me informed as to your progress.'

'I know it seems like I should stop, now that I'm not working for Douglas any longer, but Barbara is, well, not exactly a friend, but I care too much to drop her like that. Besides, I'm helping the police on this and another matter.'

She smiled like a proud mother. 'Quite the lady detective!' she said as she took a dainty spoonful of the hot soup without pressing me for more information. I like that about Mildred: she isn't your typical nosy parker.

In twenty minutes, we'd finished our meal. We parted on the sidewalk and went our separate ways – Mildred to her marketing, me to buy a newspaper and head home. I watched her go, wishing with all my might that I would see her tomorrow. Monday morning, back at the studio. Back at the job I'd loved so much. In a way, it reminded me of the insecurity of vaudeville: one day you had work and were living high, the next day your act split up or the manager handed you your pictures and you scrounged for every nickel. 'There's always another job on the horizon,' my mother used to say. I looked up the street toward home. Unfortunately, I couldn't see the horizon from where I stood.

What I could see startled me. Across Santa Monica and a block to the east, a movie theater was emptying out. People spilled out the double doors, jostling one another as they turned right or left on the wide sidewalk. At first, I didn't believe my eyes. I blinked and stared. One small figure stood alone at the edge of the curb, looking both ways for traffic before crossing to my side of the street. It was Kit.

She reached the sidewalk and turned away from me, heading

in the opposite direction. The direction I was going. She didn't see me, I was certain.

Well, that was one mystery solved. Now I knew what Kit was doing when she wandered off during the day. I should have thought of it before now. The pictures were something a deaf person could enjoy as much as a hearing person. She'd miss the music, sure, but none of the plot or the dialog, as long as she could read the titles, and Kit was a great reader for her age. For any age. I had been amazed at the books she'd been taking home from the library.

Instinct overrode common sense, and I called out to her to wait, forgetting she couldn't hear me. So I hurried along in the same direction, losing sight of her for minutes at a time, but seeing her when the crowd thinned. The sidewalk was crowded with Sunday strollers and shoppers, but I'd catch up to her at the streetcar stop ahead. Meanwhile, it was interesting to watch her walk along, not too fast, pausing occasionally to look at a window display.

The house on Fernwood was more than two miles away, but she kept walking past the streetcar stop. Perhaps her pocket money didn't stretch that far.

I trailed her for a few blocks before coming alongside her. I laid one hand on her arm. She jerked it away and spun around, then smiled her recognition. It was a lovely smile, and it served to remind me how seldom I saw it.

'Are you going home?' I asked.

She nodded.

'May I walk along with you?'

Another nod.

Since it was impossible to have a conversation without facing one another, we threaded our way through the Sunday strollers in silence for a while. When we paused at a corner stop sign, I took the opportunity to face her and ask, 'What film did you see?'

'*The Lost World.*'

'Oh, yes, I've heard of it, but I haven't seen that one yet. What did you think?'

She shrugged. 'Childish. But I liked the part at the end, when the professor gets his revenge.'

Not for the first time did I sense an eerie maturity behind Kit's solemn manner, and I wondered, not for the first time, how an eleven-year-old could be so unlike any eleven-year-old I'd ever known. And I'd known a lot of them. I'd been eleven myself for many years through several different acts, and I flattered myself that I knew how they spoke and thought and behaved. Kit didn't act like a kid that age. She couldn't be eleven.

'How old are you, Kit?'

'Eleven.'

The direct approach having failed, I shifted gears. We walked for another few blocks as I plotted the next scene and kept an eye out for a drug store. The second one we passed fit the bill – I caught sight of its soda fountain through the plate glass window.

I touched Kit's arm. 'Now here's good luck! Just when I'm thinking about root beer, I spy a soda fountain. How 'bout it? My treat.'

Nod.

We went inside and settled onto two stools. A skinny boy who looked about fourteen bustled up. 'What'll ya have, girls?'

'Two root beers, please.'

'Floats?'

I looked at Kit. She nodded. 'One float, one plain.'

'You know, when my mother was headlining in vaudeville, we could afford treats like this every day. Then after she died, I went years without the taste of a root beer or a soda. So now I really appreciate them.'

Kit gave that some thought before asking, 'You were all alone?'

'Vaudeville is kinda like a family. The people managing whatever act I was with kept an eye out for me. But I had no family.'

'No pa?'

'My father died before I was born. He had some family, but I didn't know about them until last year. My mother's family disowned her when she went on stage. They thought performing was sinful. She never had anything more to do with them, never talked about them, never even wrote to tell them I was born.'

She frowned as she stirred her float with the straw. 'How old were you when she died?'

'Twelve, I think. I'm not always sure of my age. Back when I was in vaudeville, it changed so often, I didn't always keep up with the true number. In my younger days, when my mother was singing and I was working song-and-dance acts, we had to pretend I was older to dodge the Gerry Society, so my mother would make up my face and dress me in older-girl clothes before I'd go before the judge.'

'What's Gerry Society?'

'A bunch of pinched-faced do-gooders who think children under sixteen should be banned from the stage. The law didn't exactly forbid all performance – it said kid performers couldn't move about on the stage. They could sing or recite poetry but they couldn't dance or move. So the Gerry spies would sit in the audience and report to the cops any young-looking kid who moved.'

She was visibly intrigued. 'Did you get put in jail?'

'The object wasn't to jail the kids; it was to run them out of the business. The cops would take the kids before the judge, and the kids would swear they were sixteen. If the judge didn't believe them, they'd get fined.'

'Did you ever have to go to court?'

'We got caught any number of times – some states enforce the laws more vigorously than others – but usually Mother paid someone off before we had to appear in court. I remember once in Alabama we were making such good money, she just paid the $25 fine each day. "The cost of doing business", she called it. Whenever I had to appear before a judge, Mother would make me up to look older, covering my freckles, putting lipstick and rouge on my face and red lacquer on my fingernails, and I'd wear a padded brassiere, until sixteen didn't look so unbelievable, even when I was twelve.'

The image made Kit giggle.

'Then when I got older, it was the reverse. I was working kiddie acts and needed to look younger than my age, so I'd accentuate my freckles, wear my hair in braids, flatten my chest, avoid make-up or nail lacquer of any sort, and wear little girl sailor dresses.' I waited to see if she would take the bait. She did.

'So how old are you really?' she asked.

'Guess.'

Kit frowned in concentration for a minute before she replied, 'Twenty-one.'

I shook my head. 'Twenty-six.'

Her eyes couldn't have gotten any wider if I'd said *seventy-six*. 'I thought you and Myrna were the same age.'

I shook my head. 'I've always looked a good deal younger than I am. I'm the oldest one in our house. Myrna's only twenty. Helen's twenty-four, and I think Melva and Lillian are twenty-two or twenty-three. What about you? How old are you, I mean, how old are you *really*?'

An uncomfortable silence followed. I waited, my hands clasped in my lap, my head cocked to one side, and my gaze fixed on her face until she gave in. After all the information I'd shared with her, it must have seemed stingy not to be honest in return. At least, that's what I was betting on.

'Thirteen.'

My original estimate when we'd first met had been twelve, but as I'd come to know her better, I'd revised that upwards, so her response seemed believable.

'I know why I lied about my age all those years,' I said. 'But why did you? You're not on stage.'

'If I was younger, Ma could be younger. She wanted people to think she was younger, especially after she met Joe. When we moved to Joe's house, she wanted him to think I was younger so he wouldn't bother me.'

That explained why the child looked like something out of the Oz book, with her mismatched clothing and sexless haircut.

'Well, there's no need to lie about it any longer. Wouldn't you rather be thirteen?' She looked uncertain at first, then she gave her trademark nod. Taking advantage of what was, for Kit, a chatty mood, I continued with my questions. I wanted to know about this Joe person and how long he'd been in the picture. 'Have you and your mother lived in Los Angeles all your life?'

'Where her job was, we lived. San Francisco or Sacramento,

other cities. Once she started being Joe's girlfriend, we didn't move around any more.'

'Why not?'

'Joe's boss of most clubs in LA. He got Ma gigs in any one she wanted. That's how she met him, singing in one of his clubs.'

'A long time ago?'

'A few years. Two, maybe.'

That piece of news meant I wouldn't have to ask an awkward question: whether this Joe fella was her father. If he'd only been around for two years, that was unlikely, but not, I reflected, unthinkable. He could have fathered a child thirteen years ago and come back into the picture recently. But like as not, Kit was illegitimate, like me. Like David.

I wanted to know more, in case there was a chance of finding more of her relatives. 'So what do you think of this Joe? What's his last name?'

She shot me a mean look before turning to her float. She fished out a few bites of ice cream and I figured I'd pushed the interview off the cliff. But no.

'Joe Addy Zone,' Kit said. At least that's what it sounded like she said. Addison, probably. I could look it up in the city directory. 'At first, I liked him 'cause Ma liked him 'cause he was rich and had the prettiest house you ever saw. Then I hated him 'cause he was mean. He didn't like me either.'

'Is that when your mother started telling people you couldn't speak?'

'She didn't tell people that. I just never said anything. She didn't know I could read lips so good. And there was nothing to say. She was asleep when I was awake, or she was with Joe. She didn't tell Joe anything about me, 'cept how old I was and that I was deaf. He decided I was a moron all by himself. I saw him tell people I was too dumb to go to school. That's what everyone thinks, so I just let 'em think it. You thought it too. I know you did.'

'Well, you're wrong. I didn't think you were a moron. I thought you were rude.'

That arched her eyebrows but quick. I pressed my advantage.

'So I take it you know your address?'

The dramatic roll of her eyes answered that question louder than words.

'Very well then, shall we stop by and pick up some of your things?'

She shook her head. She had relied so long on gestures to speak for her, she didn't waste words when a shrug or a nod would do.

'Why not? Surely you have clothes and other things you'd like, and some of your mother's stuff?'

'That's all gone by now.'

'It's only been a few days since her death. Suppose we go see?'

She shook her head again.

'If you have a key, we could go when Joe wasn't there.'

She shook her head violently.

'Can you tell me the address, so I could go? By myself, I mean.'

Another severe shake of the head. I had no choice but to let it drop. Still, I might have enough information now to find an address if I read through all the entries in the city directory that started with AD. AT, maybe it began, maybe Addyzone. Artyzone? Ardesone? Ar . . . Then it hit me. Ardizzone. If you didn't know how the Italians pronounced the last letter of the word, if you had only read it and never heard it spoken, you would say it the way Kit did: Ar-dee-zone.

Rose Ann's sugar daddy was the gangster, Joe 'Iron Man' Ardizzone.

TWENTY-FIVE

Bringing Iron Man Ardizzone on stage certainly changed the plot. I telephoned Carl Delaney when I reached our house, as soon as I was certain Kit had gone upstairs. Nonetheless, I turned my face to the wall as I spoke, in case she passed through the back hall on her way outside. I heard him give a low whistle after I'd finished relaying what Kit had told me.

'Are you thinking what I'm thinking?' I asked Carl.

'If you're thinking that Iron Man Ardizzone killed Rose Ann Riley, I'm thinking what you're thinking.'

'The puzzle pieces fall into place, don't they? Rose Ann left Los Angeles looking for work. She couldn't take Kit so she dropped her off with a huge suitcase at the home of a cousin she barely knew. I think she wanted out—'

'—and her lover had other ideas.'

'You know about him?'

'Iron Man? All too well. We pick up his gang's dead bodies on a regular basis. He's a ruthless sonofa— excuse me, ma'am.'

'Kit said he was mean. She didn't define that, but maybe he was beating Rose Ann or threatening her. Rose Ann ran off to look for jobs so she could move far away from him. She wasn't even planning to come back to Los Angeles to get Kit; she was going to send for her. I thought that irresponsible at the time – now I think it was prudent.'

'Iron Man must not have appreciated her streak of independence. So he hunted her down in San Diego, sent someone to knock her around a little for discipline's sake, and maybe when she wasn't biddable enough, decided to teach her and any future ladies a lesson. Drinking wood alcohol would kill her in a way that would look like an accident. No questions asked.'

'Poor thing – she didn't run far enough away.'

'I'm not sure any place was far enough away. A big city crime boss like that has contacts all over the country he can call for favors.'

'You know what I just thought? It must've been Ardizzone who hired that gunman from Chicago who came here last year and shot Bruno Heilmann, that director. Remember? We figured out he was from Chicago, but never could connect him with anyone here.'

'Like he was calling in a favor from a boss in another city.'

'Right. Doesn't Ardizzone control all the bootlegging and dope in this city?'

'Except for the Chinese and their opium.'

'Carl, can you find out the address where Kit lived? She said the house belonged to Ardizzone, but it wasn't his wife's house.'

'I can try, although if he was trying to hide a house he bought for his mistress, it'd be as easy as putting it in some other name. Why do you want to know? Tell me you aren't thinking about going over there.'

'No, not any more. At first I wanted to go with Kit and get some of her things, but she wouldn't spill the address. She said there was no use in going, that all her things would be gone by now.'

Out of the corner of my eye, I saw Kit pass by on her way to the kitchen. I heard her rummaging around in the pantry. Pure instinct caused me to lower my voice even though I knew she couldn't hear a word I said. 'Listen, Carl . . . Don't say anything about this in front of Kit. I'd rather she continue to think her mother's death was accidental poisoning.'

'You think she doesn't know who Ardizzone is?'

'I'm not sure. She knew his name and said he owned lots of clubs. He's in the newspapers now and then, and she reads them every day.'

'Yeah, sure, but no one in the papers describes him as a gangster boss. They wouldn't dare. He's never been convicted of anything, not even a traffic violation. Reporters use the word "businessman" when referring to Iron Man. We know who he is, and we'd love to nab him – so would the Feds – but he's slipperier than a greased eel. Besides, there are plenty of places Kit could have seen his name besides the newspapers. A piece of mail, a laundry ticket, a light bill, an engraved cigarette case.'

He made a good point.

'I'll see if I can turn up his whereabouts the day she was killed,' he said.

I was sure a man like Iron Man would have an iron-tight alibi.

On Monday the postman brought another batch of letters from vaudeville friends about transfigurators. A ukulele musician told me that the Great Fulgora had been playing in New York last year – something that astonished me because I assumed a man who had not been young when he performed with my mother in the 1890s would be long dead or at least retired by now. 'I don't think he's still working,' wrote my ukulele friend, 'in any event, he's not listed in *Variety*, but he was going strong when I saw him last March. He opened in street clothes and, in full view of the audience, made ten changes in costume, leaving the stage dressed in women's clothing and in less than five seconds, he reappeared in full masculine evening clothes.' I'd have liked to see that!

Another letter came from an Irish clog dancer I'd known in my teenage years. She wrote of three men who staged a protean act where they portrayed a dozen different characters in a play. Barton, Hicks & Hicks, they were called, and they were playing the Keith circuit. A friend who did dramatic poetry recitations wrote that she'd run across a Small Timer in Boston a couple years ago. 'If I knew his name, I've forgotten, but he called himself the Ace of Hearts or maybe it was the Ace of Spades, something about playing cards. He was foreign-born, Turk or Hungarian maybe. I thought his quick-change act was pretty good, but I heard he left it for an acrobatic act.' My friend in Comedy Cockatoos wrote that he had played alongside Alexander Kids, an act billed as 'a remarkable exhibition of dancing and costume changing by tiny youngsters', but I was confident the killer hadn't been a child. Two more letters regretted they knew no transfigurators, and that was the last of my inquiries.

I telephoned the police station and left a message for Detective Carl Delaney to ring me up. The next thing I knew, he was knocking at the front door.

'No moss grows on your stone, does it?' I asked.

'No, ma'am. The Los Angeles Police Department aims to please all the upstanding citizens of our fair city. And I'd be mightily pleased if you offered me a cup of coffee to go with this fine morning.'

Kit somehow divined his arrival and clattered down the stairs just as I was heading into the kitchen to brew a fresh pot of coffee. I returned in a few minutes with a tray of coffee and sugar cookies and handed Kit a cup with lots of milk and sugar, the way she liked it. When I gave Carl his, I positioned myself with my back to the porch swing where Kit was curled up and said, 'There are a few things I want to tell you that I can't say in front of Kit, but I'll hold those for later.'

'This reminds me of elevenses in England,' Carl said, looking directly at Kit so she could read his lips. 'When I was soldiering during the war, before we got to France, we spent some weeks in England where people had coffee or tea and a cookie – d'you know they call 'em biscuits there? They did that at about eleven o'clock, like we're doing now. A good custom, don't you think?'

Kit nodded her agreement.

'What do you have to report?' he asked me.

'I got the last responses to the transfigurator letters Kit and I wrote last week. Several were stamped Return to Sender, so they missed their targets – I can try again with those. Most replied promptly. One told me the Great Fulgora was still performing last year, but he's pretty old and would hardly fit the descriptions of the killer. Neither would the colored protean on the TOBA circuit – the killer was always described as a white man – or the Alexander Kids act that features tiny tots. My best prospects are the Great Rudolpho, a magician who does a trick that involves quick-change; Vesa Leka, a foreigner who seems to have left Big Time six months ago; Barton, Hicks & Hicks, an acting team of proteans who perform a short play; and an unnamed foreigner who recently swapped his quick-change act for an acrobatic one – without a name, though, so he's impossible to trace.'

I pulled out my copy of *Variety*. 'I bought this last week. The Great Rudolpho is playing in the Midwest now. There is no listing for Vesa Leka, which means he either quit – an idea that surprised my friend since his act was getting a good reception – or he dropped to Small Time. Small Time circuits aren't listed in *Variety* or *Billboard*. Barton, Hicks & Hicks are playing the Keith circuit up in Canada at the moment.'

'So, the Great Rudolpho could have murdered people when he was working in New York, St. Louis, and here.'

'Theoretically, but unlikely. No circuit goes from coast to

coast. The distances would be too expensive and travel too time-consuming. And he couldn't have played three different circuits within a few months' time. Two maybe, but not three. Performers are typically booked for tours that last several months or even years.'

'If he was working the Midwest, he could have gone through St. Louis, then. Could he have taken a week off and traveled to the east coast to kill the cook?'

Sometimes it amazed me, how little civilian people understood vaudeville. I'd grown up in the trade, so it was all second nature to me, but regular people, I'd learned, had little knowledge of how the system worked. 'You can't just take a week off, even if you don't need the money. You'd be fired. And he's still working. So I know he didn't take time off.'

'So we can scratch the Great Rudolpho. What about this Leka fella?'

'I'd be happier if his name ended in "–itch" like the others, but he's a good possibility, if for no other reason than because he disappeared from the circuit around the time of the first murder.'

'His name might have been shortened from something like Lekavitch.'

'Possibly,' I said. 'Could you please ask Officer Marks if Leka seems like a Serbian name?'

'Sure. And what about the proteans? What was their name?'

'Barton, Hicks & Hicks. We would have the same problem here as with Rudolpho, except with three performers, they could have adapted the act to two and released one to go on a coast-to-coast killing spree with none the wiser at Keith headquarters. Believe me, I've shaved acts before.' Like last summer.

'So it's Leka or B, H & H.'

'Or someone else we've missed entirely. I'm not finished asking around.'

'What now?'

'Now I go to the library and get back issues of *Variety*, to see whether those two acts were playing in New York, St. Louis, or Los Angeles during the weeks of those murders. My assistant here,' I gestured to Kit, 'can help me.' She nodded eagerly.

At that moment, a neighbor lady walked by holding the leash of a small puppy whose legs were pumping briskly, trying to match its owner's stride. The woman called a hello and waved as she passed, and that was all it took. Kit sprang up and dashed to the sidewalk. The neighbor paused as Kit plopped down on the ground and pulled the little creature onto her lap to cuddle.

No sense in wasting a heaven-sent opportunity.

'I've lost my job at Pickford-Fairbanks.'

Carl showed no surprise.

'You knew?' I asked.

'Read it in the paper. I was wondering if that would cause you to stop working on the Joe Petrovitch murder, but you didn't say anything, so I didn't either. What are you planning to do about it?'

'Find another job.'

'Good luck. You'll do it.'

'And I have some other news,' I said, as Kit returned to the porch and her spot on the swing. 'Related to that. I am going to move into David Carr's empty house.' It felt disloyal talking to Carl about David, but the subject couldn't be avoided any longer. He'd need to know where I was living as we continued with these investigations. I recited my new telephone number. He already knew the address – he'd been there once a couple of months back when we used modern sound technology to trap a murderer. Carl took the news with his usual calm, and I continued, a bit defensively, 'I can live there for free while I look after the place until David gets out. It's not wise to leave a house empty.'

'You are right about that. When are you moving?'

'Tomorrow.'

'Need help? I can bring around a police car.'

'Thanks, but I don't have much to move.'

'More than you can carry on a Red Car, I'll wager.'

'True enough. I was planning to make several trips, but all right, thank you.'

'I'm off at six tomorrow night. I'll come directly here.'

TWENTY-SIX

Moving out reminded me of a vaudeville act splitting up – an all-too-frequent occurrence in my life. The bachelor girls who had been sharing the old farmhouse on Fernwood for the past year were going their separate ways. Sad, sure, but with a future that held promise for everyone. Helen was getting married and heading to Yosemite National Park; Kit was going to Mrs Reynolds's home in Riverside; I was moving to David's house in Whitley Heights. It was inevitable. But I had an idea that would make the break-up even more disruptive – I wanted Myrna Loy to come with me.

'Myrna,' I said when she came home from Warner Bros. that evening. A glance at her told me she was all done-in, but there was no postponing this. 'Could I talk to you privately, please? In my room?'

'Sure, I've gotta climb those stairs anyway . . . somehow . . . although I don't think I could make my legs obey if my bed wasn't up there. Geez Louise, work is killing me!'

'And you pined for the life of a Hollywood film star!'

She grinned and punched my arm playfully. 'Yeah, that's me all right, the glamorous movie star. I'm nothing but a professional extra, bouncing beach balls on the sand and pouring wine into Roman legionnaire's cups. I'm a dancer and know how to slink, so they are playing up my sexy image – can you believe it? Me! A vamp! So, why don't you come in my room so I can flop on my bed?' she asked, and I followed, turning the wooden chair in front of her dressing table around and sitting on it astride, like a cowgirl on a horse.

'I have a proposition for you,' I began.

'You and two of the Roman legionnaires.'

'Oh dear, really? Well, get used to it.' Hollywood men on the make were not going to ignore a girl as enchanting as Myrna for more than two blinks of the eye.

'What is it? Don't ask me to cook dinner. I don't care if I ever eat again, I'm so tired.'

'I want you to know I've decided to move into David's house while he's in prison. He asked me to do that for him. An empty house is an invitation to thieves, and he has no one else to mind it for him.'

'Gosh, so you're leaving and Helen's leaving.' She sat up, fatigue forgotten. 'I'll miss you both very, very much!'

'That's what I wanted to talk to you about. David's house has three bedrooms and, well, it's a big house, and I hate to think of living there alone, so I was wondering . . . if you'd consider moving in with me.'

'Gosh, I'd—'

'Before you say anything, let me tell you that there would be no rent. David owns the house free and clear, and he's set aside money to pay the electric bill and the telephone and any other expenses like taxes' – that was the understatement of the year, I thought, picturing in my mind's eye the valise stuffed with cash. 'I know you're making decent money now at Warner Bros., but it would go a lot farther if you could avoid paying rent and utilities.'

'I'll say! Are you kidding me?'

'No, I'm bribing you. I want you to move in with me.'

'There's no catch?'

'Well, like here, you have to do your share of the cleaning and cooking, but we'll work that out. I'll hire a neighbor kid to mow the grass, so there won't be any outdoor work. It's a bit of a hike to the nearest streetcar stop, but I'm going to buy a motorcar. A cheap one, a Ford. Maybe a Runabout. I had a Ford last year when I lived in Oregon, and I know how to drive those babies, so we'll have a vehicle when we need it. And we aren't leaving Melva in the lurch. She says there's such a housing shortage, she can rent our rooms an hour after the ad comes out.'

'Jessie, gosh, I don't know what to say.'

'Yes would be good.'

'Yes.' She barked a loud laugh. 'Free rent in a nice house? I'm the luckiest girl in the world! When do we move?'

'I'm moving tomorrow. Our favorite detective is coming

over in the evening to help. Why don't you come with us then
and have a look at the place? Pick out which bedroom you
want. We'll need to order some furniture before you can move
– the extra bedrooms are empty at the moment – but David
has money to pay for a bed and chest of drawers and whatever
else we want. As soon as those can be delivered, you can
move in.'

'Gosh, Jessie, I feel guilty being so excited at David's
expense. Are you very, very sure he won't mind?'

'I'm very, very sure.' I stood up and gave her a hug. 'And
I'm delighted you'll come with me. I was glad to move – it's
what David wanted – but I hated to be there all alone. So
thank you.'

'Thank *me*? Applesauce!'

'Look, why don't you have a nice, long soak in the tub,
and I'll bring you up a sandwich? Then you can go straight
to bed.'

'Gosh, that sounds like heaven. You're the darling-est person
in the whole world.'

I was hardly that, but I was relieved not to be moving by
myself. I'm not afraid of being alone, but I am afraid of
being lonely. I'd never lived in a regular house until the
Fernwood farmhouse, and I'd never lived alone anywhere,
ever. Thankfully, it was something I didn't need to worry
about now.

Seconds after delivering Myrna the promised sandwich, I heard
noises below. Melva was talking to someone on the porch. It
sounded like Carl. I went downstairs at once thinking he'd
mixed up the moving day.

'Why, Carl, I thought we said six o'clock *tomorrow*! I'm
not ready to move tonight.'

'I'm not here for that. This is business. Hop in the car and
I'll explain.'

As soon as we were in the police car and able to speak
freely, he said, 'I got an address for Rose Ann Riley's house.'

'How did you do that?'

'I went to the tax assessor's office and looked up Ardizzone.
There he was, owner of two houses. If he'd put it in another

name, it wouldn't have been as easy. It was almost too easy . . .' he said uneasily. 'Anyway, the house we're going to was the one he'd purchased just a few years ago – the other he'd held for ten years, so I figured this was the one he bought for his mistress. I thought we'd pay a call, tonight, before someone cleans it out.' He reached to start the ignition; I stayed his hand with mine.

'Wait a minute. What are we going to look for? How are we going to handle this?'

'I figure we'd knock at the door. If there's no answer, I'll force the lock, and we can search the place. Maybe we'll find something that would tell us about Ardizzone and whether or not Rose Ann's death was murder.'

'Like what? He won't have left a signed confession.'

'The way I see it, Rose Ann was killed a week ago, and her death wasn't picked up by the newspapers here. So if her house has been emptied out, it means someone with access to it knew she wasn't coming back. Who else but Ardizzone had access to her house? Who else would touch his mistress's stuff?'

'Which means, her death was probably murder.'

'And Ardizzone probably the murderer. Indirectly anyway.'

It made sense. 'What if someone answers the door?'

'We pretend to be friends looking for Rose Ann. See what they say. Find out who they are, what they know, how long they've been living there. And what they know about Joe Ardizzone.'

'Uh, Carl . . .'

'What?'

'No one will talk to us. They'll know we're from the police.'

'How?'

'To start with, we'll be driving up in this police car.'

'Give me some credit, girl! I was going to park around the corner and walk up.'

'Uh . . . car or no car, anyone can tell you're a cop.'

'I'm not wearing a uniform anymore.'

'I hate to be the one to tell you this, but you radiate cop from a hundred yards away.'

'How's that?' he asked, dumbfounded.

'Your military-style haircut, your suit, your sense of authority, the way you stand. It's not any one thing, but the package says cop in capital letters.'

'Oh.' He looked crestfallen. That's what I like about Carl: he can go from sharp to dull in under a minute. 'Can I do something about that?'

'Yeah, sure, but not tonight. Wait here,' I said, climbing out of the motorcar. 'I won't be long.'

Melva was waiting on the porch for me. 'You just had a telephone call from Barbara Petrovitch. I told her you were busy, so she said to please return her call. She wanted to invite you to come over for dinner tonight with her sister and a friend. I forget her name.'

'Geez Louise,' I groaned, remembering the tedious evening I'd spent ten days ago with Barbara, Bunny, and boring Mrs Shala. 'I can't suffer through another night with those three, and I really don't have time to talk with her. Would you be a lamb and call Barbara back? Tell her I'm busy tonight with the police. Thanks, Mel.' I gave her a quick hug.

It took no time to find Kit. She was on the patio, her bare legs crossed at the ankle and a book in her lap. I tapped her knee until she looked up.

'I need to borrow one of your dresses. Just for an hour.'

Her expression telegraphed the unspoken question, 'Why?'

'Carl's waiting for me – no time to explain, but I need to look young, and fast.'

TWENTY-SEVEN

In some parts of Los Angeles, it would have been unwise for a girl to walk alone at dusk, but this was a nice section of Highland Park, where nice people lived in nice houses, so the man walking his poodle along the curb did not think it the least bit odd to pass a young girl going in the opposite direction. He bade her a cheery 'Evening!'. So did the woman carrying a sack of groceries from her motorcar to her house, when she crossed the girl's path. 'Good evening, dearie,' she said. It wasn't quite dark, but even in poor light, it was obvious the girl was young, perhaps in her early teen years. She bounced along with an occasional skip, her footsteps echoing in the night air.

At the house numbered 201, she climbed the steps to the porch. Light shone through the eyelet-curtained windows, indicating a family at home. The girl reached for the doorknocker and gave three timid raps, like a child would do, not the sort of firm, confident raps an adult would make. Someone inside peeked through the curtains and saw the girl rocking back and forth from toe to heel as she waited. An overhead bulb clicked on.

A stocky, dark-haired woman with a splotchy rash on her cheeks opened the door. There on her porch she saw a figure dressed in a smocked, sky-blue dress partially covered by an overcoat. On her head she wore a Tam o' Shanter that looked as if someone had knitted it in a valiant attempt to use up all the remnants of yarn in their sewing basket.

'Yes?' she said, not rudely, but clearly irritated to have been disturbed by this unfamiliar young person.

'Oh. Excuse me, I must have come to the wrong house in the dark.' The girl stepped back a few feet, looked up at the house, and frowned in confusion. 'No, this is right. I've come to see Kit Riley. Is she here?'

'There's no one here by that name,' said the woman, and she started to close the door, when the girl spoke up again.

'I was here just two weeks ago, and she was here then. I'm sure this is the right house.'

'Well, hon, it probably is, but the Provenzanos live here now. We just moved in.'

'When?'

'When what?'

'When did you move in?'

'Almost three weeks ago, so you couldn't have been here two weeks ago.'

'It seemed like two weeks ago. I guess it was more than that. Well, I'm sorry to bother you, Mrs Provenzano, but can you tell me where the Rileys moved to? My friend borrowed

two books from me, and I came to get them back. She didn't
say anything about moving when I saw her last.'

The woman softened a little. 'I don't know the Rileys, so
I can't say where they went. Sorry.'

'Were there any books left here?'

A deep voice with a heavy Italian flavor called from inside
the house, 'Isobel, what the hell's going on? I'm hungry!'

'Just a neighbor girl, Georgio. I'll be right there,' she
screeched, then to the girl, she said, 'No, there was nothing
at all left here when we moved in on November third. Every
room was empty. Now, I'm sorry about your books, hon, but
that's all I can do for you.' She closed the door and clicked
off the porch light.

I retraced my steps until I turned the corner where Carl had
parked the police motorcar. He was pacing beside it like a
nervous father waiting for his unchaperoned daughter to come
home after a party.

'How did it go?' he asked.

Without answering, I climbed into the car. No need advertising our business to the world. You never knew who was
listening beside an open window.

'Bingo,' I said, once he was sitting next to me. 'The Georgio
Provenzanos have lived there for nearly three weeks. Which
means our friend Iron Man cleared out the house shortly after
Rose Ann did a flit.'

'Which means he knew she wasn't coming back,' he said,
starting the motor and pulling away from the curb.

'Which means he had no intention of finding her and
bringing her home. He knew she was gone. He must have
been furious. Here's how I see it: he knew she would be
looking to support herself the only way she knew how – with
her voice – so he put out the word to every speakeasy and
cabaret on the west coast to contact him if Rose Ann came
looking for work.'

'So he tracked her to San Diego and tried to get her to come
back—'

'I don't think so. I doubt he wanted her back at that point.
He'd have been furious. Humiliated. I think he wanted her
dead. He wanted revenge.'

'Hmmm. So he tracked her to San Diego and made her drink "smoke" to kill her.'

'That's my guess,' I said.

'Georgio Provenzano. Sounds very Italian.'

'Like Ardizzone.'

Carl nodded. 'No sense in letting a good house go to waste. Betcha Iron Man junked Rose Ann's things and moved in one of his trusted paisanos.' As I nodded my agreement, he made a right-hand turn and headed back toward Hollywood.

I was reading in bed later that night when the door to my room opened. I knew who it was before I saw her face peering around the door – anyone else would have knocked. Without waiting for an invitation, she came in and sat at the end of my bed, folding her skinny legs beneath her, Indian-style. I guessed she wanted to talk about her mother or maybe Mrs Reynolds. I was wrong.

She stared at me in a vaguely hostile way, as if I had interrupted her and not the other way around.

'What is it, Kit?' I asked, finally.

'You're moving,' she began, in her oddly-modulated voice.

'So are you. So is Helen and Myrna. We'll still see each other. We'll get together for holidays and reunions. No one will be far away, except Helen.'

'Why did you want my clothes?'

'I needed to look young so I could ask some questions without looking suspicious. I can't tell you more than that. Sorry.'

'Did it work?'

I smiled. 'Yes, it did. Thanks for your help.'

'I have more help. I know why your friend David can't get out of jail.'

'Really?' I said, setting aside my book. I realized the girl had been present during some of the conversations between Mike Allenby and me, so she was aware of David's trial and sentence. It was sweet of her to give thought to his case, so I gave her my full attention, as if I expected to hear something significant.

'I saw men talking about someone named David a few

weeks ago.' She scrunched up her face and corrected herself, 'No, longer ago than that. I didn't know it was your David. Now I know. Some government men and Joe's men made a deal to get rid of him. Joe's men wanted to kill him, but the government men said no, let us have a trial and put him in prison so we look good, like we're fighting bootleggers, and you get rid of him that way.'

Our roles had reversed. Now it was I who stared at her in wide-eyed silence, unable to speak. Finally Kit took pity on me and explained further.

'That's why the bribes weren't working for that lawyer to get David bail,' she continued, patient as a teacher with a dull pupil. 'It was them that told the judge about the bribed jury so he got a different jury.'

'H-how could you possibly know this?'

She gave a modest shrug. 'Some things I read in the news-paper. Most I saw at our house when men came there to meet Joe. Everyone thinks I'm deaf and dumb, and that deaf people are simps, and I'm just eleven, so I sit in the corner of the room when the men come and draw their faces and watch their lips. I know lots of things.'

'Who – what men?'

'Joe's men. The bootleggers. You know Joe Ardy Zone. He's the bootleg boss of the whole city.'

And her mother was his mistress. 'I know that, but . . . he lived with you?' I asked, aghast.

She shook her head in disgust at my slow uptake. 'Of course not. He's married. He got Ma a nice house and came to visit when he wanted to. Lots of times he would meet men at our house 'cause he didn't want them at his real house and 'cause it was nicer than his office.'

'And . . . and government men came there too? Who are they? Do you mean federal prohibition agents?'

'Yeah, I guess. They were getting pushed around by some lady boss in Washington they hated.'

'Mabel Willebrandt?' I asked, thinking of President Coolidge's much-loathed Assistant Attorney General, a woman who had the audacity to take her job seriously. She vigorously prosecuted thousands of prohibition cases every year to enforce the Volstead Act. Some thought she was a hero, but not everyone.

Kit shrugged. The name didn't seem to register.

I continued. 'I've read about her in the papers. She likes to fire men who don't have good records putting bootleggers in prison.'

'That's her, then. These government men said a big win would get her off their backs. They don't like women telling men what to do. They do what Joe tells them because he pays them lots of money, lots more than the government, so that's how they knew Joe's men wanted to kill David.'

'But . . . but,' I sputtered. 'Why would Joe Ardizzone want to kill David?'

Another shrug from Kit.

By now my brain was grinding gears. 'It's because he sells whiskey in his drug stores, isn't it? His is medicinal whiskey, so it's legal. And their whiskey isn't. David must have been cutting into their business. But . . .' I paused, confused. Thousands of drug stores all over the country sold legal, medicinal alcohol without interference from the local gangsters – or the local gangsters owned the drug stores. What was it that made David and his stores a particular target?

The brand of whiskey. Old Grand-Dad. David had thousands of cases of the top-shelf hooch, so much that it was drawing too many people into his drug stores, not because it was a legal product, per se, but because they preferred the real McCoy to the lousy bathtub gin at the speakeasies.

'Legal, not legal. They don't care. Only about money. Get it?'

I got it. In crashing Technicolor, I got it. David had undercut sales for southern California's biggest crime boss, 'Iron Man' Ardizzone. Ironically, I remembered David telling me once that he would never try to muscle into the territory of an existing gang, because he understood the likely consequences. He must have thought selling legal whiskey wouldn't interfere with the gang's regular bootleg business – a logical, if some-what risky, assumption. He'd been caught up in a collaboration between gangsters who needed to rid themselves of a rival and federal agents who needed to look effective. Oddly enough,

I was grateful Mabel Willebrandt had browbeaten her agents into this high-profile prosecution, because it had saved David's life. Without her, the competition would have ended with a bullet in his brain.

I understood now why Allenby couldn't get his appeals to work. Why no one in the governor's office returned his telephone calls. Everyone had been warned, either by the gangsters or by the federal agents, to not interfere with David's case.

And I understood something else. David Carr was not going to get out of prison early, no matter how angelic his conduct behind bars. No appeal, no parole, no visitors, no time off for good behavior. He would serve the entire three and a half years – probably longer if they could figure out a way to add time on some trumped-up charge – and when he came out – if he came out – he would be a changed man.

Thank heavens we girls could afford a telephone! The past few weeks had seen me burning up the wires. I put a call through to Mike Allenby at once, expecting him to be elated to learn the truth behind his logjam. I blurted out the basics and asked him to stop by my house or to meet me someplace so I could fill in the details and discuss our next move. To my astonishment, he refused.

'Too busy. Just tell me everything now.'

'Well, it's complicated,' I began. 'I've learned the reason you couldn't get David off was because the federal agents were working with "Iron Man" Ardizzone to put David away. The agents are in the pay of the Ardizzone gang. The gangsters didn't like David's medicinal whiskey competing with their bathtub hooch, so Ardizzone was going to have him killed until the feds convinced him to let them put him behind bars in a big win so they could look good with their lady boss in Washington, Mabel Willebrandt.'

'The Assistant Attorney General. Yeah, yeah, everyone's heard of her. A real battleax. Where did you get this?'

'Someone overheard them talking about it. I can't say who.'

'Yeah, well, don't say who, and keep it to yourself too. If this got out, you and your snitch would be dead. And the story rings true. Top-notch, bonded whiskey is going to cut into the sales of the crap the bad boys peddle. And Iron Man has bought his own distillery, so now he's both buyer and seller in the great game we all play. Seems Mr David Carr was a threat on more than one front. So what do you want me to do?'

'What do you mean, what? Now you know the federal agents are in bed with the bootleggers. Doesn't that give you some leverage in your appeals or in getting David's sentence reduced? What about a parole now?'

He heaved a long sigh. 'Look, sweetheart honey. Your boy David is lucky to be alive. He might not be if I got him out.'

'Get him out, and he'll leave town.'

Another sigh. 'There's nothing I can do with your information, see? Everyone in the chain – judges, clerks, prison officials, whoever – everyone on both sides is being bribed or threatened by either Iron Man or by the feds. No one's going to stick his neck out on this one. You need to come to grips with the cold, hard fact that your boy is going to stay where he is until his sentence runs out. He's stuck. Be glad it's not forever. But when he does get out, please remember that he'll need to leave Los Angeles within the hour or he'll find himself in an even smaller cell six feet under.'

'But—'

'Okay, listen. Let this blow over, and I'll look into the situation again in a year or so. Maybe the players will have changed, and we can do something. But we can't do anything now. Okay?'

I swallowed the lump of anger and tears that clogged my throat. 'Can I see him?'

'Maybe in a few months. We'll try then.'

'Can *you* see him?'

'Sure. I'll be going to the prison tomorrow to see another client. I can see Carr then too. You want me to take him a message?'

'Yes, please. Tell him I've decided to move into his house, like he wanted.'

'Good girl. That'll make him happy.'

'Tell him I got his message and will make every effort to take care of his belongings. Got that?'

'Sure.'

'Repeat it to me, to make sure.'

'You got his message and will make every effort to take care of his belongings. That it?'

'That's it.'

TWENTY-EIGHT

T urns out I didn't move into David's house the next day after all. Tuesday found me on a crowded northbound train to San Francisco and, instead of sleeping in David's bed on Tuesday night, I was at my grandmother's house in Pacific Heights, where I had stayed last year after the Oregon impersonation swindle went wrong. As I sipped raspberry cordial in her very Victorian parlor in front of all the photographs of my father's family, I poured the story of my investigations into her discerning ears.

'. . . and so early this morning I got a telephone call from Barbara Petrovitch, the widow who'd invited me to dinner Monday night. She wanted to tell me the Western Union boy had delivered a telegram during their dinner. I could tell by her voice she blamed me for not being there when he came, but I was with Carl Delaney investigating Kit's mother's death. Anyway, this telegram was the only response Barbara has had thus far from the obituary Carl placed in Serbian-language newspapers across the country. We were hoping some pals of Joe Petrovitch would notice an obituary about him and maybe lead us to some clues about who would want to kill him and why.'

I paused as she refilled my cordial glass, took a sip, and continued my story. 'The telegram was from a man named Paul Pavlovitch in San Francisco. It didn't say much. He merely sent his condolences to the widow and said he had known Joe years ago in Serbia. That's all. I telephoned the police station to let Carl know I was going to San Francisco to find Pavlovitch, but he wasn't there. They'll give him the message when he calls in. I thought he might want to come up here with me, but honestly, it isn't worth his time, and I told him so in my message. All I'm going to do is hunt up this Pavlovitch fella and ask him a few questions – and warn him that someone's shooting certain Serbian men who served in their military before the Great War.'

Grandmother listened intently, absorbing details like a dry sponge soaking up water, her shrewd eyes fixed on my face, her hands clasped in her lap. Not for the first time, I wondered how old she was. I would never have dared ask, but that didn't prevent me from adding twenty to the approximate age of my detestable Uncle Oliver, her eldest, which let me peg her at around eighty.

Until last year, I hadn't known I had any relatives at all, and their discovery still amazed me. Having blood relations provided a sense of belonging that tethered me to the present in a way I hadn't realized I'd lacked and gave me confidence about the future. Relatives meant security. No matter what horrible turn life took, there was someone who cared about me, someone who would stand by me to the best of her ability. When I'd needed a place to recuperate from a broken leg, Grandmother had taken me into her house for two whole months, using the time to stuff my head so full of Beckett family history that I could almost forget I'd never actually known my father or his people. Others had grandmothers who were sweet and soft and sang them lullabies. My grandmother suffered no fools and took no prisoners. I adored her.

Steadying herself with an ivory-handled cane, Grandmother made her way to her desk where her telephone sat. She pulled a city directory out of the top drawer and, without comment, handed it to me.

Flipping to the Ps, I ran my finger down the list of names and addresses. 'Pavlovitch, Paul. Here he is! What does "mtrmn" mean?'

'Motorman,' she said. 'It means he's a gripman on one of the cable car lines.' My blank look brought a slight crease to her brow. 'Come now, Jessie, you've ridden the cable cars. You've surely noticed that each car has two men, a gripman and a conductor. The gripman is the main brakeman; the conductor handles the money and the passengers.'

'I see. Here's his address. I'll go there first thing tomorrow.'
I gave a great yawn. 'Meanwhile, I'm bushed.'

The twelve-hour train trip had left my muscles crying for
release. With Douglas Fairbanks no longer fronting first-class
tickets, I was back where I belonged – in a thirteen-dollar seat
in a crowded, second-class car. The Daylight Limited traveled
the four hundred miles between Los Angeles and San Francisco
without a single stop, but there was only one of them a day,
so I was lucky to get a seat at all. This good fortune did not
prevent me from grousing about wailing infants, rambunctious
children, and the quarrelsome couple behind me who, had they
been on stage, could have been heard in the highest balcony.
Fortunately, I'd snagged a window seat on the left-hand side
so I could lose myself in the spectacular coastal scenery.

'If you are no longer working for Mr Fairbanks, why do
you continue to pursue the Serb murder investigation?'
Grandmother asked tartly, ignoring my attempt to escape to
my bedroom.

'I suppose because I owe it to Barbara Petrovitch. She's a
good person, and I do feel sorry for her. And I'm working
with Carl on that other case, too, about Kit's mother. I can't
very well tell him I won't help him any more with the Petrovitch
murder but please help me with Rose Ann's murder, can I?'

'I suspect you could tell this Carl to dance an Irish jig, and
he'd do it.'

Ignoring that bit of insight, I drained the last drop of cordial
before continuing. 'Besides, I feel like I'm closing in on this.
Finally, a live Serb I can actually talk to! The other three were
murdered before I could question them. This one will surely
have something to say.'

But only if I could find him, which proved harder than
anticipated. I thought it a simple matter to go to his address,
which I did first thing the next morning. However, the
disheveled woman who answered the door at the boarding
house told me Paul Pavlovitch had left more than six months
ago.

'Would you happen to know his new address?' I asked.

'I'm sorry, I don't. He may have skipped town for all I
know. Probably did. Are you a relative or something?'

'No, I've never met him,' I said. 'I'm merely looking for some information.'

'Well, if you run the bum down, tell him I'm still waiting on that last two week's rent he owes me.'

'Yes, ma'am, I'll do that.'

Wednesday was a cloudy, drizzly, thoroughly unpleasant day, however, there was nothing to do but start riding cable cars and asking questions. I began with the nearest line – Market Street. It made sense that he would get a room near the line where he worked, but after riding three cars and speaking to three conductors who had not heard of Paul Pavlovitch, I switched to the Powell Street line and started anew. San Francisco had eight cable car companies operating a variety of lines, and I only hoped I would not run out of nickels before I'd discovered which one employed Mr Pavlovitch. If, indeed, he still lived in San Francisco.

It quickly became clear that I would not be able to speak to Mr Pavlovitch while he was working. Conductors dealt with money and made sure passengers did not disturb the gripmen with frivolous chatter. Watching them work, I understood why. Brute strength and intense concentration were required to keep the cable cars from colliding with other vehicles or pedestrians and to release and reattach the car to the underground cable when crossing perpendicular lines. Once I'd found Mr Pavlovitch, I would need to wait until his shift was over to talk with him.

Several hours later, including a noontime break for fish-on-a-bun, I reached the California Street line, and – at last! – a conductor who recognized the name Paul Pavlovitch.

'Yeah, sure, I know him. He's been a gripman for a few years.'

'Do you know how I might find him?'

'Well, if you ride down to the turntable, you can wait as each car comes in and spot him then.'

'What's he look like?'

'Uh, lemme think. Big guy. Dark hair. Usually squints.'

Thanking the man with a half dollar, I sat down to ride to the end of the line. Once there, I posted myself on a bench near the turntable. From that vantage point, I could see each cable car arrive at this end of the line and align itself on the turntable. As I watched, the conductor and the gripman jumped off and gave a fierce heave-ho against the side of the car to start it turning, and then, when it was pointed in the opposite direction, climbed back on and allowed passengers to board. As each car rotated, I approached one of the men and asked if he knew Paul Pavlovitch. Each time, the man said yes, but he hadn't seen him today. Finally, one of the conductors said, 'I think he's on second shift today.'

'I just need to ask him a few questions. When's second shift?'

He indicated the powerhouse with his chin. 'See if them in there can help you.'

Them could. Pavlovitch would be working a shift that was over at about ten o'clock that night, many hours from now. I tipped the man, then fished in my purse for another nickel, boarded yet another cable car, and made my way back to Grandmother's house to spend the next few hours in the comfort of her parlor and dining room. Relatives, I'd learned, were always keen to feed you.

TWENTY-NINE

I am sensitive to being watched. Whenever someone's eyes rest overlong on me, a prickly awareness flushes across my neck and shoulders. It comes, I am sure, from a lifetime spent on the vaudeville stage, honing the subtler tricks of my trade – the toss of the head, the lift of the chin, the flutter of the fingers – whatever pulls the audience's attention. I can tell when someone is staring, and someone was staring at me as I sat in a three-sided shelter beside the turntable of the California Street line, waiting for the end of Paul Pavlovitch's shift.

I'd been there almost an hour. I'd picked out the dark, scowling Pavlovitch as his cable car came through on its previous run. I had approached him as he and his conductor strained to rotate their vehicle on the turntable.

'I'm a friend of Joe Petrovitch's widow,' I began, 'and I was hoping to ask you a few questions about Joe on her behalf.'

He squinted at me with distrustful eyes, but he didn't say no.

'Over a drink, maybe? I picked up a bottle of whiskey at the drug store.' I didn't have a doctor's prescription for this 'medicine', but a friendly young man in line had an extra he was willing to part with for five dollars.

The mention of whiskey brought a friendlier expression to Pavlovitch's face. 'I punch out after one more run,' he said. 'Wait over there.' He pointed to a sheltered bench.

So I waited. It was cool – not cold – and damp – not wet. As I waited, I felt tickled again by this sense of being watched. Of course it could have been a masculine admirer, but that sort is easy to spot, mostly because they want to be spotted. I looked about – not in an obvious way; I'm no amateur. I stood and stretched, gazed about innocently, then bent to fiddle with my shoelaces before standing again and scanning the people behind me, all without seeing anyone the least bit suspicious.

The streets were lightly populated. At this late hour, fewer than a dozen passengers were riding each cable car, and the line waiting for the next car was short. I saw nothing fishier than a man walking his dog, a mother balancing a large package in one arm with a baby in the other, a policeman rocking back and forth on his heels, a couple strolling hand in hand, a gaggle of giggly flappers toddling on high heels toward the corner speakeasy, and businessmen striding across the wet pavement with conspicuous self-importance, all with umbrellas up or down as the mist turned to drizzle and back to mist. But the feeling of being watched persisted.

I remembered having felt the same tingling sensation when I came north on the Daylight Limited train yesterday. Unable to shake it then, I'd left my seat and strolled the length of the rail car not once but twice, as if I wanted nothing more than to stretch my legs on the long trip, moving slowly, checking every passenger, male and female. Most were dozing. I found nothing amiss. No one looked the least familiar.

I sacked my overactive imagination and reclaimed my bench

seat. There was nothing to worry about – a second policeman had recently joined the lone officer on the corner and a third was ambling his way from the opposite direction, swinging his nightstick like a circus baton, so I was well protected from any malefactors. Besides, no one knew I'd gone to San Francisco. No one except Barbara Petrovitch and Carl Delaney.

Fewer cable cars were needed at this time of night, which explained why, at about ten o'clock, Paul Pavlovitch drove his car onto the turntable and from there, off to a sidetrack to let it sit until the morning rush called it back into service. He disappeared into the powerhouse, emerging a few minutes later, lunch pail in hand, and joined me beneath the shelter. The mist had turned to gentle rain. Streetlights cast a glow around the terminus. Other lights at nearby intersections pushed back the shadows.

'Finished at last?' I asked. 'You gripmen work hard.' Pulling the bottle out of my purse, I passed it to him. 'I'll bet a shot of whiskey would go down nice about now.'

'Sure would, lady. Sure would.' He put the bottle to his lips and took a swig before holding it out to me. I shook my head. David's bonded Old Grand-Dad had spoiled me forever.

'Name's Jessie Beckett. And the bottle's yours.'

'Thanks, Miss Beckett. What can I do for you?'

He had an accent, but nothing heavy enough to make him hard to understand. I concluded he'd been in America a good many years to have reached this level of easy fluency.

'You can tell me about your friend, Joe Petrovitch,' I said. 'His grieving widow hopes to learn something that would let her get in touch with his relatives back home to notify them of his death. I take it you knew Joe in the Old Country? What country was that?' I knew the answer, but that was the way to start questioning someone. If you know the answers, you can see if they are telling the truth.

'Serbia,' he said, putting his mouth to the bottle again. 'We were in army together.'

'And you came to America when?'

'After we got out. 1913.'

'And did Joe leave family behind?'

'No. No family. The war . . . you see, you don't understand

over here about how is war. Families dead or disappeared. Gone for good. Mine too. No one can know what happened or find them.'

'You and Joe had other Serb friends who came to America with you.'

I'd moved too fast. The gripman's eyes narrowed into hard slits, closing him off from my too-probing question.

'Thank you for this bottle,' he said, standing. He turned up his coat collar against the rain, which was coming down harder now. 'That is all I can tell you about Joe's family.'

'Then perhaps I can tell you something. Something important. Joe Petrovitch didn't die of illness or accident. He was murdered. His friends Ilitch and Jovanovitch were murdered too. Gunned down. I think you may be in danger as well.'

He stared straight ahead into the darkness, then, inhaling a long swallow of the whiskey, sat down again beside me. I interpreted that as a request to continue.

'You came to America with the other men in 1913. Jeton Ilitch was shot a few months ago in New York City at the restaurant where he worked as a cook. Al Jovanovitch was killed – shot – not long after that in St. Louis at the automobile factory where he worked. And Joe Petrovitch was gunned down last month at the theater where he was a projectionist. I believe the same man killed all three. Each time, he pulled the trigger three times, then vanished. Would you have any idea who might have done this and why?'

The longer the silence, the stronger the need to fill it. I waited through several more swigs of whiskey until Pavlovitch had worked through exactly what he was going to tell me about those years. Starting with a grunt, he said, 'It was four or five of us, soldiers, just privates. In the battle, we got lost from our unit. Then at night, some men attacked. We fired at them and killed two. We found their bodies in the morning. They were officers from our own Third Army. This is very bad, to kill our own officers. A big accident, but we would be shot. So we walk many days to coast, steal a fishing boat and get to Bari in Italy, then to New York. We split up after a few months and don't see each other again. Maybe . . .' His voice trailed off.

'Maybe what?' I prompted.

'Maybe some guy find out about dead officers and come for revenge.'

'How could anyone know?'

He shrugged. 'Maybe they see us from far away.'

'How would they know who you were or where to find you?'

He shrugged again and fell silent.

Sometimes even the most improbable of stories carries a whiff of sincerity that overcomes doubt. This was not one of those times. Pavlovitch was lying. Or maybe dissembling was the better way to describe it. Rather than go meekly into the night, I hoped to jar him into further revelation, and so I said, 'Well, I don't believe your story, but if that's all you care to tell me, I'll go now.' And I stood.

My little gambit failed. Pavlovitch offered nothing more. He stood too and, nodding goodbye, left the shelter, heading away from me and the cable car stop toward the street corner.

I had turned to go when, without warning, a man brandishing a gun leaped out of the shadows to block the gripman's passage. The stranger shouted some brief, unintelligible slogan, fired three shots into Paul Pavlovitch's chest from a no-miss distance of about six feet, and took off running.

THIRTY

What astonished me most was how fast everything happened. Before Pavlovitch had even crumpled to the pavement, I heard shouts and saw two plain-clothesmen draw guns and break into a run. Detective Carl Delaney and Officer Steve Marks were heading pell-mell into the screams of women and the shouts of men that ripped the night air. I didn't recognize them at first. I thought they were local policemen, so I called out, 'There! Over there!' and pointed in the direction of the assassin as he dashed toward the powerhouse. Poor Pavlovitch lay in a sodden heap beside the cable car track.

More shots rang out. At first, I thought they had missed their mark, then I saw the assassin lurch and fall, clutching his leg. That was the moment I realized Carl was there and that he was the one who had brought down the assassin with a well-aimed shot. The man was still moving but the leg wound made flight impossible. Carl dropped to Pavlovitch's side, motioning for his partner to follow through with the wounded killer. Warily, Marks crept toward the wounded man, his gun drawn.

Meanwhile, the three local policemen on the scene launched rather belatedly into action. One headed toward Carl and Pavlovitch with his gun drawn, and Carl called to him, 'Hold your fire, we're police!' The other two moved more cautiously in the direction of Marks and the assassin. Before they could reach Marks, more shots pierced the night as Marks fired on the downed figure, who must have refused to lay aside his gun. The San Francisco policemen caught up to the action and, unsure of which man was the good guy and which was the bad, shouted that they would fire on whoever didn't lay down his gun at once.

Marks laid his weapon on the pavement and raised his arms. 'We're police!' he said, echoing Carl. The assassin lay without moving.

The entire drama took less than ten seconds.

Shedding the spectator's role, I became an actor and ran onto the scene toward Marks and the downed assassin. 'Don't shoot,' I called to the local cop as I dropped to the ground beside the killer. I'm not sure who they thought I was, but no one made any effort to intercept me, a harmless female. Kneeling on the pavement, I turned the assassin over, hoping that I would recognize him. He was still alive.

And he was a total stranger.

Glancing over my shoulder for Carl, I saw that the officer who had taken his gun was now handcuffing him. No surprise – these cops didn't know Carl from Adam, and he'd shot a fleeing man. Neither he nor Marks were wearing uniforms. Beside me, one of the local cops retrieved Marks's gun and ordered him to stand aside while the other fished out his handcuffs. I figured they'd work out the details sooner or later, so I focused my attention on the assassin.

His appearance was exactly as witnesses had described: average. His height and weight were unremarkable. His dark hair had been cut in a common style, and his suit and shirt (now marked with a blood stain that grew larger with each passing second) were neither cheap nor expensive. His fingers were bare of rings. Even in the dim light, I saw no scars or moles on his face, no gaps in his teeth, nothing that would stick in someone's memory. He wore the thin mustache that half the men in America wore, a mustache that I might have tried to pull off had I been bolder, to see if it were fake as I suspected. Otherwise, there was nothing remarkable in his description, which is why no one had ever remarked on any descriptive detail. The man was perfectly ordinary. The sort of person who crept into your consciousness and out again without leaving the slightest trace. The perfect villain.

One of the policemen had hustled to a callbox to ring for an ambulance, which came clanging down the hill within minutes.

'You with him, lady?' asked a voice close by.

I looked over at the polished shoes and up at a blue uniform topped by a brimmed cap. Honesty was not going to get me anywhere.

'I'm his sister.' Damnit, too late, I realized what a mistake that was. I should have said cousin. I did not bear the slightest resemblance to this man.

'We got an ambulance on its way. What happened? Who shot who?'

I understood that nothing was clear to those unfamiliar with the history of our murderous drama, and a befuddled scenario worked in my favor.

'I have no idea, officer,' I answered in a pathetic trembling voice. 'I want to go to the hospital with him.'

'Sure, why not? We'll be taking the both of them. Hospital's not but a few blocks away. He'll be fine, don't you worry.'

Next thing I knew, the cop was pushing back a small clutch of curious spectators who had gathered now that the shooting was over. 'Make way for the ambulance, people,' he said. I spared a nervous glance at Carl Delaney, who was being held some distance away with Officer Marks by several San

Francisco cops. With an eloquent look in my direction, Carl gave me to understand that he blamed everything on me. I thought it prudent to disappear until he'd cooled off.

Two men in white coats leaped from the ambulance. Dragging a stretcher out of the back, they went first to Pavlovitch – who wasn't moving and whose eyes were closed – and carted him into the truck. Next they came our way. Lifting the assassin, they laid him on the stretcher and hoisted it into the opposite side of the truck.

'I want to come with him,' I repeated.

The driver looked at the policeman who nodded his permission. 'Up front with me then, miss,' he said. The other man – the one I figured for a medic – rode in back between the two stretchers.

We reached the hospital in minutes. Before I could climb out of the front seat, a nurse and two men in white coats busied themselves pulling the injured men out of the back with commendable efficiency. The policeman who had followed the ambulance joined us, probably to make sure neither of the wounded men did a flit.

The closest I'd ever come to a hospital had been on the set of Mary Pickford's *Little Annie Rooney* where we'd filmed the poignant blood transfusion scenes. I'd imagined a real hospital to be a noisy confusion of nurses and doctors rushing from crisis to crisis, so the calm atmosphere of the real thing came as a surprise.

'Who's worse?' someone asked. I inched closer to the assassin.

'This one's dead,' said the medic, pointing to Pavlovitch.

A moment's examination confirmed that diagnosis, at which point the trio shifted its attention to the assassin who had by this time been lifted onto a gurney. I stepped back, content at present to be ignored, as the nurses pulled his shirt tails out to reveal the belly wound inflicted by Officer Marks – and something unexpected: an odd roll of dark red fabric bunched around his waist. Frowning slightly with confusion, the nurse pulled it out of the way and concentrated on the injury. I alone recognized it for what it was – part of a transfigurator's quick-change costume. Had Carl Delaney and Officer Marks not shot him, he'd have transformed into a woman by unrolling a dark red skirt and walked calmly away from the scene of the crime.

The medical trio read each other's minds better than any vaudeville psychic act I'd ever seen, exchanging no more than a couple grunts as they examined the killer's wounds. The nurse bound his leg wound and then ignored it in favor of the more serious belly wound. Lights made the entry brighter than it had been at the cable car terminus, which meant I could study the man's features more closely. Still, I saw nothing familiar about him. For one brief moment, he opened his eyes and took in his surroundings with an indifference that said plainer than words that he couldn't have cared less where he was or what had happened to him. I looked into his eyes and felt a little jolt of surprise. Familiar eyes. Brown, with gold flecks like the sun's rays.

Startled, I racked my brain trying to remember where I'd seen those eyes before. Or was this a coincidence? Just how common were brown, yellow-flecked eyes?

Two men hustled the gurney down a long hall and banged through swinging doors. I stood staring stupidly after them, rooted to the spot, consumed by those eyes, until another nurse approached me with a clipboard.

'You're the patient's next-of-kin?' she said, putting a gentle hand on my arm to pull me out of my daze.

'Yes!' I shouted, not as a response to her question. I hardly heard her. Yes, I remembered those eyes! Julia Shala's eyes. The woman who befriended Barbara Petrovitch in her grief, brought food to her house, and sat beside me at dinner that night. Julia Shala! Julia Shala?

I must have been blind not to see past Julia Shala's disguise. The truth hit me like a slap in the face. The killer had posed as *Mr* Shala at the Petrovitch funeral and as *Mrs* Shala when he brought food to Barbara and hung about so he could learn how the investigation was proceeding. That's how he learned about other Serbian friends – by attending their funerals and talking with their grieving relatives.

His nondescript appearance was the key to his ability to change sex. His size made him slightly smaller than the average man, slightly larger than the average woman. His neutral face shaved clean could be feminine; adding a beard or mustache made it masculine. His short hair was easily covered by a woman's wig. He was a killer with no remarkable features. None that were visible from a few feet, that is. To notice those unusual eyes, one had to be very close – something that almost never happened. When the witnesses all agreed they'd seen a man, the last thing police would be looking for was a woman. Besides, everyone knows women don't shoot people in cold blood.

The pull on my arm by the persistent nurse brought me back to earth. She probably thought I'd been struck dumb with grief. 'There now, dearie,' she said, oozing sympathy, 'he'll be fine. The doctors will take care of everything. You can't be any help to them in the operating room. But you can certainly help us here at the admitting desk. I need you to fill out this patient-information form.' She guided me to a chair and handed me the clipboard and a pencil. I drew a deep breath, sat, and stared at the form without seeing it.

I was responsible for Paul Pavlovitch's death. The assassin had known I was looking into the murders. He'd learned everything at Barbara's house. He knew I was making progress, drawing the murders together, understanding that they were all related. He had been waiting for me – *me!* – to track down the fourth Serbian victim, with Barbara's help. He'd wormed his way into Barbara's confidence and probably knew everything she knew. He'd been there the night Barbara received the telegram from Pavlovitch – the night I was with Carl posing as a child to visit Rose Ann's house – so he learned about the man in San Francisco. But he didn't know where, so the bastard followed me, letting me do all the work of finding the gripman so he could kill him. I had all but pulled the trigger myself, by guiding the hunter directly to his prey. I couldn't have made it easier. Julia Shala was really a man. I had sat right beside her – him – that night at Barbara's house. How could I have been so blind?

The policeman who had followed the ambulance was standing nearby. A nurse offered to get him a cup of coffee. He accepted and told her he wouldn't be there long, just until he learned whether the second man survived surgery. She threw a glance in my direction and shushed him before coming quietly to my side. 'As soon as you finish with that form, dear, you can go in to the waiting room.'

My eyes focused on the busy room for the first time. This wasn't a waiting room? She read my confusion.

'This is admitting. The waiting room for relatives is down the hall. It's quieter. Private. You'll be more comfortable there while you wait for the doctor to come out of surgery.' She put her hand on my shoulder as I started to stand. 'But you must finish this first.'

The first blank was the hardest. Patient's name. Julia Shala? Of course not, that was an alias. So was Mr Shala. *What difference does it make?* None, really, but I wanted to get it straight for myself. We'd narrowed the possibilities to two, Vesa Leka and the protean act of Barton, Hicks & Hicks. Vesa Leka was reputed to be a foreigner. The names Barton and Hicks did not sound like foreign names. Touching the tip of the lead pencil to my tongue, I wrote 'Vesa Leka' in the blank.

From there, it was easy. I made up an address in San Francisco, estimated Mr Leka's height, weight, and age, and gave him his real profession: vaudeville performer. After handing the completed form to the nurse on duty, I was directed down the hall to a small room where I was the only occupant, and I settled in to wait for the doctor's report.

It wasn't long before the doctor entered the room. Young, with bright red hair, spectacles, and cheeks dotted with freckles, he approached me with a solemn face that did not bode well for Mr Leka.

'You are the patient's sister?'

A safe assumption. I was the only person in the room.

'Cousin,' I said, correcting my earlier blunder.

'I am Dr O'Flaherty,' he began. Behind the spectacles, his eyes sagged with fatigue. 'I'm sorry to bring bad news. The bullet went through the upper abdomen, piercing the kidneys and liver. We hoped to find minimal damage that could be repaired, but it was not to be. I never say no hope, because there is always hope, but there is nothing a surgeon can do for such a serious injury. Your cousin is still alive, but I'm

afraid she will not survive for long. How long? It is impossible
to say. A few hours, a few days. It's in God's hands now. The
ether is wearing off, and she is coming around now. I recommend you call a priest or clergyman, if that would ease her
mind.'

She?

I glanced behind me in case the doctor was talking to
someone who had just entered the room, but I still was the
only person there. He could not be addressing the wrong
relative.

The assassin was a woman.

THIRTY-ONE

I hadn't spent twenty-four years on a vaudeville stage without
learning how to react to the unexpected. Like the time little
Darcy Darling danced off the edge of the stage into the
pit, or the orchestra opened our act with a waltz instead of
ragtime, or a dogfight in the wings spilled onto the stage during
our finale. Some things in life can't be anticipated, and this
was one of them, in spades.

Not once had I figured the killer for a woman masquerading
as a man. How could that have sailed past me? Instinctively
I dropped my head into my hands, the tried-and-true method
of covering any expression of shock I might be unable to hide.
The doctor took it as grief and laid a comforting hand on my
shoulder.

'You should sit down,' he said. 'I'll have a nurse bring you
some water.' His solicitous tone changed as he snapped out
orders to a nurse coming down the hall. 'Now, maybe you can
enlighten me. I'm quite confused. Was your cousin an innocent
bystander? Who shot whom? Not that it matters as far as her
care is concerned, of course.'

If he wondered why a woman was wearing a man's getup,
he was too shy to ask. I figured he'd learn the truth about the
shooting soon enough from the police, so I didn't hesitate to

respond. 'She shot the other man. A policeman shot her. I
don't know why,' I added to forestall his inevitable next question. It was the truth.

The surgeon shook his head in disbelief. 'Women aren't
violent by nature. Only one with a severe mental illness could
have done such a thing. Was your cousin exhibiting other signs
of mental illness?'

'Not that I was aware of.'

'Well, it's cold comfort perhaps, but at least she won't have
to pay the price for her crime.' Meaning she wouldn't live
long enough to go to prison or hang. 'Excuse me, now, I must
give my report to the police.'

The nurse brought a glass of water. 'We've put the patient
in Room 7,' she said. 'Down the hall to your right.'

The hospital was quiet as a morgue as I walked the hall,
past two nurses – no wonder, it was the middle of the night
and most patients were asleep. I had lost all sense of time. In
Room 7, the weak bulb in a wall sconce gave off enough light
for me to make out the killer lying on his back – *her* back – in
a narrow bed. A simple table and a straight wooden chair
completed the décor. No clock. Behind a curtain, a second bed,
table, and chair – all empty – were pushed against the wall.

I sat in the chair closest to the bed, where I had a good
view of the patient, and she of me when she emerged from
the ether. I wished someone would offer me a cup of strong
coffee instead of water.

After a long while, I don't know how long, her eyes opened.
She gazed about the room, blinking rapidly, but her eyes were
soon clear and intelligent. She seemed mindful of her surroundings and not at all surprised to see me sitting beside her bed.
We stared at each other for a long while without speaking.

'Is your real name Vesa Leka?' I asked at last.

Her response sounded like a hiss. I took it for a 'Yes' and
continued, somewhat foolishly, 'Good. That's what I wrote on
the hospital admitting form. I don't suppose I need to tell you
my name.'

She blinked.

'You killed him. Paul Pavlovitch. He's dead, in case you
were wondering.'

Her lips turned up at the corners.

'He's the fourth you've killed, isn't he? The fourth that I know of, anyway.'

'Yes.' This time she said the word clearly. 'Water?'

A burly police guard stationed outside the door to Room 7 gave me a wordless once over as I passed him on my way to the nurse's desk. I found a nurse and asked if the patient could have water. For an answer, she took a piece of ice from an icebox, placed it in a clean towel, crushed it with a hammer, and shook the pieces into a glass. 'Not water, no, but she can suck on these. I'll be down in a few minutes to look in on her.'

I fed Vesa Leka bits of ice until the nurse showed up. She felt her patient's pulse and forehead, propped her head up with a second pillow, and murmured the usual clichés about feeling better soon. 'The doctor will be in shortly, dear.' By the time she left us alone again, Vesa Leka had found her voice. Rough and soft at the same time, it came with an accent, but her English was pretty good.

'I will die, yes?'

'I'm sorry. The doctor said he couldn't do any more for you. The wound was too serious. He said a few hours, or a few days at most. He suggested we ask for a priest. Are you Catholic?'

'No.'

'Greek Orthodox?'

'No priest.'

'Wouldn't a priest make dying easier?'

'I am not afraid to die. Everyone dies. I will join my family again. I regret only that I die before I have finished.'

'Finished what?' I was afraid I knew the answer.

'Killing.'

'Isn't four men enough?'

'Five is enough.'

'Why did you kill them?'

She closed her gold-flecked eyes, signaling her refusal to answer as clearly as if she had telegraphed the words. Thinking she did not believe me about the seriousness of her wounds, I waited for the doctor. Maybe once she understood she really was dying, she would ask for a priest. Maybe then she would talk – to him or to me.

Fortunately, I've had little to do with doctors in my life, save for the year my mother died. I saw more doctors that year than I ever want to see, a new one at nearly every town we played. All were stern, hard men, but young as I was, I understood that their brusque manner stemmed from anger at their own helplessness in the face of the disease that was destroying my mother. They could cut off a crushed limb and save a life, but cancer had them licked. The young red-haired doctor here was cut from the same mold. He was sorry, he told Vesa Leka when he came into the room, but there was nothing more he could do. He repeated the same lines about never saying 'no hope' and that she was in the hands of God and would she like a priest, and she answered him as she had me: no.

'Are you in pain?' he asked.

'Some.'

'I'll tell the nurse to get you opium. As much as you like.'

He left. The nurse reappeared and spooned a large dose of white liquid into the patient's mouth. Then Vesa Leka and I were alone again.

'You're Julia Shala,' I said.

Her eyebrows lifted. I had surprised her with that observation. 'How did you know?' she asked.

'Your eyes. I saw them up close at Barbara's house that night and again in the admitting room. They are unusual.'

'Tiger's eyes, my father called them.'

'Is there a family member I can notify about your injury and . . . death?'

'No.'

'This may be the last chance you have to explain. You must have had a reason for killing those men. Don't you want us to understand why you did what you did?'

She said nothing.

'Are you Serbian?'

'No!' she snapped. And then, a little calmer, 'Pigs.'

'What, then?'

'Albanian.'

'Tell me.'

After a long wait, I gave up. I made ready to leave. Perhaps Carl Delaney and Officer Marks were in the admitting room by now, wondering what had happened to me. I should try to find them. And my grandmother, if she were still awake at this hour, would be worried about me. I could come back to the hospital tomorrow and see if Vesa Leka had survived the night. Maybe she would talk then. Maybe never. Some secrets go to the grave.

Then she began talking, slowly at first, as if each word hurt to come out, then faster.

THIRTY-TWO

'Our farm, it was small but good. We lived there, my mother, my father, my uncle, my brother, and me. Fighting comes often to our land. For us, the Great War started not in 1914 but in 1912.'

She coughed and clutched her stomach as a spasm caused pain. After a minute, she marshaled her strength and continued.

'One day five soldiers came to our farm. Serb deserters. They want food. My mother was frightened so she gave it. Then my father and brother came from the field. The soldiers shot them. Even our dog. My brother was ten. I was fifteen. They rape my mother and me. Five men. Then two more soldiers came. Good soldiers, officers looking for the deserters. The five said they would not go back to the army, and they shoot their officers. They shoot my mother and me, but I did not die. My uncle came home that night and find all of us dead except me. I wanted to die too, but he made me live.'

Her voice sank to a whisper. She licked her cracked lips and motioned with her fingers for the ice. I handed her more shards to suck on. After a moment, she resumed her story.

'My uncle, next year, he sends me to New York where lives a cousin and no one knows of my dishonor. I become apprentice to my cousin, a tailor. This cousin makes clothes for many people, some on the stage. One customer is the Great Fulgora, the famous transfigurator. I learned the tricks of making clothes that come off and on very fast. Fulgora himself taught me some of his secrets. I practiced. I went to vaudeville to make more money than a tailor. It is a good life, vaudeville. Better than tailor.'

She paused for more ice chips. Her story horrified me. It shouldn't have. Like everyone else, I'd read about the atrocities inflicted on the Belgian women and children by the invading Huns during the Great War – babies bayoneted, women defiled and decapitated – but that was far away, and I knew none of those people. Here was one I knew who had suffered unspeakable violence. Something Carl Delaney had said once came to mind: that he wished men could satisfy their lust for war by shooting at each other from their trenches and leave civilians alone.

'I'm so very sorry.' It sounded pretty feeble, but I didn't know what else to say.

'In our culture, avenging wrongs is important. I never thought I would have the chance to avenge my family. Then God showed me He had not forgotten. One afternoon, I was on stage in New York and the audience showed me a face, in the front row, a face I could never forget if a thousand years would pass. He was one of the soldiers at our farm that day. He was one who raped my mother and me and killed my family. It was a message from God.

'I rush off stage and got by the door when the audience let out. I follow the man. He went to Italian restaurant near the theater, but not to eat. The kitchen was his place of work. I sat at a table and ordered food, even though to think of eating made me taste vomit. I asked the waiter, was the cook Italian? No, he said to me, the cook is Serbian. I asked did he have a wife and children, for it made me uneasy to think to kill a man who would leave a wife and children to starve. He said no. That was the moment I knew I would kill him.'

She looked at the ceiling, as if gathering strength from something on the plaster. She swallowed hard several times, and her mouth opened and closed as her lips struggled to form words. When she continued, she spoke to the ceiling, almost as if she was watching the events take place up there, almost as if she had forgotten I was beside her in the room.

'I go again to this restaurant to look and plan my revenge. I plan it as I would plan my act on stage – entrance male, action, exit female. I brought a gun. I went in the kitchen, I pointed my gun and told him who I was. The fear in his eyes warmed me. He knew he would now pay for his sins. I shot three bullets, one for my mother, one for my father, and one for my brother. Then I transformed into a woman and screamed the killer ran out the back door.

'I was so happy with my success. For the first time since the farm, my life had purpose. I thought of the other four soldiers. Were they in America too? How to find them? I knew their names but nothing more.'

'How did you know their names?' I asked.

'My uncle, he search pockets of the two dead officers to maybe find money. He found a paper with five names. The deserters' names. I did not know if the other four had died in the war or come to America like the cook, but now I think it possible they could be in New York. They cannot stay in their own country, even if our murders were never known. Deserters can never go home. So I go to this man Ilitch's funeral and pretend to be a friend of Ilitch. I went as a woman, because people talk more to women. I learned there was a friend of Ilitch who lived in St. Louis.'

'So you quit your vaudeville act and went to St. Louis,' I continued for her, to let her rest. 'You found the small Serbian immigrant community there and a man named Jovanovitch. When you learned he worked at a motorcar factory, you got a job at that factory.'

She gave a thin smile. 'Yes. I clean floors and water closets, I watch and listen, until I knew which man was Jovanovitch. While I clean, I plan his death and my escape, just as before. Then I had revenge with three bullets for my family. You know this. You were there. I heard you tell Barbara Petrovitch.'

'You were the man who paid for his funeral, pretending to be a distant cousin, weren't you?'

'I paid his funeral with his own money what I took from his apartment. I search his papers until I found one with the address of two men, one in Los Angeles, one in Detroit. I also find his hidden money – two hundred dollars. This was good, because cleaning women earn little wages. I went to Detroit, but he was not there. There was another at his address who said he left several years before. So I went to Los Angeles and found the man who showed films. I found him at his home and followed him to his work. I go two times to the theater to learn how to come and go quick. His face when I shot him made my soul rejoice. I went to his funeral. I was sad for his wife, but people say he beat her, so it was good to spare her more beating.'

'Barbara,' I said. 'She's a good person.'

'I bring her cake one day and learn you are helping find her husband's killer. She told me about the letter from St. Louis – she told me everything. I knew you would soon understand the connection between the killings. So I watch and listen to Barbara tell me of your progress. I hoped you would lead me to the two men I wanted to kill. You did. One, anyway. Now he is dead too. So, you see, I do not need a priest. I have nothing to confess. I did not murder anyone. I avenge my family and honor them. My father will be proud. I am only sorry to leave one alive.'

Only a stone could fail to be moved by her story, and I was no stone. But I was torn. On the one hand, what she did was clearly wrong. On the other, how else was justice to be served? American police could not arrest men for murders and rapes committed thirteen years ago in a far-off land. American courts could not prosecute foreign men for foreign crimes. If the men returned to Serbia, they would be shot for desertion and the murder of the two officers, which is, of course, why they fled that country in the first place. Were they to be excused with an 'Oh well, never mind?'. Murder was wrong, but this seemed to be something other than murder. I sympathized with Vesa Leka. Hers was a rough, Old West sort of justice, but it was the only justice available.

'You don't know about another Serb, do you?' she asked hopefully.

'I'm afraid not.'

'The last one's name is Stefan Markovitch. He lived in Detroit but moved someplace else.'

'There were no letters or telegrams that mentioned such a name. He must not have kept in touch with the others. Would you like me to get you more – Oh!' In my excitement, I leaped to my feet.

'What?'

My mind raced. 'Did you point a gun at the cop who shot you?'

'No, the gun I dropped when I fell with my leg bleeding. I didn't have any gun.'

'That cop who shot you in the chest. His name is Steve Marks.'

She understood instantly. 'Stefan Markovitch? You think he is Stefan Markovitch?'

'No wonder he tried to kill you when it wasn't necessary! He must have left Detroit and come to Los Angeles years ago with Joe Petrovitch!'

Stunned at the implications, I sat back down and dragged my thoughts through the past few weeks, collecting the bits and pieces that involved Officer Marks. 'He heard about Joe's death and volunteered to translate letters. One time, I remember, he didn't translate the entire message until I pressed him. He denied being Serbian; he claimed to be from Macedonia. He knew all about the investigation. Oh my god, I left word with Carl where I was going, and Marks must have volunteered to come to San Francisco with him so he could have a chance at killing the killer before his turn came.'

'He tried to kill me once, on our farm, but I lived then. He tried again tonight. When I die, will he not go to prison for shooting me?'

'I doubt it. He's a policeman.'

'Ah, but this is America. In America, policemen cannot kill who they please, no?'

'He was chasing the person who had just shot and killed a man. He should have tried to capture you alive, but he can always say you pointed your gun at him so he had no choice but to shoot in self defense.'

'I had no gun then.'

'He can say that anyway. They will find your gun nearby and believe him.'

She thought this through before sighing. 'So this time he will succeed in killing me.'

She must have seen the stricken look on my face, for she gave a weak smile. 'Do not be sad. I have revenge on four of them. It is no small thing. I honor my family.'

'I – I'm just . . .'

The nurse made another brief appearance. She checked on her patient, then turned to me. 'Two men are waiting for you in the admitting lobby, dearie. And we have another patient coming in here shortly. I'm sorry – the police wanted you to have a private room, but all the other beds on this hall are full.'

'Thank you. What time is it?'

'Quarter past two.'

After she had left the room, I turned to Vesa Leka, 'That will be my friend, Detective Carl Delaney, who came here with Officer Steve Marks. They will want to know what happened and how you are. I don't know how I can face him.'

'You were in vaudeville, like me, no? You will know how to act.' We fell silent for a time, until she spoke again, her voice soft with hesitation. 'This detective, is he a bad man?'

'He's probably the only honest cop in Hollywood.'

'You are honest person too. You are vaudeville, like me. I cannot kill Markovitch. I will die soon. But if you help me, I can avenge my family. If you help me. Will you help?'

'Me? No!' But then, to my dismay, curiosity trumped good sense. 'Help how?'

THIRTY-THREE

'To start with,' I said, sitting across from Carl and Officer Marks, 'he's a she.'

Carl nearly spat out his coffee. Marks's eyes widened. Clearly neither man had any idea they were dealing with a woman.

'Are you sure?' Carl asked.

A smile tugged at my lips. 'I think the surgeon would not mistake that detail. She is Vesa Leka, a vaudeville transfigurator until a few months ago.'

I watched Marks's expression closely when I said her name. It meant nothing to him. I began to think Vesa Leka might be wrong . . . just possibly, Marks really was what he claimed to be – a Macedonian who happened to read Serbian. The similarity of the two names could be coincidence. Yet if that was the case, would he have shot the unarmed person? He knew the person on the ground was responsible for killing his comrades. But did he make the connection to the Albanian farm family? Did he know who she was? I didn't think so.

'Vesa is a girl's name,' observed Marks without emotion.

I nodded, wishing I'd known that tidbit earlier. 'I told them I was her cousin, so I could stay close.'

'Good thinking,' said Carl. 'The locals aren't too happy with Marks and me right now. Did you learn anything?'

I took a deep breath. 'I sure did. Vesa Leka is out to avenge her Albanian family who was murdered back in 1912 during the war over there. That was the war that came before the Great War. Five men, all Serbian army deserters, came to their farm, raped her and her mother, and killed her whole family. She alone survived.' I watched Marks's face as I spoke and saw recognition flush his face. His eyes widened and he gave a soft cry. Carl mistook it for horror. I knew better. He was Stefan Markovitch. No doubts remained. I wanted to spit on him.

'Sometimes I think war is worse hell for civilians than it is for soldiers,' Carl said with a shake of his head. 'Law and order is the first victim. When that disappears, the strongest man with the biggest gun gets away with doing whatever he wants to because there's no police, no jails, no courts, no consequences.' And his own army experience in France during the Great War was, I knew, the reason he had decided not to return to the farm but to become a cop.

I went on. 'The five men also murdered two officers who had come looking for them. Vesa Leka learned the names of the deserters from papers one of the officers was carrying. She hadn't come to America to search for the deserters; it just happened that she recognized one in a vaudeville audience while she was performing in New York City one day and followed him to his restaurant and shot him. His funeral led her to find the others, one by one. Her training allowed her to shoot and change her appearance so quickly that she was never caught.'

'How did you know she was coming to San Francisco?' Carl asked.

'I didn't know. I found out from Barbara Petrovitch that one of the five soldiers was living here – Paul Pavlovitch – and I came to see what I could learn from him. And to warn him, of course. Vesa Leka wormed her way into Barbara's confidence and has been tracking our investigation all along. I had no idea she was following me. I led her straight to him. I feel like a chump.'

Carl reached over and squeezed my shoulder for reassurance. 'So we know about four of the men she killed. Did she get the fifth too?'

'No. She doesn't know where he is, only his name. And she knows she won't be able to track him down now.'

'We heard she was going to die.'

I stole a glance at Marks. He was staring at his hands like someone who wasn't paying attention, but I could almost see his ears stretch toward our conversation.

'Well, that's old news. She looked to be in pretty bad shape when she came in, but luckily, Marks's bullets missed the main organs, and the doctor was able to repair the critical damage. She's stronger already. I don't pretend to understand the medical details . . . but now it looks like she'll go to trial after all.'

'And hang for four murders. Or spend the rest of her life in prison.' Clearly, he believed the former outcome more likely.

I nodded. 'But her testimony will come out at the trial, of course, and while she won't be able to track down the fifth deserter, all that publicity will shine a spotlight on him. You know the newspapers in New York, St. Louis, Los Angeles, and here will play up the story like mad – she'll become a national sensation. After all, she has a very sympathetic tale to tell. And she plans to start telling it now. The public will eat it up raw. She wants me to arrange for a reporter from the *Chronicle* and the *Examiner* to come to the hospital as soon as the sun's up. Someone, somewhere is bound to know him.'

Carl gave this some thought before adding, 'He may not be in this country. Hell, he may not be alive.' I noted with some satisfaction that the man-who-might-not-be-alive was wringing his hands.

'If he is alive, could he be tried for those murders?' I asked, hoping to pour salt in the wound.

'Not in America,' said Carl. 'There's always a possibility that he could be arrested and shipped back to Serbia for justice there. Slim, I grant you, but a possibility. They'd probably shoot him for desertion before they bothered about any civilian deaths, though. That's the way war works, I'm afraid.' He sighed and checked the clock on the wall. 'I guess there's nothing more we can do here.'

'You're right. Vesa Leka isn't going anywhere. There's a policeman built like an icebox guarding the door to Room 7 and a night nurse keeping watch on the hall. The doctor has gone home. All the other third-floor patients seem to be asleep. Me, I'm going to faint from hunger. The nurse told me there was an all-night diner around the corner. What say we head there for some early breakfast?'

Carl considered my proposal. 'It'll be daylight in a few hours, and the southbound express leaves at eight. We could eat, and then go straight to the station. Marks, you and I could be home this evening.'

Marks spoke up. 'What about our guns?'

'The San Francisco police confiscated them,' he said in response to my questioning look. Then he turned back to Marks. 'They're not going to give them back to us today, that's for sure. They'll probably ship them back to headquarters when they're good and ready. We don't need them now.' Carl stood, stretched, and yawned. 'You coming with us, Jessie?'

'To the diner, but not on the train. As long as I'm in San Francisco, I think I'll spend some time with my grandmother and come home in a day or two.'

I stood. Officer Marks remained in his wooden chair, a vacant stare in his eyes. He was, I knew, ruined. He knew it too. The thought gave me a thrill of satisfaction. His best hope now was to vanish, but would he? As soon as the newspapers got hold of Vesa Leka's story and the additions to it that I intended to make, his respectable job with the Los Angeles police would be over. He'd have to change his name and move to another state. Maybe another country. Canada or Mexico, perhaps. Or somewhere in South America. In one sense, he'd escape justice, but he'd never land safely anywhere. He would be forever isolated, looking over his shoulder, unable to mingle with the decent Serb immigrant communities where he would be despised for having deserted their army and for killing his officers. Living alone, without family or friends or familiar surroundings, would be its own kind of verdict. And that was his best hope. There was always the chance that he could be shipped back to Serbia for trial. But I was pulling for a third ending to this sordid drama.

'I'm more tired than hungry,' said Marks, his eyes fixed on his shoes. 'I'm going to the station and sleep on a bench until the train comes.'

Carl nodded. I smiled, and we left the hospital.

The all-night diner served a limited menu after midnight, but the breakfast special appealed to us both. A waitress poured us strong coffee and jotted down our order for the cook. Too tired to chatter, I cradled my coffee cup and tested various bits of opening dialogue in my head. Carl wasn't going to like this – he was the sort of man who put a high price on honesty. I realized how much I valued his good opinion, now that I was about to lose it. He deserved the truth at the first possible moment, but I stalled, thinking it prudent to wait until our food came, and then convincing myself to get a few bites into my stomach in case the meal was interrupted. When I swallowed the last mouthful of potatoes, I knew I'd run out of excuses.

'So, Carl,' I said, fixing my gaze on the knot in his tie. 'Something happened that you should know about.' I paused for him to make a comment, but he was a man of no unnecessary words. I could feel him tense.

'Well, okay, here it is. Everything I said about Vesa Leka wasn't exactly true. Most things were, but not every single thing.'

Still no comment from Carl. It was time to rip the adhesive tape off with one quick motion.

'For one thing, she knows who the fifth deserter is. He's here in San Francisco. He followed us. His name was Stefan Markovitch. Now it's Steve Marks.'

As I watched, Carl turned his thoughts inward. His brown eyes stared through me, unseeing, as if he'd been sitting alone at the table. He was, I knew, sifting through what I'd said, analyzing it piece by piece, the way he did everything. I knew he'd fitted enough of the puzzle pieces into place when he gave a low cry and leapt to his feet, his eyes snapped into focus.

'He's going to kill her. Before she has the chance to talk to the reporters. It's the only way he can save himself. You knew who he was! What he was capable of! Why in hell did you tell him that?'

He fumbled in his wallet for money and threw two dollars on the Formica table.

'Wait. There's more.'

'No time.' He threw on his jacket and bolted toward the door, leaving me no choice but to follow. We moved so fast I was sure the waitress would take us for eat-and-run dodgers.

'Listen,' I gasped as I ran along side of him, our footsteps echoing eerily on the damp pavement. 'Vesa Leka is not going to recover. The bullets tore up a couple of organs. She's dying. Very soon. The only weapon she has left is her life. She is luring him to her room. She wants him to kill her. Then he'll be charged with her murder. That's how she'll get her revenge.'

We were too late. Two police cars blocked the hospital entrance where lights blazed. Hospital staff were milling helplessly about the admitting area. Marks was nowhere to be seen.

And Vesa Leka was dead.

THIRTY-FOUR

'Looked at the right way, the plan was a success,' I told my grandmother the next afternoon.

It was like a scene from some absurd farce: two ladies sipping tea from dainty porcelain cups in a fussy Victorian parlor as if they were prattling on about the weather, when we were talking about death and violence of the most gruesome sort. But Grandmother was a tough old bird. There was no need to shade the details, so I left nothing out of the history of Vesa Leka.

'By the time Carl and I reached the hospital, it was too late. Marks had gotten hold of a white coat – someone speculated that he must've gone around to the employees' entrance and snatched one from the changing room. The police guard said Marks walked right past him into Room 7 with a confident step and a short greeting, and he didn't suspect a thing. Whether Vesa Leka was awake or not, we'll never know, but he smothered her. Evidently it takes a good while to smother someone, and while Marks was holding the pillow on her face, the guard looked in and saw what was going on. He grabbed for the pillow and tussled with Marks, but as big as that cop was, Marks was tougher. He nearly knocked the guard out. The commotion alerted the night nurse who called for help, but by then, Marks had run out of the hospital. The police are looking for him now.'

'Another cup please, Jessie.' I poured from the silver teapot and stirred in sugar and milk the way she liked.

'Since Carl was Steve Marks's partner, the police suspected him of being in on the plot. They took him to the station for questioning. I hope he's been released by now.' I winced as I considered what Carl would have to say to me when we next met. Whatever affection he had for me would have dried up like raindrops in the desert. I told myself I didn't care. I was David's girl, and Carl was just a friend. But it hurt.

'What about you? Did the police not suspect you as well?' I shook my head. 'No, Carl made sure of that. He distanced himself from me quickly, saying he'd been at the diner alone and was just coming back to the hospital to fetch Marks. I had already told everyone I was Vesa Leka's cousin, so they had no reason to think I was involved with these out-of-town policemen. I said I'd just stepped out for some fresh air. Then I told them her story, about how she was seeking revenge on the five Serbian deserters. A newspaper reporter arrived and began scribbling furiously, so I expect to see the story in this afternoon's papers.'

'That should help direct public attention to Marks. I hope they catch him soon. A dangerous man like that who has murdered so many people . . .' She made a 'tsk, tsk, tsk' sound with her tongue and then said, 'I suppose we will be overrun with newspapermen after the first account appears.'

'I didn't give the police this address. I said I was staying at a hotel in the theater district. I've told them everything I know about Vesa Leka, except my own part in her plan, and I think it best if I fade away. I'll leave on tomorrow morning's train to Los Angeles.'

'Good, then you'll be here for today's dinner. It has probably slipped your mind, but this is Thanksgiving Day, and Delia is preparing a small turkey in honor of the occasion. That and a good night's sleep should restore your spirits.' Grandmother set her cup down and folded her hands in her lap. 'Miss Leka's plan wouldn't have worked had you not played your part. How does that make you feel?'

Trust Grandmother to hone in on the key issue.

'I've been asking myself that question all day. Did I help Vesa Leka commit suicide? Is it suicide when you have only a few hours to live? Or did I arrange a murder? I'm afraid I wanted Marks to pay for his crimes badly enough . . . and she was going to die very soon . . .' I sighed and shook my head. 'I just don't know.'

'She was the bait.'

'I helped her get what she wanted, and she wanted to be murdered. Without me, she would have died in her hospital bed, probably before talking with any reporters, and Marks would have gotten clean away. When she realized that Marks wouldn't be arrested for having shot her down in the street, she had to revise her plans. A police officer who shot a fleeing man who had himself just shot another man would get a medal, not a noose. Once she realized Marks was going to get away with killing her a second time – those were her words – she devised a way for him to kill her for good the third time. She persuaded me to tell Marks that she was going to recover from her wounds and would tell her story at her trial and to the newspapers. She made it plain – through me – that she knew who he was and that his exposure was imminent. I "accidentally" gave him the necessary details: her room number, the floor, and the layout of the people on duty. She lured him there fully expecting him to kill her. And in doing so, he ensured his own death – or at the very least a life sentence – which let her have her revenge on the fifth deserter. It was not merely vengeance. It was about honor.'

'They'll have to catch him first,' she said primly.

They caught Steve Marks the following day at the train station, when he tried to buy a ticket to Vancouver. The ticket seller recognized him from the artist's sketch in the newspaper and notified the police, who arrived in force to pry him off the northbound train and charge him with the murder of a hospital patient.

Carl was released after a day in custody, with stern warnings from the local police never to return to San Francisco. Then they told him to be back for the trial or else. When asked if he knew the whereabouts of Vesa Leka's cousin, the I-cannot-tell-a-lie detective said he didn't know she had a cousin.

THIRTY-FIVE

The bride wore green – a pale, leafy green that would naturally appeal to an outdoorsy girl like Helen. The groom wore a double-breasted, dark gray sack suit with a pale green shirt to match his intended's dress. She carried a nosegay of wildflowers we had picked for her that morning at the edge of town. Kit acted as Helen's attendant, looking . . . well, if not exactly cherubic, at least presentable, and holding a matching nosegay. We'd put a little curl in her stick-straight hair and brushed her cheeks with rouge. I had the distinct impression that given time, she would grow into an attractive young woman. Larry's brother, who served as his best man, flipped the records on the borrowed Victrola from solemn orchestral music for the bride's entrance to lively jazz afterwards.

Mrs Reynolds, Helen's mother, blinked back tears during the brief ceremony. 'Oh dear, I'm such a cry-baby,' she laughed, 'always weepy at the happiest events. To think, my little girl . . . married. It seems like yesterday that she—'

'—caught her first frog?' interjected one girlfriend, to much laughter.

After the minister had tied the knot, the guests sent up a cheer and descended on the refreshments prepared by Helen's friends. I had prepared two bowls of fruit punch, one for the wets and one for the drys. It was easy to tell which was which. In the corner, Helen and Larry busied themselves opening their gifts.

'An electric iron!' Helen exclaimed, holding the gift aloft like a trophy.

'I got you this nice new one so you could leave your old one with us,' teased Melva.

'And oh, Jessie, thank you for the towels. How lovely and soft!'

'Open mine next,' urged Kit, handing her cousin a small box.

'Why, Kit, this is the most practical gift yet – a sturdy clothesline.'

'And clothespins too,' Kit added, in case she hadn't seen them.

'Trust you to understand how much a girl like me appreciates those practical items! I'll be using this every wash day and thinking about you each time I do.'

I stood at the edge of the patio beside Mrs Reynolds. 'I'm

so glad I was able to get back in time – I wouldn't have missed this for the world! Will you be taking Kit home with you tonight?' I'd miss the girl. We'd all grown rather fond of her, in spite of her difficult ways.

'No, not tonight,' said Mrs Reynolds. 'The newlyweds are going to spend a short honeymoon at the beach, did you know that? A friend of Larry's has lent them his cottage. They'll return Wednesday to pack the motorcar and leave Thursday morning for the long drive to Yosemite, driving Kit home to me in Riverside as they go. If that's all right with all of you?'

'Whatever you and Helen have worked out is perfect for us.'

'I'll miss my little girl . . . but she and Larry promise to come home at least once a year. And I'll have Kit for company.'

When it was time for the newlyweds to go, Myrna passed around a bag of rice, and we lined the front walk to shower the couple as they ran to Larry's motorcar. Helen threw her nosegay and Lillian caught it. 'Gosh – and I don't even have a fella!' she protested.

'I'm free,' teased Larry's brother.

As the last guest drifted away, Myrna announced, 'Come on, girls, many hands make light work. Let's put on our aprons and whip this place back in shape before dark!'

In an hour, no one would have dreamed we had just hosted a wedding. I poured everyone a glass of leftover fruit punch – from the spiked bowl, of course – and we kicked off our shoes and freed our tired toes. Just then, a voice from the other side of the front-door screen echoed through the empty house.

'Anybody home?'

'That sounds like Carl Delaney,' I said. Kit saw my lips and jumped up before I could move. The moment of reckoning had arrived. I polished off my glass of punch for fortification.

I called, 'Come on through, Carl. We're all out back, recu-perating from Helen's wedding.' Kit flew through the house and met him at the door.

'You're welcome to leftovers and punch,' said Myrna when he had joined us.

'Don't mind if I do,' he said genially, helping himself to a large slice of cake. He seemed calm, just like his usual self. I was the one who was perspiring. 'Evening, ladies. Congratulations, Mrs Reynolds,' he said to Helen's mother, giving her a charming bow. 'I trust the event was a success?'

Carl chatted amicably with everyone for a few minutes, then turned down the volume of his voice and said to me, 'Might we go out front for a while?'

Lowering his voice prevented the other girls from hearing him, but it couldn't prevent Kit from reading his lips. No sooner had we excused ourselves than she marched out and joined us.

'It's okay,' said Carl when I raised my eyebrows pointedly. 'I only wanted to fill you in on the latest news from San Francisco. Nothing secret. I just didn't want to interrupt the festivities with unpleasant talk.'

Kit settled herself on the porch swing where she had a clear view of both our faces.

'Carl,' I began. 'Let me just say, first, that I want to apologize for not sharing Vesa Leka's plan with you that night. I couldn't. I knew that if you knew, you'd prevent it, and try to have Marks arrested yourself, and, well, we wanted . . .'

To my astonishment, he waved off my halting explanation. 'I didn't come here to scold you. I admit, I was pretty steamed that night, and I wish you'd confided in me sooner, but at least give me credit for understanding the position you were in.'

'Then you don't think I was wrong?'

'I didn't say that. I think we could have handled it differently, but it's over now, and Marks's murder trial is slated for January. That's what we just heard from San Francisco.'

'I didn't know anyone at the San Francisco police department was on speaking terms with you,' I said.

He grinned. 'They aren't. But they'll talk to our captain. And things are friendly again. They were furious that we barged into their territory, guns blazing, no less, ignoring protocol, but when they found we *had* followed the rules and that *they* had routed the message to the wrong desk, they cooled off and shared this information to our chief a few hours ago. They've charged Marks with first-degree murder. The defense will argue that Vesa Leka was already dead when he came into her room, but the night nurse will testify that she was alive moments earlier when she checked on her, and the police guard will testify that he heard her moaning when Marks was suffocating her. That's what brought him into the room. So I think our Serbian deserter is headed for a long prison sentence at the very least.'

'Good.'

Carl gave a satisfied nod and stood to leave.

Kit broke in. 'Wait. What about my mother's killer?'

'I think,' I began carefully, 'that we've come to the conclusion that her death was a tragic accident . . .' but she brushed my words aside with a wave of her thin hand.

'You're just telling me that to make me feel better. Ma didn't accidentally drink rotgut. She didn't drink hooch, not hardly at all. And never at strange places where she didn't know where it came from. I know. I used to be with her in lots of those places. And I saw her face. Someone tried to cover up the cuts and bruises but they didn't. Stop treating me like I'm stupid. Being deaf doesn't mean I'm stupid.'

'No one thinks you're stupid, Kitty Kat,' said Carl before I could protest. 'We think you're young.'

'So I'm not old like the rest of you, so that means I can't know the truth? Joe Ardy Zone was mean. He used to hit my mother and call her names.'

'You saw him do that?' I asked, horrified.

'I never saw him do it, but I saw her bruises, and I saw her crying.'

'Kit,' said Carl in a gentle tone of voice she could not hear. 'I've considered all that. We know he's a gangster. I'm sorry your mother ever got mixed up with him – he's a very bad man, no doubt about that. But I checked on his whereabouts the day your mother died, and he was definitely in Los Angeles, not in San Diego. He couldn't have killed her.'

'Where was he?'

'At home with his wife. There are plenty of witnesses, and not all of them gangsters on his payroll.'

'Elsie. That's his wife. Joe doesn't like her, but they can't get a divorce because they're good Catholics. Isn't that funny?

He can kill people and beat up people and break laws, but he can't get a divorce because he's so religious.'

Carl and I were silent. She was too young for such cynicism.

'So what?' she continued, louder. 'Who cares where Joe was? He doesn't kill people himself. He gets other people to kill for him. Mostly Danny Boy. Find out where Danny Boy was the day Ma died, and you'll find the man who killed her. I know some other people Danny Boy killed. Do you want to know their names?'

'Sure.'

'Carl . . .' I warned.

He held up his hand to forestall my objections. 'Sure, Kit, I'd like to know.'

'Heck Stetson is one. Rube Frankel. Little Man Dragas. Frank Capriano and his brother whose name I forget. You want more?'

'Sure.'

'Are you going to arrest Danny Boy?'

'I don't have any proof.'

'What do you need proof for? Everyone knows he's a killer. Why don't you just shoot him in the head? That's what he does.'

'Because he's one of the Bad Guys and we're the Good Guys. We have to follow the law or it will be nothing more than two groups of Bad Guys. And I don't want to live in a city where two groups of Bad Guys are duking it out for control. Do you?'

She sniffed with disgust.

'Look, Kit, we've tried to get at Danny Boy and others in the Ardizzone gang, but they're always a step ahead of us. In cases like these, sometimes the best we can hope for is that they'll have a falling out and kill each other. It happens more often than you think. But we're bound to catch a break sooner or later.'

'No, you won't. Not ever. You know why? Because Joe always knows what the police are going to do. You know why? Because there's a stool pigeon inside your headquarters who tells him.'

Carl came out of his chair like a shot. 'Who?'

She squirmed in her seat. 'I don't know,' she admitted.

'Are you sure?'

She nodded. 'He tells Joe everything.'

'You said "he". It's a man?'

'I don't know.'

Carl started pacing. Kit pushed one bare foot against the porch railing to rock the chain swing back and forth. I could tell she was pleased with her own importance.

'Did you find all this out by reading lips?' he asked uneasily.

'I sat in the corner and drew portraits while I watched their lips,' she said, as if it were the simplest thing in the world. 'I didn't have anything else to do.'

'That's how she learned why David Carr's trial went so badly,' I added.

'Because Joe hated David's medicine whiskey,' she explained, forgetting that Carl was already aware of the details. 'It made their lousy hooch look even worse. Their own sales went lower on account of David.'

Carl nodded his understanding. 'I'd heard about the appeals being stonewalled and wondered . . . that is, not many people come to trial on charges involving liquor, let alone get convicted and sent to the pokey, unless someone is making a point, so we figured Carr had run afoul of someone big. Just didn't know who. It wasn't us locals. Makes sense that it was the feds in cahoots with Ardizzone's boys. An unbeatable partnership.'

'Joe had so much hooch coming in and not much going out, Joe said it was backed up. No more room. He said they would have to find another Fort Knox.'

'Fort Knox?'

'That's what they call their warehouse where they keep all their hooch and dope. I looked up Fort Knox in the encyclopedia. The real Fort Knox is where they keep all the gold.'

'You, ahhh, you wouldn't happen to know where this Fort Knox is, would you?'

'Kentucky.'

'I mean, Ardizzone's Fort Knox.'

She smiled at her own joke. 'I'm just razzing you! But no,

I never went there, sorry. But I saw them talk about a warehouse, and I know it has a blue door, because sometimes Danny Boy or Joe would tell someone to come to the blue door at Fort Knox.'

I couldn't remain silent any longer. 'Carl, this scares me. If this is a great secret and you raid that warehouse, they'll know the information came from inside, and they may think of Kit and come looking for her. She wouldn't be hard to find – there aren't many deaf girls her age around. They may already know Rose Ann dropped her off here . . .'

'Give me some credit—'

'They won't think of me,' Kit interrupted. 'No one knew I could read lips, and they all thought I was a simp. But you can't raid Fort Knox. The stool pigeon will just warn Joe, and he'll move the stuff or figure out how to stop the raid.'

'Not if I don't tell anyone at headquarters – not a blessed soul. I can arrange to meet federal agents and cops somewhere without revealing where we're going until the last minute. And afterwards, when I write up the report, I'll say I heard the information from an informant who can't be named.'

'And even if the police chief or someone really important asks you who gave you the information, you mustn't ever tell!' I said. 'Even if they fire you! We can't know who's on Ardizzone's payroll. It could be the police chief himself, for all we know. We can't trust anyone!'

'Hell, half the force is on Ardizzone's payroll. That's the problem. But the stool pigeon at headquarters . . . that's one name I'd like to have.'

'I think Fort Knox is a good name for a secret warehouse,' said Kit with a cherubic smile, 'don't you? Be sure to write that name in your report.'

Inside the house, the telephone bell rang. A moment later, Myrna came onto the porch. 'Jessie,' she whispered conspiratorially. 'It's Douglas Fairbanks.'

My heart pounded as I went to the back of the hall and reached for the receiver. What on earth could he want? Was he going to explain why he had to let me go? Apologize, maybe?

'Hello?' I said in a tone I hoped sounded like a self-confident girl who was unfazed about being fired because she had so many other prospects beating down her door.

'Jessie! Douglas here. Take a bow, my girl! Just heard the news from the chief of police. Another feather for your cap. I know Barbara Petrovitch will be comforted to know her husband's killer is dead. And a woman! Who would've thought it? Good work, good work. So when can we expect you back at the studio?'

THIRTY-SIX

Turns out it was all a misunderstanding – Douglas was just trying to throw the newspapermen off my trail. He hadn't meant me to take those newspaper articles seriously, and he wanted me back at work as soon as I could get there. 'The pirates need you,' he said. He thought a name change would be in order, so I returned under my mother's stage name, Randall. And my new address at David's house would play into that quite well. Jessie Beckett on Fernwood who had testified at David Carr's trial would effectively disappear. Jessie Randall worked for Pickford-Fairbanks and lived at a fashionable Whitley Heights address.

I wanted to believe him. I pretended to believe him. But deep down, I pretty much knew that he'd shifted gears because of my sleuthing success and because the studio was no longer on the hot seat as regards David's trial. Scandals had short lives in Hollywood. David's was ancient history. So ancient that Douglas could afford to be magnanimous and have me back. So two and a half weeks after I read in the newspaper that I'd been fired, I was back at work.

The next day was Sunday, a good day to move. Now that I was a Pickford-Fairbanks employee again, I was allowed to borrow the studio flivver. With that, I drove my and Myrna's meager belongings to David's house. My house. It was half mine, David had said when he first bought it, and from now on, I would remember that.

'Are you very, very sure that furniture isn't too much money?' Myrna asked as we lugged our boxes up the steps. 'I wouldn't want David to be unhappy with me.'

'Nonsense, Myrna. He'll be thrilled when I tell him. He wants us to furnish the empty rooms in the house, and twenty-five dollars for a nice iron bed is perfectly reasonable, especially since it includes the mattress. I'm glad they delivered on a Sunday. You'll have a bed to sleep in tonight, but you'll need to pick out a dresser and vanity and night tables as soon as possible. Find something you like and have it delivered one evening when we're home.'

Monday morning found me almost giddy to be walking through the Pickford-Fairbanks arch. I understood that, with my own Fort Knox residing cozily under David's bed, I need never work another day in my life, but I loved my job at Pickford-Fairbanks and couldn't imagine staying home . . . doing exactly what? I had never for an instant contemplated not working.

With a wave to the guard, I returned to my desk where someone had placed the biggest bouquet of roses I'd ever seen in my life. 'Welcome home,' the card read, signed Mary and Douglas. I nearly skipped to the pirate set on the back lot where we were filming one of the complicated scenes on the pirate ship, a scene that involved scores of extras. The set was swarming with light men, make-up girls, cameramen, set managers, grips galore, assistants, and assistant assistants. Script girl Julia Girone wasted no time bringing her assistant – me – up to speed.

'Good morning, Jessie,' she said, her voice crisp with tension. 'Handle wardrobes for these extras, please.' She handed me a long list. I needed no further direction. The extras were arriving as we spoke, and their costumes had to be made ready, costumes that matched the ones they wore last week. Extras wouldn't be seen that clearly in the final film version, so we could have gotten away with some variation, but Douglas was a perfectionist in all aspects of his films. No detail was too small.

'Barbara!' I called as I caught a glimpse of her in the hall between Make-up and Wardrobe.

'Oh, Jessie! I heard the news yesterday from Mr Fairbanks. He says it will be in all the newspapers tomorrow. I'm eager to hear the details from you as soon as you can spare an evening to come to my house for dinner. I want to know everything. I knew you could do it! I knew you would find Joe's killer.'

'Did Douglas tell you—'

'That it was a woman? Yes! So shocking! Who would think a woman could do such violent, horrid things?'

'Did he tell you the woman was posing as Julia Shala?'

Barbara's shocked expression told me better than words that Douglas had not shared that. She stopped cold in the middle of the hall, speechless, her arms full of wigs.

'Yes, her name was Vesa Leka, but she pretended to be Mr Shala at Joe's funeral, and later she came to your house as his wife, Julia Shala. She was masquerading in order to learn more about other friends of Joe's that she wanted to kill. I'll tell you all about it later.'

And I would, too. But I would leave out the part about Joe's former life as a Serbian army deserter, rapist, and murderer. That information would do Barbara no good at all. I would say that Vesa Leka had a grudge against five men she believed had swindled her family back in the Old Country. If Barbara pressed for details, I would say that was all I knew. And Vesa Leka, being dead, could not gainsay my version.

After Director Parker dismissed us that night, I went straight to a Ford dealer and bought a motorcar. The under-the-bed stash meant I could have bought anything, foreign or domestic, but I'd been driving the studio's Ford for the past few months and was comfortable with that. However, the more I thought about a Ford Runabout, the more I realized the limitations of having only the one seat, so I'd set my cap for a touring car because of its spacious rear seat. The salesman was rather flummoxed at having to deal with a female customer and kept asking was I certain I didn't have a father or husband to help me?

'I'm certain. I am sorry, you will just have to deal with me.'

'No brother? An uncle perhaps?'

'I'm afraid not. I'm an orphan.'

'Oh my, oh dear, I'm very sorry. Is there not even a beau?'
I shook my head sadly. 'But I can go over to the Oldsmobile
dealer if you don't want to—'

'No, no! We'll handle everything for you right here.'

And cheat me, if he could. But he couldn't, because Carl
had told me not to go over $325 for the Ford touring car. I
got it for $314 and two dollars worth of gasoline, which filled
its ten-gallon tank.

'Are you sure you aren't interested in the weekly purchase
plan, miss?'

'I'm sure.' I exchanged David's cash for the key and steered
toward home.

THIRTY-SEVEN

D ouglas Fairbanks was an unhappy man. He stood,
arms akimbo, decked out in full pirate garb, glaring
at the lights through narrowed eyes. The crowded
scene with all the pirates on deck had not gone the way he
wanted, and he and Director Parker had their heads together
as they discussed possible solutions to the lighting problem.
Technicolor filming was so untested. Wringing the maximum
value from it involved a good deal of experimentation. Filming
in color required more light than filming in black and white,
but no one knew how much was enough. Fortunately, Douglas
regarded this as another challenge to overcome, one he attacked
as vigorously as he did the dastardly pirates. Parker showed
less enthusiasm.

'All right, everyone,' Parker called through his megaphone.
'Take an hour. We're bringing up some additional lights.'

It was late – after two o'clock – and I was as hungry as the
Starving Chinese, but I had something more important to do
than eat. Mike Allenby's law office was not far from the studio,
and I wanted news of David. In my new touring car, I whisked
over in half the time it would have taken had I hopped a Red
Car. Luckily, his secretary indicated her boss was in. She

waved me into his office, a cave-like corner room with dark leather furniture and open windows that drew in a fresh cross breeze.

'I've been out of town,' I began, 'but I'm home now, and I wanted to know how David was doing.'

'I haven't seen him since we last spoke,' he told me without inviting me to sit. I sat anyway.

'When will you be visiting him next?'

He sighed. 'Probably not until after the first of the new year. There's just no reason to. Nothing to talk about.'

'You could deliver my letter.' I placed the long letter I'd written last night on his desk. In it, I told him all about Vesa Leka and how she'd avenged her family at the cost of her own life. I told him Myrna and I had moved into his house and bought some furniture with his funds. And a motorcar. He'd know which funds I meant. I told him he should send future letters to Jessie Randall at the Whitley Heights address. I never told him I'd lost my job on account of his trial, but he'd probably figure out that bad publicity had brought about the name change.

'I'm no mailman. I can't spend half a day going all the way to the prison to deliver a letter.' I pressed my lips together so I wouldn't burst out with something I would regret later. It wouldn't help David to antagonize his lawyer. 'Look,' he said, taking in my pained expression, 'it'll get there just as quick if you put it in the mail. The guards are gonna read it either way.'

'I wasn't concerned about the guards reading it, I just wanted to hear from you how he looked. How he was doing. He hasn't written . . .'

'Lotta times they don't write. Hell, what have they got to say? Their days are all the same.'

The telephone on his desk burst forth with such a loud, harsh jangle, I jumped. The lawyer picked up the receiver and identified himself. 'Allenby. Yeah . . . yeah . . . yeah? No kidding? Yeah. Well, thanks.'

He looked at me, his lips stretched in a wide grin, as he replaced the receiver in the cradle.

'Well, this is good timing, you being here. You'll like this.

Remember that Joe Ardizzone fella who set your boy up for a fall? Well, listen to this: cops raided a big warehouse this morning down on East First and seized thousands of cases of liquor and more dope than you could imagine. They're still counting. Evidently it was his gang's main hoard. Wooo-eee!' he said, slapping his hand on the desk. 'That'll knock old Iron Man off his gold-plated throne.'

'Has he been arrested?'

Allenby shook his head. 'No chance of that,' he said. 'His lawyers will have shielded him from the warehouse. He'll claim he knows nothing about it, and there will be nothing to tie him to the liquor or the dope. But he'll suffer, that's for sure. Thank God I just laid in a couple bottles of whiskey last weekend. This'll bring on a scramble and prices'll shoot sky high, at least until the gang restocks. Could take weeks. Hell, that's news Carr will want to hear! Better add a P.S. to your letter.'

THIRTY-EIGHT

When I got back to the house at eight o'clock that evening, exhausted and hungry, I found Myrna upstairs in her bedroom, arranging her clothes in her sawdust-smelling dresser drawers 'so new they were trees last week', she'd said. I had only just taken off my sweater when the telephone bell rang.

'I'll pick up,' I called. I sat on the bench and lifted the receiver. It was Helen.

'Helen! How lovely to hear from you! How was the beach?'

'We had a fine time. Jessie—'

'Bet you're both busy as bees packing for the trip tomorrow. How long a drive is it?'

'About three days, depending on how we go. Jessie, is—'

'And is your mother there?'

'Well, no, we're going to Riverside tomorrow and say goodbye.'

'And drop off Kit.'

'Well, that's what I'm calling about. Is Kit there?'

'Here? No! Why – is she missing?'

'When Larry and I got home, the house was empty. Of course, Melva and Lillian were at work, but I thought Kit would be here.'

'She's probably gone on a walk somewhere. She goes to the pictures sometimes.'

'That's what we thought at first, but it's been several hours, and it's getting dark.'

'Geez, I haven't seen her since Myrna and I moved out on Sunday.'

Hearing my end of the conversation brought Myrna to the head of the stairs. 'Kit's missing?' she asked.

I pressed my lips together and gave a grim nod. 'You don't know where she might be, do you?' I mouthed. Myrna shook her head. 'Myrna says she doesn't know where she is either,' I told Helen.

'Lillian said she was here this morning when they left for work.'

'Have you checked the library?' I asked.

'Yes. She wasn't there, and they hadn't seen her today.'

'What about that woman down the street who has the puppy?'

'I've walked the street twice. No one's seen her today.'

Myrna had gone to the closet and was putting on her jacket. 'Myrna and I are on our way, Helen. We'll spread out to the other streets in the neighborhood. I've got my own motorcar now, so we can cover a lot of territory quickly. Someone will have seen her. Have you called the police?'

'Not yet. I was just about to.'

'Let me do that. I'll call Carl Delaney. He found her walking along the sidewalks one day a few weeks ago and brought her home on his motorcycle. He might have an idea where she's gone. And he can alert the cops on patrol to keep an eye out for her.'

Myrna handed me my jacket as I dialed Carl's desk at the police station. Luck was with me: he picked up on the second ring.

'Evening, Jessie. Did you see the newspapers?'

'I did. I heard about the raid yesterday, just after it happened. I want to hear all about it, but not right now. We've got a problem. Kit has gone missing.'

'When?' His voice took on a tense tone.

'Not sure. Helen just called me. She and Larry arrived home from their honeymoon at about five o'clock, and Kit wasn't there. Melva and Lillian saw her this morning before they left for work. They usually leave around eight.'

'What you don't know from the newspapers is that the button man, the one they call Danny Boy, was found dead this afternoon and, uh, mutilated in, uh, his private areas. They think he was murdered early this morning.'

My heart started pounding like I'd been running a footrace.

'Carl, I'm scared. What if . . . what if Ardizzone figured out who it was who squealed about his warehouse and somehow tracked Kit to the Fernwood house? What if he knew she was there all along? What if he kidnapped her?'

That was illogical. Ardizzone wouldn't kidnap Kit. There was no reason for him to do so. She had no value to him – no family money to extort, no task he needed accomplished in return for her safe keeping. If he'd grabbed her, it could only be because he'd figured out that she knew too much about his operation, and he needed to get her out of the way before she spilled anything more. And if so, he had no reason to delay – he'd kill her at once. Maybe she'd been dead for hours.

Carl's voice pulled me back from the cliff edge of despair. 'No need to jump to conclusions. Kit's wandered off before, remember, and that's probably all this is. Still, I'll put the word out on the street and start looking myself.'

'I have my own motorcar now. Myrna and I will start looking too. And Helen and them are scouring the neighborhood.'

'She probably got cold and went into some store. I'll get the boys to pay attention to the commercial streets. Maybe she's lost and can't find her way home.'

'She'd ask. She isn't that helpless.'

'No, you're right. If you find her or hear anything, call back to this number, and I'll make sure someone's close by to pick up. We'll keep in touch that way. And try not to worry, Jessie. We'll find her.'

Yes, but alive?

THIRTY-NINE

Myrna wanted to be dropped off on Sunset Boulevard near our Fernwood house. 'I'll walk the boulevard until I drop, then take a taxi home,' she said. We had no photographs of Kit but her unruly dark hair, stick-thin body, and huge eyes made painting her visual portrait a snap. And how many deaf children were walking around Hollywood alone at night?

I drove to the library for a second look and found them getting ready to close. The librarian knew Kit but hadn't seen her in days. So I turned right onto Hollywood Boulevard and drove as slowly as I could get away with, my head turning from right to left as if I were watching a game of ping pong. Pedestrian traffic was light this time of night; the sidewalks would become more crowded as the evening wore on. Motorcar traffic was light as well, light enough to let me make a U-turn at Normandie and start back toward the opposite end of the boulevard; once there, another U-turn took me back to where I'd started.

Stores were closed or closing, but restaurants and clubs provided noisy oases of activity on every block as patrons surged in and out and on to the evening's next episode, and reporters and cameramen hovered to capture any famous faces. Without the sunshine to bring up the temperature, a penetrating chill had descended on the city. I hoped Kit was wearing her jacket. For the first time in my life, the sight of uniformed cops walking the pavement did not make me twitch. I knew they were keeping eyes peeled for our missing girl. Visions of Rose Ann's battered body on the table in the San Diego morgue tortured me. I prayed her only child would not suffer the same fate at the same hands.

Twice I left the Ford idling at the curb while I stepped inside a drug store to call Carl's desk at headquarters, hoping for news. When there wasn't any, I resumed my creep down the boulevard. At one point, I saw Lillian coming out of a drug store; later I caught a glimpse of Larry and Helen speaking earnestly to a street vendor. I waved and kept going.

Cutting over to Santa Monica Boulevard, I repeated the process, driving down its long stretch first east, then west, watching both sides of the street as I crawled along. As midnight approached, I gave a pass down Sunset, hoping to see Myrna to give her a ride home. I didn't.

Back at David's house, I made a final telephone call to the police station. There was no news. By now, there was not a fiber of optimism left in me. Kit wasn't lost. She didn't get lost. She'd been snatched.

'Any word?' called Myrna as she came in the front door.

I tried to reply but couldn't speak. Tears burned my eyes, and I swallowed hard. Myrna put her arms around me and hugged, which only made it worse.

'The police are still out looking,' she said. 'They'll look all night. They'll find her, I'm sure. We need to get some sleep before we fall down. First thing in the morning, we can start out fresh.'

I threw the deadbolt on the front door and trudged up the stairs, wondering if I'd had dinner that night or not. It didn't matter. I wasn't hungry, and I couldn't have kept anything down anyway.

At the door to my bedroom, I stopped and gave a sharp cry, unable to trust my eyes. Someone was lying on my bed.

Kit. Sound asleep.

Coming up behind me, Myrna said, 'What's the matter? Oh!'

Of course, Kit couldn't hear the noise we made. I rushed to the bed and shook her. She came awake quickly, her hair sticking up in all directions and a crease from my chenille bedspread on her cheek. Looking from my face to the clock, she snapped, 'Where have you been? It's after midnight!'

Myrna, moving faster than I could, threw her arms around

the girl. 'Oh, Kit, we were so worried! We thought that horrible man had kidnapped you!'

Weak with relief, I rose. 'I'll call Carl's desk at once,' I said. 'And Helen.'

Unable to reach anyone at the Fernwood house, I left the message at the police station and trusted an officer would soon run into Helen and the other girls on the street. Mindful of the hour, I said I would bring Kit back the following morning.

'I've not been able to contact Helen,' I told Kit. 'So I left word that you would be spending the night here. You can sleep on the sofa downstairs, and I'll drive you home in the morning.'

Kit shook her head. 'I'm not going back. I don't want to live with Mrs Reynolds.'

'Kit, you can't go with Helen and Larry. Their lives will be very rough, almost like camping, and you won't have another soul to talk to or even a library for books. Mrs Reynolds is your cousin, and she has a nice house full of books and friends with children your age, and she wants you very much.'

'If you make me go, I'll run away, like from deaf school when Ma made me go there. I don't want Helen. I want to stay here. With you. You have room – I saw the empty bedroom. I can bring the cot Helen bought, so you don't need to buy furniture, and I don't eat much, so I won't cost much.'

The idea was preposterous, but I was too tired to argue. I had been operating for the past few hours on sheer terror, and now that the crisis had passed, I felt like a deflated balloon. I thought numbly of my mother – and I know I sounded like her – when I put Kit off with that old parental favorite, 'We'll talk about this in the morning.' I handed her my extra pillow and a blanket from the closet. 'Take these downstairs and sleep on the sofa.'

Myrna's exhausted eyes met mine, and we shook our heads.

Early the next morning, I drove Kit back to the Fernwood house and helped her persuade Helen and her mother to let her stay with Myrna and me.

FORTY

'She really won't be much trouble,' I explained to Carl that evening when he stopped by our house after work. We were sitting in the living room with its large picture window that overlooked the walled garden. I was still a little uncomfortable having Carl in David's house, but there was no getting around the fact that I was going to be seeing Carl now and then. I'd have to get used to the idea of him in David's domain.

'Where is she?' he asked.

'Upstairs unpacking. I ordered a duplicate of the furniture Myrna chose for her room, and they delivered it this afternoon. I wasn't here, but Kit told the men where to put everything. Now she's organizing her clothes, happy as a clam. Why shouldn't she be? She got her own way, the wretched child.'

'It didn't sound like anybody had to break your arm to get you to agree.'

I grinned. 'I guess not. I really am fond of the kid. I can see some of myself in her. We both had to grow up fast and learn things early on. Too early, but we didn't have any say in that.'

'You ready to be a mother?'

'I'm ready to be a big sister.'

'That sounds about right. Good luck to you.' He raised his gin and tonic to me in a mock toast. 'Did the newlyweds get off today as planned?'

'They drove off in Larry's truck this afternoon, I heard. I wasn't there. I was at the studio. I talked with Helen this morning though, and her mother.'

'I hope Mrs Reynolds wasn't too disappointed to lose Kit?'

'Frankly, I think she was relieved. She was willing to step up and take the child when there was no one else, but Helen wasn't exaggerating about her poor health. She really doesn't get around very well, and Kit can be a handful. Besides, we promised Mrs Reynolds that Kit would visit at Christmas and that's just four weeks away. Can I freshen up that drink, mister?'

'Sure can. Thanks.'

Myrna breezed in through the front door. 'Hi, Jessie,' she said. 'Hi, Carl.'

'Hello to you, Miss Loy. How is Warner Brothers's finest actress today?'

Myrna sent Carl one of her high-wattage smiles and kicked off her shoes. 'There's a big push on to finish up with *Why Girls Go Back Home*. They oughta call it *Why Girls* Can't *Go Back Home*, we're working so late every day. I have only a small part playing a girl named Sally Short, but I have to stay until the director dismisses us all, even if I'm not in the scene. Is there any food in the kitchen, Jessie?'

'Kit and I have eaten, but there are some leftover chicken wings.'

'Copacetic.' She padded off into the kitchen on stocking feet.

'So, tell me about Tuesday's raid,' I said when we were alone again.

'The plan worked like a charm. Not knowing who the snitch is at headquarters, I couldn't tell anyone anything. I drove the streets of the warehouse district until I spotted one with a blue door. Then, one by one, I contacted a dozen officers and had them meet me near La Grande Station, and then I did the same for some federal agents. None of them knew about the others until we had all gathered – I didn't want anyone knowing I was assembling a large force – and by then it was too late for anyone to squeal to Joe Ardizzone.'

Sometimes I wonder just how deaf Kit really is, because she seems to hear just fine whenever anyone is talking about a topic she cares about. Maybe she's just psychic. Whatever the reason, she appeared at the top of the stairs, took one look at Carl's lips, and clamored down to the living room to position herself in a chair where she could see both our mouths.

'Hello, Kitty Kat,' Carl said, raising his eyebrows at me in a question that was easy to read. Kit read it too.

'I can stay. I want to hear too.'

I nodded and Carl continued. 'The captain wasn't too happy with me for not letting him in on the raid, but he could have been the snitch for all I knew – and he still could be – so I'm not apologizing. I don't need to – he's pleased enough with the results and eager to take credit for the sting. We found the warehouse with a blue door just like you said, Kit. We surrounded it. Then we just walked inside. There were only two men there at that time of day and they couldn't put their hands up fast enough. Didn't have to fire so much as a warning shot.'

'And was it a big haul?' I asked.

'Huge. Like Kit said, this is Iron Man's main warehouse, with thousands of cases of hooch piled high plus a good deal of cocaine and heroin and some morphine and other dope.'

I couldn't help but think back on the time a few months ago when crooked detectives had stolen the dope they found at Director Bruno Heilmann's house after he was murdered and tried to sell it on the market. Much of the illegal booze that was seized found its way back into the public trough when cops sold it to speakeasies. 'How are you going to make sure all that contraband isn't stolen by crooked cops?'

'No doubt some of it will be, but we've got an army guarding the place to prevent wholesale theft, and also to prevent Iron Man's boys from trying to repossess it. So on Tuesday afternoon, I filed my report. At that point, it was too late for a stool pigeon to warn the gang, but I expect he stole a peek at it so he could learn where the information came from.'

He looked at Kit. 'Naturally, I didn't mention your name, and I never will. I said only that "an informant" told me the Fort Knox location. A gangster named Daniel O'Rourke – that's your friend Danny Boy, Kit – was later found murdered in an unusually brutal manner, so I'm figuring they thought he was the informant.'

'I wonder why,' I mused. Then I saw Kit's cherubic smile, and it hit me like a landslide. Somehow, that child had engineered this. I was certain of it. But how?

I'd seen that smug smile before. When? Where? I sorted through the file cabinet in my head until I reached Saturday night after Helen's wedding, when Kit had joined Carl and

me on the front porch and Kit was telling him everything she
knew about Ardizzone's operation. What had she said? '*I think
Fort Knox is a great name for a secret warehouse. Be sure to
write that in your report.*'

And Carl had done just that.

'Kit,' I asked, with an artlessness that I hoped matched her
own, 'was it Joe Ardizzone who thought up the name Fort
Knox for the warehouse?'

'No, not Joe. It was Danny Boy. He thought it was funny.
It was his little joke.'

'Did others call it that?'

'I don't think so,' said Miss Innocence Personified.

With nothing more than a few well-aimed remarks, this
thirteen-year-old deaf girl had crippled the biggest bootlegger
in the state while cold-bloodedly arranging the torture and
murder of the underling Ardizzone believed had ratted him
out, the same man who had killed her mother.

I looked uneasily at the child I had just taken into my life
– a child who had conned California's biggest gangster and a
savvy police detective, not to mention an experienced swindler
like myself, in a ruthless scheme to avenge her family the only
way she could. Just like Vesa Leka.

ACKNOWLEDGMENTS

When I was first discovered historical fiction as a child, I was curious to know how much of what I'd read was history and how much was fiction. Did the Scarlet Pimpernel really rescue the young French dauphin during the Reign of Terror? (Sadly no, the boy died in prison.) Was the 'Great Game' young Kim played in India real? (Yes, and some would say, ongoing.) Usually a trip to the encyclopedia would answer my questions; sometimes a biography gave me the true story. That's why I like to separate fact from fiction at the end of my novels.

My main characters, Jessie, David, and Kit, are products of my imagination, but many others are real. Mary Pickford and Douglas Fairbanks reigned over Hollywood in the 1920s and started their own studio. Myrna Loy was not yet a famous actress when my story takes place, but she really did live with girls named Lillian, Melva, and Helen (although their characters are made up). Joseph 'Iron Man' Ardizzone headed up the LA crime world for many years. He was such a nasty piece of work, his own men murdered him in 1931. His body was never found. The Great Fulgora was perhaps the most talented of all transfigurators on the vaudeville stage. Another like him was Fregoli, an Italian transfigurator. You can see his act at https://www.youtube.com/watch?v=hP_e43T4zNM? Most of the vaudeville acts I mention in passing were real acts. Olga Myra was the aunt of a friend of mine who performed in the 1920s with her unique violin contortionist act. I've seen several pictures from the newspapers of her odd act. Adele Astaire was far more famous and talented than her little brother Fred, although he is remembered today and she is not. For a short history with darling pictures of young Fred and Adele, see http://www.youtube.com/watch?v=0W5wbKffWHo. While everyone knows of Helen Keller, almost no one remembers that she performed a vaudeville act for a few years with her interpreter. She tried and tried to learn to speak – it was one of the few things she couldn't master. Hear how she sounds at http://www.youtube.com/watch?v=8ch_H8pt9M8. It might give you some idea of how Kit sounded – although Kit's deafness struck her later than Helen Keller's, which meant she could more accurately make the right sounds.

Pickford-Fairbanks was one of the highest quality studios in Hollywood; it was also one of the most innovative. Moon Motors was an important automobile factory in St. Louis in the days before Detroit had a monopoly on car production. The Great Depression put them out of business. The Busch factory and the story of Bevo are true.

I am especially indebted to Carolyn Schmid, the former librarian at Douglas Freeman High School in Richmond, VA, for sharing her own story about becoming deaf at a young age and learning to lip-read. Her help in creating the character of Kit was invaluable. Silent film buffs at the Library of Congress's annual Mostly Lost workshop helped me understand the filming techniques Douglas Fairbanks used in making *The Black Pirate*. And, as always, my thanks go to Donna Sheppard, retired editor from Colonial Williamsburg, who taught me more about writing than any professor.